She knew that Max had been badly injured; she knew he was close to death

But somehow, Maddy simply could not make her brain accept the fact that she might never see him again, that he might never walk arrogantly and irritably through the front door of Queensmead, bringing with him that highly charged atmosphere that always seemed to be so much a part of him.

She closed her eyes. Max was far too alive to be dying. Her throat suddenly closed and her body started to tremble.

"Oh, God, please let him live," Maddy prayed. Max wouldn't want to die. She tried to picture him, her husband, lying white and still in his hospital bed, but she couldn't. All she could visualize was the way he had looked the first time they had gone to bed together, when she had woken up to watch him with the eyes and the emotions of a woman deeply and bemusedly in love.

The smell of him on her skin, the taste of him on her mouth—these were sensations she would remember forever.

As she raised her cup to her lips, Maddy suddenly realized that her face was wet with tears.

Penny Jordan's novels "...touch every emotion."
—*Romantic Times*

Penny Jordan

THE
PERFECT
SINNER

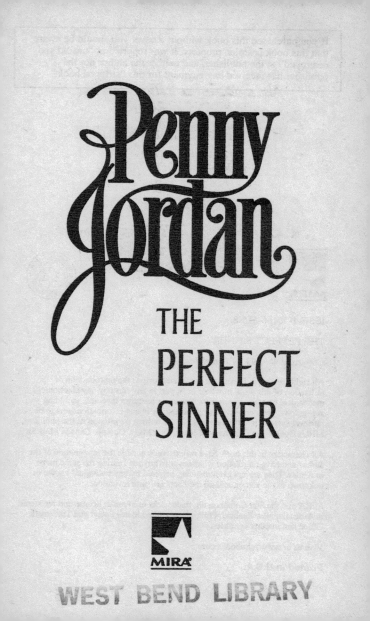

MIRA

ISBN 1-55166-515-8

THE PERFECT SINNER

Copyright © 1999 by Penny Jordan.

Visit us at www.mirabooks.com

Printed in U.S.A.

The Crighton Family

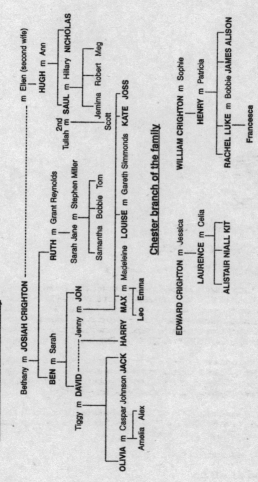

Haslewich branch of the family

Bethany m JOSIAH CRIGHTON ----------------------------------- m Ellen (second wife)

HUGH m Ann

2nd
Tullah m SAUL m Hillary NICHOLAS

Jemima Robert Meg
Scott

BEN m Sarah

RUTH m Grant Reynolds

Sarah Jane m Stephen Miller

Samantha Bobbie Tom

Jenny m JON

LOUISE m Gareth Simmonds KATE JOSS

HARRY MAX m Madeleine

Leo Emma

Tiggy m DAVID

OLIVIA m Caspar Johnson JACK

Amelia Alex

Chester branch of the family

EDWARD CRIGHTON m Jessica

LAURENCE m Celia

ALISTAIR NIALL KIT

WILLIAM CRIGHTON m Sophie

HENRY m Patricia

RACHEL LUKE m Bobbie JAMES ALISON

Francesca

1

Max Crighton, thirty years old, married, successful, sexy and the father of two healthy, energetic play school age children, and right now thoroughly disenchanted and bored with his lot, surveyed the other occupants of the ballroom of Chester's Grosvenor Hotel—presently the scene of his sister's wedding reception—with cynical contempt.

Louise, the bride and the most dominant of his two younger twin sisters, was laughing up into the handsome face of her new husband, Gareth Simmonds, while various members of the collective Crighton and Simmonds clans looked on in what to Max was grotesquely irritating sentimentality. Louise's twin sister Katie stood to one side of the bride, and slightly in her shadow.

Twins!

Twins ran through the genealogical history of the Crighton family. His own father was the younger one of one pair and his grandfather, Ben Crighton, the lone survivor of another.

Twins!

Max was eternally grateful to his parents for the fact that *his* life had not been overshadowed; that *he* had not been overshadowed by another half, another self, threatening his position of sole supremacy, and it was about the only thing he *was* grateful to them for.

As he glanced around the large room, Max was coolly amused to observe the way so many of his relatives failed to meet his gaze. They didn't like him very much, but he didn't care. Why *should* he? Having people *like* him had never been one of Max's ambitions.

The brand new Bentley Turbo convertible car he was currently driving, his position as a partner in one of London's most prestigious sets of legal chambers; they hadn't been acquired because people *liked* him. To be one of London's foremost barristers had been Max's driving goal in life, ever since he had been old enough to learn from his grandfather just what the word *barrister* meant.

Max's uncle David, his father's twin brother, had once been destined for that same golden future, but Uncle David had failed to make it. There had been a time, too, when Max had feared that *he* also might fail, when despite all the promises he had made himself, all the promises he had made to his *grandfather*, he might, through no fault of his own, have the prize he so desperately wanted snatched from him at the last minute. But he had found a way to turn the situation to his own advantage, to show those who had tried to bring him down just how foolish they had been.

He glanced across the room to where his wife, Madeleine, was sitting with his mother and his grandfather's sister, his great aunt Ruth.

While not one of his female cousins of his own generation, nor the wives of his male ones, could ever be said to be the kind of high-profile trophy wives that their partners could take satisfaction in flaunting beneath the envious eyes of other men, they were certainly attractive enough—very attractive indeed, in fact in the case of Luke's wife Bobbie—to underline Madeleine's dreary, boring plainness.

Max's mouth curled cynically as his wife glanced up and saw that he was watching her, in her eyes the look of a rabbit momentarily trapped in the dazzle of a car's headlights, before she quickly looked away from him.

Madeleine did, of course, have *one* redeeming feature as his wife. She was extremely wealthy and extremely well connected, or at least her family was.

'What do you mean, you don't want our baby,' she had faltered in shocked disbelief when she had so humbly and so adoringly brought him the news that she was pregnant with their first child.

'I mean, my oh-so-stupid wife, that I don't *want* it,' Max had told her callously. 'The reason I married you was *not* to procreate another generation of little Crightons, my cousins can do that....'

'No...then why...why *did* you marry me?' Madeleine had asked him tearfully.

It had amused him to see the dread in her eyes, to feel the fear she was trying so hard to conceal.

'I married you because it was the only way I could get into a decent set of chambers,' Max had told her coldly and truthfully, and cruelly. 'Why so shocked?' he had taunted her. 'Surely you *must* have guessed....'

'You said you loved me,' Madeleine had reminded him painfully.

Max had thrown back his head and laughed. 'And you *believed* me.... Did you really, Maddy, or were you just so desperate to get a man, to get laid, to get married, that you *chose* to believe me?

'Get rid of it,' he had instructed her, his glance flicking dispassionately towards her small, round stomach.

But Maddy hadn't done as he had demanded. Instead she had defied him, and now there were two noisy, squalling brats to disrupt his life—not that he allowed them to do so.

It had been a positive stroke of genius on his part to encourage his grandfather to become so dependent on Maddy that the old man had insisted that she was the only person he wanted around him.

Persuading Maddy to virtually live full-time in Haslewich, the Cheshire town where he had grown up and where his great-grandfather had first begun the legal practice that his own father now ran, had been even easier, a move that had left him free to pursue his own life virtually unhindered by the interference and responsibility of two turbulent children and a clinging wife.

Max felt not the least degree of compunction about the affairs he had enjoyed during his marriage, relationships that in the main, had been conducted with female clients for whom he was acting, on whose behalf he had been instructed by their solicitors to ensure that their divorces from their extremely wealthy husbands allowed them to continue living in the same financial comfort they had been accustomed to during their marriages.

It was not unusual for these women—rich, beautiful, spoiled and very often either bored or vulnerable—to feel that a relationship with the handsome young barrister who was going to make their husband part with as much of his fortune as he could was a justifiable perk of their divorce, as well as an additional small triumph against their soon-to-be ex-husbands.

It was not to be hoped, of course, that they would keep the details of such a delicious piece of vengeance a secret.

Confidences were shared and exchanged with 'girlfriends,' and Max had very quickly become known as the barrister to have if one was getting a divorce—and not just because of the wonderful amounts of money he managed to wrest from previously determinedly ungenerous husbands.

Even his marriage to Maddy, which initially he had intended should last no longer than the time it took to get himself established, had begun to be a bonus. After all, marriage to

Maddy and the existence of two small dependent children meant that all his lovers had to appreciate right from the start of their affair that it could only ever be a temporary thing, that no matter how desirable, how enticing they might be, he as a man of honour could not put his own needs, his own desires, above the security of his children. For their sakes he had to stay married.

'If only there were more men like you...' more than one of his lovers had whispered. 'Your wife is so lucky....'

Max totally agreed, Madeleine *was* lucky. If *he* hadn't married her she could have been condemned to a life of being the unmarried daughter.

There was currently a whisper that her father was being considered for the soon-to-be-vacant post of Lord Chief Justice, and it would certainly do his own career no harm at all if that whisper should become a reality.

Max knew that Madeleine's parents didn't particularly care for him, but it didn't worry him. Why should it? His own parents, his own *family* didn't like him very much, either. And he didn't particularly like them. The only member of his family he had ever felt any real degree of warmth for had been his uncle David, and even that had been tinged with envy because his grandfather doted on David. Max also felt contempt for David, because for all his grandfather's talk and praise, David had, after all, still only been the senior partner in the family's small-town legal practice.

Love, the emotion that united and bonded other people, was an alien concept to Max. He loved himself, of course, but his feelings for others veered from mild contempt through disinterest to outright resentment and deep hostility.

In Max's eyes, it was not his fault that others didn't like him, it was *theirs*. Their fault and their loss.

Max glanced at his watch. He'd give it another half an hour and then he'd leave. Louise had originally wanted to get married on Christmas Eve, but the wedding had actually taken place a little bit earlier, primarily because it was the turn of Great-aunt Ruth and her American husband, Grant, to fly to the States to spend Christmas with Ruth's daughter and her husband.

Great-aunt Ruth's granddaughter, Bobbie, and her husband, Luke, one of the Chester Crightons, were going with them, along with their young daughter.

* * *

Several yards away, Bobbie Crighton, who had observed the way Max had looked at poor Maddy, reflected grimly to herself that Max really was detestable. She had once heard his cousin Olivia remark very succinctly, 'Max is the kind of man who, no matter how attractive the woman he's speaking with is, will always be looking over her shoulder to see if he can spot someone even better....'

Poor Maddy, indeed. Bobbie didn't know how she could bear to stay in her marriage, but then, of course, there were the children.

She patted her own still-flat stomach with a small, secret smile; her second pregnancy had been confirmed only the previous week.

'I think this time it *could* be twins,' she had confided to Luke, who had raised his dark eyebrows and asked her dryly, 'Women's intuition?'

'Well, one of us has got to produce a set,' Bobbie had pointed out to him, 'and I'm the right age for it now. Mothers in their thirties *are* more likely to have twins....'

'In their thirties? You are only *just* thirty,' Luke had reminded her.

'Mmm... I know, and I rather think that these two were conceived on the night of my thirtieth birthday,' she had told him softly.

Luke was one of four children—two boys and two girls. His father, Henry Crighton, and his father's brother, Laurence, were the senior partners, now retired, in the original solicitors' practice in Chester. Over eighty years ago there had been a quarrel between the then youngest son, Josiah Crighton, and his family, and he had broken away from them and gone on to found the Haslewich branch of the Crighton firm and family.

While Luke's brother and sisters and the other Chester cousins and their Haslewich peers were extremely good friends, Ben Crighton, the most senior member of the Crighton family in Haslewich, was still obsessed by the family tradition of competitiveness with the Chester members, even if it was now in spirit only.

It had been a burning ambition of Ben's all his life that initially his eldest son and then, when that had not been possible, his eldest grandson, Max, should achieve the goal that had been withheld from him and be called to the bar.

All through his growing years, Max had been alternately bribed and coerced by his grandfather to fulfil this goal, his naturally competitive spirit sharpened and fed by his grandfather's tales of the injustices suffered by their own branch of the family and the need to restore the family's pride by proving to 'that Chester lot' that they weren't the only ones who could boast of reaching the higher echelons of the legal profession.

When Max had announced to his grandfather that he was to join one of London's most prestigious sets of chambers, he had made Ben Crighton's dearest wish come true.

As Bobbie surveyed the Grosvenor's ballroom now, she couldn't help remembering the first time she had attended another family occasion—Louise and her twin Katie's coming of age, an event to which she, as a stranger then to the family, had been invited by Joss, Louise and Katie's younger brother.

Max had behaved very gallantly towards her then. Too gallantly for a married man, as Luke hadn't hesitated to point out. Conversely, she and Luke had clashed immediately, equally antagonistic towards each other.

She was glad that Louise had brought her wedding forward from Christmas Eve so that they could all attend. She would have hated to have missed the celebration, but she was looking forward to spending Christmas with her parents and sister as well. Her mother, Sarah Jane, would be thrilled when she told her about her pregnancy, and so, too, she hoped, would Sam.... A small frown touched her forehead as she thought about her twin sister.

Something was wrong with Sam's life at the moment. She knew it, could sense it with that extraordinary magical bond that made them close....

In a small anteroom just off the ballroom, the youngest members of the Crighton family were having a small party all of their own, not so much by design as by accident. From her seat within watching distance of the door, Jenny Crighton was keeping a motherly eye on the events, though she knew they could come to no harm.

Who would have thought in such a short space of time that the family would produce so many little ones, a complete new generation.

Olivia, her husband's niece and the eldest of his twin brother David's two children, had started it all, and now she and Caspar, her American husband, had Amelia and Alex. Saul, Ben's half-brother Hugh's elder son, had Jemima, Robert and Meg from his first marriage and now a baby from his marriage to

Tullah, and of course her own daughter-in-law, Maddy, had Leo and Emma.

Maddy... Jenny could feel her body tensing as she took a quick look at her daughter-in-law, who was seated between her and Ruth, her head bent down. Maddy might seem to the unaware onlooker calm and serene, but Jenny had seen the tears sparkling in her eyes several minutes ago and she had known who had been the cause of them.

Even now, after all these years, she still hadn't come to terms with the reality that was her eldest son, and it hurt her unbearably to know that it was Max, flesh of her flesh, hers and Jon's, who was the cause of so much hurt and pain.

She ached to ask her son *why* he behaved in the way he did. *Why.* What it was that motivated him to be the person he was, but she knew that if she even tried to talk to him he would simply give her that half mocking, half sneering contemptuous little smile of his and shrug his shoulders and walk away.

She had *never* been able to understand how she and Jon had ever produced a person like Max, and she knew that she never would. She knew, too, that every time she looked at her daughter-in-law and witnessed the pain her marriage was causing her, she was overwhelmed by guilt and despair.

Maddy was everything that she, Jenny, could have wanted in a daughter-in-law, or a daughter, and as such she was dearly loved by her, but Jenny would had to have had far less intelligence than she did have to be able to convince herself that Maddy was the kind of wife that Max should have gone for.

Max thrived on opposition, challenge, aggression. Max wanted most what he could have least, and poor Maddy just wasn't...just couldn't... Poor Maddy!

At her mother-in-law's side, Madeleine Crighton had a pretty fair idea just what Jenny was thinking and she couldn't blame her in the least.

Max had only arrived home at Queensmead this morning, the lovely old house that belonged to his grandfather and where Maddy and the children had now virtually made their permanent home, with only an hour to spare before the wedding began, having assured Maddy that he would be there early the previous evening. Not an auspicious start, and to make matters even worse, Leo was going through a belligerent and rather touchingly possessive phase where his mother was concerned. Unlike his father, Leo didn't seem to realize that her looks made it a visible implausibility that any man could ever feel possessively jealous about her—and he had glowered at Max when he had arrived, refusing to leave her side to go to his father.

In private Maddy knew that Max couldn't care less whether the children ignored him or not. In fact, if the truth were known, the less he had to do with them, the happier he was. After all, he had never wanted either of them.

But in public, it was different. In public, in front of his grandfather and others, his children had to be seen to love their father, which Leo, quite plainly at the moment, did not. And then Emma had been sick. Not, fortunately, badly enough to harm her dress, but certainly enough to cause the kind of delay that had Max swearing under his breath and telling Maddy with chilling cruelty that she was as useless as a mother as she was a wife.

Maddy knew what the true cause of his anger was, of course. It was a woman. It had to be. She knew the signs far too well now not to recognize them. Max had left a woman behind in London whom he would far rather be with. And no doubt *she* was the reason he had not come down to Haslewich last night as they had agreed.

Maddy told herself that his infidelity didn't have the power to hurt her any more, but deep down inside she knew that it wasn't true.

Maddy knew that her mother-in-law and the rest of Max's family felt very sorry for her. She could see it in their eyes, hear it in their voices, and sometimes, when she looked at Max's cousins and their wives with their families and saw the love they shared, she felt positively rent with pain for all that she was missing out on, although she tried to tell herself stoically that what you never had you never missed. She had certainly never been loved as a child as she had longed to be. Her mother was a peer's daughter who had always given Maddy the impression that she considered her marriage, and with it her husband and her daughter, as somehow slightly beneath her. She held herself slightly separate from them and spent most of her time on a round of visits to a variety of relatives while Maddy's father, a career barrister, made his way via the Bench towards his goal of being appointed Lord Chief Justice.

Maddy, their only child, had not featured very significantly in her parents' lives. Now that she was married she hardly saw them at all, and to come to Haslewich and discover that there was not just a home waiting for her with Max's grandfather, but also a role to play where she was really genuinely needed had, for a time at least, been a comforting salve on the open wound of her destructive marriage.

Maddy was, by nature and instinct, one of life's carers, and when other people grimaced over Max's grandfather's tetchiness, she simply smiled and explained gently that it was the pain he suffered in his damaged joints that caused him to be so irascible.

'Maddy, you are a saint,' she had been told more than once by his grateful relatives, but she wasn't, of course, she was simply a woman—a woman who right now longed with the most ridiculous intensity to be the kind of woman whom a man might look at the way Gareth Simmonds, her sister-in-law Louise's new husband, was looking at Louise, with love, with pride, with desire...with *all* the things Madeleine had once mistakenly and tragically convinced herself *she* had seen in Max's eyes when he looked at her, but which had simply been mocking and contemptuous deceits designed to conceal his real feelings from her.

Max had married her for one reason and one reason only, as he had told her many, many times in the years since their wedding, and that reason had been his relentless ambition to be called to the bar; an ambition that she had discovered he might never have fulfilled without her father's help.

'Maddy, why do you put up with him? *Why* on earth don't you divorce him?' Louise had asked her impatiently one Christmas when both of them had sat and watched Max flirting openly and very obviously with a pretty young woman.

Maddy had simply shaken her head, unable to explain to Louise why she remained married to her brother. How could she when she couldn't really explain it to herself? All she could have said was that here at Haslewich she felt safe and secure...wanted and needed.... Here, while she had a task to complete, she felt able to side-line the issue of her marriage, to pretend to herself, while Max was away in London and she was here, that it was not, after all, as bad as it might seem to others.

The truth was, Maddy suspected that she didn't divorce Max because she was afraid of what her life might be, not so much without *him* as without his family. It was pathetic of her, she knew, but it wasn't just for herself that she was being what others would see as weak. There were the children to be considered as well.

In Haslewich they were part of a large and lovingly interlinked family network where they had a luxury not afforded to many modern children, the luxury of growing up surrounded by their extended family—aunts, uncles, cousins. The Crighton family was part of this area of Cheshire, and Maddy desperately wanted to give her children a gift that she considered more priceless than anything else; the gift of security, of knowing they had a special place in their own special world.

'But surely if you lived in London, the children would be able to see much more of their father,' one recent acquaintance had commented to her not long ago.

Madeleine had bent her neat head over the buttons she was fastening on Leo's coat so that her hair fell forward, concealing her expression as she had responded in a muffled voice, 'Max's work keeps him very busy. He works late most evenings....'

Luckily the other woman hadn't pressed the subject, but as she ushered Leo towards the path that cut across behind the building where he attended play school classes three mornings a week—Madeleine refused to use the car unless she absolutely had to, one of the pleasures of living in a small country town was surely that one could walk almost everywhere—Madeleine had felt acutely self-conscious. Within the family it was accepted that Max remained in London supposedly mostly during the working week, but in reality for much longer stretches of time than that, so that she and the children could often go weeks if not months on end without really seeing him.

Although her marriage was a subject that she never discussed—with anyone—Madeleine knew that Max's family had to be aware that it wasn't merely necessity that kept Max away.

Sometimes she was sorely tempted to confide in Jenny, Max's mother, but the natural reticence and quiet pride that were so much a part of her gentle nature always stopped her, and what, after all, could Jenny do? Command Max to love her and the children; command him to...

Stop it, Madeleine hastily warned herself, willing her eyes not to fill with tears.

Max was already in a foul-enough mood without her making things any worse. He might not be the kind of man who would ever physically abuse either his wife or his children, but his silent contempt and his hostility towards them were sometimes so tangible that Madeleine felt she could almost smell the dark, bitter miasma of them in the air of a room even after he had left it.

The first thing she always did after one of his brief visits to Queensmead was to go round and open all the windows and to breathe lungsful of clean, healing fresh air.

'Where's that husband of yours?' she remembered Ben asking her fretfully recently as he shifted his weight from his bad hip to his good one. The doctor had warned him the last time he had gone for a check-up that there was a strong possibility that he might have to have a second hip operation to offset the wear-and-tear caused to his good hip by him favouring it to ease the pain in his 'bad' one.

Predictably he had erupted in a tirade of angry refusal to accept what the doctor was telling him, and it had taken Madeleine several days to get him properly calmed down again.

But despite his irascibility and his impatience, she genuinely liked him. There was a very kind, caring side to him, an old-fashioned protective maleness that she knew some of the younger female members of his family considered to be irritating, but which she personally found rather endearing.

'I do not know how you put up with him,' Olivia had told her vehemently only the previous week. She had called to see Madeleine, bringing with her Christmas presents for Leo and Emma, and she had brought her two small daughters, Amelia and Alex, with her.

'Daughters! *Sons,* that's what this family needs,' her grandfather had sniffed disparagingly when she had taken the girls in to see him. 'It's just as well we've got young Leo here,' he had added proudly as he gazed fondly at his great-grandson.

'I will not have him making my girls feel that they are in any way inferior to boys,' Olivia had fumed later in the kitchen to Madeleine as they drank their coffee.

'He doesn't mean anything by it,' Madeleine had tried to comfort her, pushing the plate of Christmas biscuits she had baked that morning towards Olivia as she spoke.

'Oh, yes he does,' Olivia had told her darkly as she munched one of them, 'and *I* should know. After all, I heard enough of it when I was growing up. He never stopped making me feel...reminding me...that as a girl I could never match up to Max, and my father was just as bad. Sometimes I used to wish that Max had been my father's child and that Uncle Jon had been *my* father....'

'Jenny's told me how dreadfully Gramps spoiled Max when he was growing up,' Madeleine remarked quietly.

'Spoiled him is exactly right,' Olivia had agreed forthrightly, momentarily obviously forgetting that Madeleine was Max's wife. 'Anything Max wanted he got, and Gramps was forever boasting about him to everyone else. Whenever we had a get-together with the Chester lot, there was Gramps singing Max's praises, and woe betide anyone who tried to argue with him.

'I hate to think what it would have done to Gramps if Max hadn't got a place in chambers. I know that it was touch-and-go for a while, and of course, the fact that your father is so influential obviously helped in the end.'

'Yes,' Madeleine had agreed. She knew Olivia far too well to suspect her of any kind of malice or unkindness. She was simply stating what she saw as the facts, and her opinions were quite naturally tainted by her dislike of Max. She had always been completely open with Madeleine about her feelings for her cousin, explaining that they went back a long way, and that much as she liked Madeleine herself, she doubted that she could ever pretend to feel anything other than wary acceptance of Max.

Did Olivia know that the only reason that Max had married her had been to further his career? Madeleine hoped not. Olivia was basically very kind-hearted, and Madeleine knew she would never have deliberately hurt her by raising the subject if she had known the whole truth.

'Gramps is going to be putting an awful lot of pressure on Leo to follow in Max's footsteps,' she started to warn Madeleine, but Madeleine stopped her, shaking her head calmly.

'Leo isn't *like* Max,' she told Olivia quietly. 'I think if he takes after anyone, it's Jon, and I suspect that if he does go into the law he will be quite happy to follow Jon into the Haslewich practice.

'To be truthful, I think if any of the babes *are* destined to be real high flyers, it's going to be your Amelia....'

Olivia had smiled lovingly at her elder daughter.

'She is very quick and very determined,' she

had agreed, 'but life doesn't always turn out as we expect it to. Look at Louise. We all thought that she was going to be a real career girl, and look at her now. She and Gareth are so very, very much in love, and Louise is already talking about having a family and putting her career on hold. Now it's Katie, whom all of us have always thought of as the quiet twin, the one who would probably settle down the first, who looks as though *she's* going carve out a career for herself.'

Olivia didn't say anything to her about the fact that *she*, Madeleine seemed to have no interest in anything outside her domestic life and her children, she noticed rawly.

'Mmm...these cookies are delicious,' Olivia had suddenly confounded her by saying. She added, 'You could cook professionally, Maddy. I'm not surprised that you manage to coax Gramps into eating so well.'

Madeleine had said nothing, just as she had said nothing about the kitchen cupboards that were brimming with the fruits of her labours over the long summer and autumn—literally. She enjoyed gardening as well as cooking, and with Ruth's expert tuition and assistance when she was in Haslewich, Madeleine had resurrected Queensmead's neglected kitchen gar-

den, with its espaliered fruit trees and its
newly repaired glass house along its south-
facing wall. She was presently cosseting the
peach tree that had been Ruth and Jenny's
birthday present to her and that she hoped
might bear fruit next summer.

Since moving into Queensmead, she had
quietly and gently set about bringing the old
house back to life—dusty rooms had been
cleaned and repainted, furniture mended and
waxed. She had even made the long trip north
to Scotland to persuade her maternal grandparents to part with some of the sturdy country furniture not deemed grand enough for the
lofty, elegant rooms of their Scottish castle and
currently housed in its attics, but which she
had known immediately would be perfectly at
home at Queensmead.

Guy Cooke, the local antique dealer with
whom Jenny had once been in partnership,
had whistled in soundless admiration when he
had visited Queensmead and been shown the
newly revamped and furnished rooms.

'Very nice,' he had told Madeleine appreciatively. 'Too many people make the mistake of
furnishing houses like Queensmead with antiques that are far too grand and out of place,

or even worse, buying replicas, but these... you've definitely got an eye, Maddy.'

'It helps having grandparents with attics full of furniture,' Madeleine had laughed as Guy turned to examine the heavy linen curtains she had hung in one of the rooms.

'Wonderful,' he had told her, shaking his head. 'You can't buy this stuff now for love nor money. Where...?'

'My great-great-grandmother had Irish connections,' Madeleine had told him mock-solemnly. 'I found it...'

'I know, in the attics,' Guy had supplied for her.

'Well, not exactly,' Madeleine had laughed again. One of her third cousins had apparently been aggrieved to discover that Madeleine had made off with the linen from one of the many spare bedrooms, having earmarked it for some expensive decorating project herself.

'I'm so looking forward to Christmas this year,' Jenny suddenly said to her. 'You've done wonders with Queensmead, Maddy, and it's going to make the most wonderful venue for the family get-together. That's one thing that the Chester family doesn't have that I suspect they rather envy....'

'Mmm... Queensmead is a lovely home,' Madeleine agreed.

'Jon's had a word with Bran,' Jenny told her, 'and he's arranged for the tree to be delivered the day after tomorrow. I'll come round if you like and give you a hand decorating it.'

'Yes, please,' Madeleine accepted with alacrity. The Christmas tree that was to go in Queensmead's comfortably sized entrance hall was coming from the estate of Bran T. Thomas, the Lord Lieutenant and a close friend of the family. Elderly and living on his own, he had been invited to join the family for Christmas dinner. Madeleine liked him. He had a wonderful fund of stories about the area and talked so movingly about his late wife that Madeleine often found her eyes filling with tears as she listened to him.

'I think Louise is getting ready to leave,' Jenny warned her daughter-in-law now, disturbing Madeleine from her reverie.

As she glanced towards the newly married couple, Maddy's heart suddenly missed a beat. They seemed so happy, so much in love, Gareth looking tenderly down into Louise's upturned face and then bending to kiss her. As they reluctantly broke apart, Maddy could quite plainly see the look of shimmering joy illuminating Louise's face. It wasn't that she begrudged Louise her happiness—how could she? It was just...it was just... Swallowing hard, Maddy looked the other way.

Obligingly Madeleine got up and went to separate her own two children from the happy mass playing in the adjacent anteroom.

Leo, who had been a page boy, had conducted himself with aplomb, and Emma had swiftly recovered from the morning's bout of nausea, but they were tiring now as Madeleine's experienced maternal eye could tell.

As Bobbie, Ruth's granddaughter, came to find her own daughter, she grimaced at Madeleine and confided, 'I'm not looking forward to a transatlantic flight on top of this....'

'But it will be worth it once you're with your family,' Madeleine reminded her.

'Oh, heavens, yes,' Bobbie agreed fervently.

As Luke came to join her and picked up their small daughter, cradling her tired body in his arms, Bobbie couldn't help reflecting on the differences between Luke and Max.

Her Luke was a tender, loving father and an equally loving husband, while Max... Max might pretend in front of others—especially his grandfather—to be a caring human being, but Bobbie could see through that pretence.

Poor Maddy.

2

---▶ ◀━━━

Poor Maddy. She had heard herself so described so often that sometimes she thought she ought to have been christened thus, Maddy reflected several hours later, unwillingly recalling hearing Bobbie whisper the two words under her breath as she had turned to smile at Luke.

Leo and Emma were safely tucked up in bed, their stories read and sleep not very far away.

Ben had gone to bed protesting that Maddy was fussing unnecessarily and that there was nothing wrong with him, even though it was perfectly obvious that he was in pain. Tiredly Maddy headed for her own bedroom. Supposedly it was the room she shared with Max on his rare visits home, but in reality... Max might deign to sleep in the large king-size bed alongside her, but for all the intimacy, the love, the natural closeness one might expect to be shared between a married couple, they might just as well have been sleeping in separate beds and at opposite ends of the large house.

On this occasion, though, Max was not intending to stay the night and had already left for London. Maddy had long since ceased to struggle with the pretence that their marriage was either happy or 'normal,' just as she had ceased to question the fact that Max was returning to London ostensibly to 'work.'

And the worst thing about the whole horrid situation was not that Max cared so little for her, but that she cared so much. Too much. What had happened to the dreams she had once had, the bright shining hopes, the belief that Max loved her?

Her maternal ears, forever tuned, picked up the sound of a soft cry from Emma's room. Tiredly she slid out of bed. Emma was going through a phase of having bad dreams.

Having parked his Bentley at the rear of the smart mews house he had bought with the wedding cheque given to them by Maddy's grandparents, Max unlocked the front door and headed for the bedroom, dropping his overnight bag on the floor and stretching out full length on the bed as he reached for the telephone and confidently punched in a set of numbers.

The woman's voice on the other end of the line sounded sleepy and soft.

'Guess who?' Max asked her, tongue in cheek.

There was a brief silence before she responded.

'Oh, Max... But I thought! You said you were going to a family wedding and that you'd be staying for the weekend....'

'So, I changed my mind,' Max told her, laughing. 'What would you like for breakfast?'

'Breakfast... Oh, Max... I don't... I can't...'

She sounded more alert now, and Max could picture her sitting up in bed in her Belgravia house, her tawny hair down round her shoulders, her skin honey gold from her recent holiday in Mauritius. He had flown out to join her there for five days.

'Some client conference,' the solicitor who had originally instructed him had commented enviously when he had handed Max Justine's fax.

'When you're playing for millions, the cost of flying your barrister out for an urgent conference is pretty small beer,' Max told him carelessly.

Justine was the wife of a millionaire, soon-to-be billionaire corporate raider. The first thing she had done when she had discovered that he was having an affair with one of her 'friends' was to instruct her solicitor that she wanted him to hire Max as her barrister, the second was to arm herself with as much evidence as she could of her husband's business affairs, including his complex and often adventurously artistic interpretation of the tax laws.

Max had decided appreciatively that she had enough on him to make it a piece of cake for them to get her the kind of divorce settlement that would make her virtually as comfortably wealthy as his ex as she had been as his wife, and to get *him* the kind of publicity that would ensure that he maintained his position as the country's foremost divorce barrister.

'Divorce isn't really the kind of thing we like to specialize in here in chambers,' the most senior member, a QC and one of the country's foremost tax law specialists, had advised Max stiffly when he had originally joined them. 'It's not really quite us, if you know what I mean.'

Max had known exactly what he meant, but he had also been acutely aware of the fact that it was only his father-in-law's name that had got him a place in the chambers at all. He also knew that the only reputation he had then to gain him the clients who would bring him the kind of high profile and even higher income he craved so desperately was one of being unwanted and rejected by his previous 'set,' where he had been allowed to work only as a tenant and on the cases that no one else wanted to deal with.

His new chambers attracted a clientele who wanted and expected only the best barristers whose names and reputations they already knew, and so Max had seen a niche for himself in the one field where the chambers didn't already have a specialist—matrimonial law.

That had been several years ago, and now Max's reputation had grown and his name on a case was likely to strike dread in a wealthy husband about to enter the divorce arena.

The extremely high fees Max charged for his services weren't the only benefit he earned from his work. Max had quickly and cynically discovered that newly divorced and about-to-be-divorced women very often had an appetite for sex and the male attention that went with it, which ensured him a constant turnover of willing bed mates.

One of the main advantages of these relationships, from Max's point of view, was that they were always relatively brief. While his female clients were going through their divorces, he provided a comforting male shoulder to lean on, someone with whom they could share their problems as well as their beds. But once everything had been finalized, he was always able to very quickly and firmly detach himself.

If any of his lovers showed a tendency to cling and become possessive, he suddenly became far too busy with 'work' to be able to take their calls—they soon got the message. A new client, a new lover—it was time for Max to move on.

The affair with Justine, because of the extremely complex nature of her husband's financial affairs and the huge amount of money potentially involved, had lasted considerably longer than usual, and as yet Justine's husband had not been served with any divorce papers.

'I've got at least two friends who got damn all out of their ex's,' Justine had told Max, showing him her expensive dental work in a very sharp, foxy smile.

'I have no intention of allowing *that* to happen to me. Here is a list of the assets I intend to make a claim on,' she had told Max, handing him an impressively long typed schedule.

They had been lovers for more than two months, and Max had to admit that he was impressed. He doubted that Justine had a single ounce of emotional vulnerability in her entire make-up. She was one of the most sexually demanding women he had ever had, abandoning herself completely and totally to the sexual act and not allowing him to stop until she was completely and utterly satisfied. But once she was, she was immediately and instantly back in control; her mind, her brain, were as sharp and dangerous as an alligator's teeth.

Her husband would be lucky to escape with even half of his fortune intact, Max had decided as he listened to her plans for using her knowledge of his tax affairs to blackmail him into settling and giving her what she wanted.

'I don't intend to file for divorce until after this new deal he's working on has gone through,' she had told Max candidly. 'It's worth almost five hundred million, and I want to make sure I get my share of it.'

'Look. I... I can't talk now,' he heard her saying quickly to him now. 'I'll meet you tomorrow. I'll come round to your place....'

She had rung off before Max could object,

leaving him angrily aware of his sexual frustration and even more importantly, with a sharp sense of unease.

It was going on for two o'clock in the morning, but he felt too restless for sleep. Max's instinct for survival was very acute and very finely tuned. It had had to be. As his grandfather's favourite he had spent his growing years fighting off any potential claims on his position from his siblings and cousins, and as a young adult he had had to strive to maintain that position.

Now that he was married to Madeleine, his grandfather's favour didn't matter in quite the same way. Madeleine's trust funds were worth considerably in excess of his grandfather's assets, but it wasn't just the desire for wealth that drove Max. He had another need that in its way was just as intense, and that need was to stand apart from his peers, to set himself above them, to be envied by them. Friendship, affection, love, none of these interested Max nor mattered to him.

Supremacy, that was what Max craved. Supremacy and the security that came with it. The supremacy of being the best divorce barrister, the best QC, the best head of chambers in the best set of chambers. In Max's opinion, there were two ways to gain those goals. The first was through merit and skill, the second—sometimes the more subtle—was an underhanded method of gaining power, which made its acquisition all the sweeter. To emerge as top dog was important when others had openly derided one's fitness for such a role.

It had amused him recently to bump into Roderick Hamilton, the barrister who had beaten him on a vacancy they had both applied for in his last set of chambers and who had none too subtly crowed his victory over him.

Max had invited Roderick to join him for a drink and over it had encouraged him to talk about himself. He had learned that Roderick had married somebody from the county set, the lower echelons of the upper classes of whose acquaintanceship he had once boasted to Max.

His wife, to judge from the photograph he had shown Max, was the plain horsy type, and no, they had no children as yet...but they were trying.... His dream, it turned out, was to buy himself a small country house.

'But they're so damned expensive, old chap, and Lucinda's wretched horses cost the earth to keep.'

Max had smiled and casually mentioned his own two children. Maddy's grandparents' family seat was also dropped into the conversation along with references to its history and its decor; not too much, just enough to ensure that Roderick realized that he, Max, was living the life-style that the other man so desperately wanted, that he had fathered the children that Roderick so far had not.

And sweetest of all had been when he had given him a lift home in his new Bentley, to coolly refuse the invitation extended for him and Maddy to join Roderick and his wife 'for supper one evening.'

"Fraid no can do, old chap,' Max had told him, giving him his crocodile smile. 'We're pretty fully booked right now.'

Revenge indeed.

Max couldn't really remember when he had first discovered this power he had within himself to hurt others. What he could remember, though, was the sickening sense of anger and fear he had felt when he had once overheard his father and his uncle David talking about him.

He had been about ten at the time and already feeling the effects of Louise and Katie's arrival on his relationship with his parents.

Max had never been the kind of child who liked being held or touched. Even before he could walk he had wriggled out of the reach of adults who would have picked him up and fussed over him, resenting, too, his cousin Olivia's challenging presence in the arena of his life. Olivia, who was always cuddling up to his mother. Olivia, whom his mother seemed to like more than she liked him.

'You've got a fine boy there,' he could remember hearing his uncle David say enviously to his father. 'The old man thinks I'm letting the side down by not giving him a grandson. Mind you, I've got to say, Jon, that you and Jenny don't seem to realize just how lucky you are.

'If Max was mine... Perhaps he should have been mine,' David had said very softly. 'Dad certainly seems to think so. He says that Max is far more like me than you. You know, Jon, sometimes it seems to me that you and Jenny don't like your son very much.'

The two men had moved out of earshot before Max could hear any more. What had his uncle David meant? Why didn't his parents like him?

Deliberately Max had begun to test them,

anxious to discover if what his uncle David had said was the truth.

He asked for a new bicycle and he was told he couldn't have one, but the twins were given new tricycles for their birthday.

Max had 'borrowed' one of them, and when it had 'accidentally' been pushed under the wheels of a delivery van and smashed, he had told his stern, grave-eyed father that he hadn't meant to push the bike, he had just let go of it at the wrong time.

The other tricycle had mysteriously disappeared, and when questioned about it Max had stubbornly refused to say a word.

His sharp eyes began to notice how much more time his mother spent with the twins than she did with him, how much more fuss she made of Olivia.

He told her that he didn't want her to take him to school any more and that he was going to ask his grandfather to tell uncle David to take him. This was despite the fact that more often than not it was Jenny who took Olivia to school, David being far too self-engrossed to consider doing anything so mundane as the school run.

Max began to listen keenly to the way his grandfather compared his two sons, praising

David and speaking contemptuously of Max's own father, Jon. His father, Max had discovered, was a man to be despised and ignored. His grandfather and his uncle David became the pivotal male role models in his life. To cloak his childish fear of his parents' rejection of him, he began to cultivate a protective wall of indifference to any kind of adult emotion, and at the same time he started to learn how to manipulate it to gain his own ends.

In much the same way as he had learned to distrust his parents—his father might speak of chastising him out of love for him, but Max knew better: his father did *not* love him, his father did not like him. Max had heard his uncle David saying so—so Max also learned to distrust and alienate his peers. Better to protect himself by cultivating and inciting their antagonism than to risk the pain of being rejected by them.

Now, twenty odd years down the line, if anyone had suggested to Max that it was out of the seeds of his extreme emotional sensitivity and vulnerability as a child that his adult persona had grown, he would have laughed at them in cynical mockery.

He was as he was; he liked being as he was,

and for those who didn't like it or him—then too bad!

It irritated him that Justine had put him off instead of inviting him to go straight round, as he had expected her to do.

He had been looking forward to the release he knew that having sex with her would have brought him; not just for his sexual desire but also from the anger and sense of ill-usage that being with his family always caused him.

Madeleine, with her pathetic humility and eternal self-sacrificing; his parents with their well-mannered 'niceness'; his cousin Olivia with her smug self-satisfaction; Luke with his arrogant superiority; and Saul, the perfect father and husband. God, but they all irritated the hell out of him. He knew how much they disapproved of him...disliked him.... How sorry they felt for 'poor Maddy,' how they talked about him behind his back, but *he* was the one whose name was beginning to appear with flattering regularity in the society columns; *he* was the one whose income was running very satisfactorily into six figures; *he* was the one who never lacked a willing sexual partner—a *variety* of willing sexual partners. Well, at least not normally!

Tomorrow he would have to punish Justine

a little for tonight, to point out to her that he had virtually walked out on a family gathering just to be able to spend the night with her—it didn't matter that he would have left, anyway; *she* wasn't going to know that. Yes, just a small cooling off on his part; a discreet hint of withdrawal should be more than enough to make her come running, eager to appease him.

He had a meeting in chambers to attend in the afternoon, which would give him an excuse to cut short the time he spent with her, further reinforcing and underlining the stance he intended to take with her. It was their final chambers meeting before they closed down the office for the Christmas and New Year period.

Apart from Justine's proposed divorce, Max had no other major work currently in progress, but that did not concern him too much. Early spring was always a good time for new briefs; the forced conviviality and intimacy of the winter months *en famille* often proved to be the breaking point for a marriage under strain. Also, Justine had already dropped several hints about inviting him to join her when she went skiing. Max had no particular love of either the sport or the cold, but he had to admit that the thought of Aspen and its social life, its socialites, was extremely tempting.

He would tell Maddy that it was business, of course. Getting off the bed, he started to strip off his clothes before heading for the shower.

Like virtually all other male members of his family, Max was a stunningly sexy man. Tall, broad-shouldered, with a naturally well-muscled torso, he shared his male cousins' dark-haired and very masculine good looks. However, in Max they possessed a certain almost magnetic intensity that one of his smitten victims had once described as making her completely spellbound, like standing in the path of a ten-ton lorry, knowing it had the potential to destroy you and yet being so hyped up on the mixture of adrenaline-induced excitement and fear that knowledge produced that you simply couldn't move out of its way.

'It's that look of cold ruthlessness in his eyes,' she had continued, shivering sensually. 'You just *know*, the moment you look at him, that he doesn't give a damn about you or your emotions, but somehow you just can't help yourself.'

There was a sharp ache in Max's body, which he knew from experience could only be alleviated by sex. He smiled grimly to himself as he turned on the shower. He should, after all, have taken Maddy to bed before he left Haslewich. Although he would never have told her so, despite her lack of self-esteem and her plainness, there was about Maddy a very rich vein of sexual warmth and generosity, a femininity, a womanliness that Max knew perfectly well most men would have found extremely alluring, all the more so because her own unawareness of it meant that it would be a secret that only a lover would have access to, just as only one lover would have access to her body.

Maddy had been a virgin when he had first taken her to bed, inexperienced and unknowing, untutored, but her body had surrounded him with a softness, a warmth as instinctive and natural as her protective mother love for her children.

She didn't receive him with that same innocent generosity and warmth any more, of course. On the rare occasions when they did have sex, he could feel how much she resented his ability to arouse her and how hard she strived to resist her physical desire for him. It amused Max to let her. He knew he could make love to her more often and easily turn her resistance into molten liquid acceptance and desire, but what was the point? The last thing he wanted was for Maddy to be sexually demanding or sexually possessive.

He showered himself briskly, then stepped out of the cubicle, smoothing his dark, wet hair back sleekly off his face as he reached for a towel.

If he was going to go to Aspen he would need to buy himself some suitable clothes. He had read that a lot of the Hollywood set went there for the season. He started to smile as he rubbed his body dry and then padded naked across to his bed.

Max was going through some paperwork when he heard the front doorbell ring. On his way to answer it he quickly checked his appearance in the hallway mirror. He was wearing the expensive after-shave that Justine had given him and the Turnbull and Asser shirt, which had been another present from her. The gold cuff links had been a gift from another grateful client. He glanced at his watch, a Rolex that Maddy had given him as a wedding present. Justine was earlier than he'd expected her. Well, she was still going to have to make due reparation for last night and wait a little for her sex. Yes, and plead with him for it, too!

Max opened the door.

'Crighton, may I come in?'

Without waiting for Max's assent, Justine's husband stepped determinedly into the hallway.

Max had met him on only one previous occasion at a dinner party given by a friend of Justine's to which he had been invited.

Although not as tall as Max and certainly a good twenty years older, Robert Burton nevertheless possessed that aura of power and forcefulness common to most entrepreneurially successful men. He might not walk with a deliberate swagger nor verbally boast of his achievements or his wealth, but he most definitely had about him that air that warned other males that he considered himself to be their superior, and as he eyeballed Max with cool aggression as he marched past him, Max was immediately and acutely aware of a relentless dislike he could feel emanating from him.

To give Max his due, though, apart from a small betraying distortion of his pupils and a reactive tensing of his muscles, he gave no other sign that his visitor was not the person he had expected to see, even managing a passably plausible, polished wave of his hand in the direction of his sitting room as he invited,

'Robert. Good to see you, old man. What can I do for you…?'

On the verge of walking into the sitting room, Robert Burton turned round and thoroughly scrutinized Max.

'I'll say this for you, Crighton, you've got nerve,' he commented tersely. 'I'm a very busy man and I don't have time to play verbal games. Justine has told me what's been going on and…'

'Ah. Good.' Max cut in on him smoothly. 'I did counsel her to tell you that she wanted a divorce. These things are always better when the two parties concerned discuss them as adults, and—'

'Better for the bank balances of their lawyers, yes,' Robert Burton cut him off acidly, 'but let's not get side-tracked. It isn't your *professional* relationship with my wife I'm here to discuss.' He paused meaningfully. 'I do know, like I said, what's been going on. A friend tipped me off. Apparently you've got quite a reputation for bedding your female clients.…'

Max gave a small shrug. 'When a marriage is breaking down, people become emotionally—'

'Vulnerable,' Robert Burton supplied darkly before Max could finish. 'But it's hardly professional behaviour to use that vulnerability against them, is it, and I should have thought that a man in your position would have to be very careful about guarding his professional reputation. After all, that's really what a barrister has to sell, isn't it? His *reputation* is his product. Unless, of course, you've decided that it's more financially profitable for you to trade on your reputation in the bedroom rather than in the courtroom. Rumour does have it, of course, that it wasn't so much your *legal* skills or qualifications that got you into your chambers in the first place. Does your wife *know* that you regularly bed your female clients?'

'It's a very pleasant bonus to my work,' Max acknowledged with a taunting smile and a small shrug, 'and I can't deny that it is a perk that I do find very enjoyable...after all, what normal heterosexual man would not?'

It was one of Max's greatest assets that he possessed a remarkable gift for turning the tables on his opponents and sending back the arrows they fired at him with devastating speed and accuracy, and he could see from the betraying narrowing of Robert Burton's eyes and the hard edge of colour seeping up under his skin that he had succeeded in getting him off guard.

'In your shoes, I'd be rather careful about what I admit to,' he warned Max. 'I doubt very much *you'd* enjoy being on the other side of a lawsuit....'

'No, I wouldn't,' Max agreed, and added urbanely, 'but then I doubt that very many men would like to stand up in court and admit that their wives preferred *me* as a lover. Which reminds me, since I am acting for your wife in the subject of her divorce, I really should advise you that it is quite unethical for you to approach me....'

'There isn't going to be a divorce.'

Max stared at him in disbelief.

'Justine and I have had a little talk,' Robert Burton told him with heavy irony, 'and we've decided that we're going to give our marriage a second chance. I think that what Justine really needs is to be a mother. A woman needs a child, children, and they do say, don't they, that the conception and birth of a child cement a couple more closely together than anything else. You've got children, haven't you?'

He gave Max a challenging look.

'Divorce can be an extremely expensive and messy business, and as Justine now agrees, it makes sense for the two of us to stay together. Oh, and by the way, there's no point in you trying to get in touch with her. She flew out to New York on Concorde this morning.

'I hope I've made myself understood,' he told Max as he turned round and opened the door, 'but then, I know you'll have got my drift, won't you, Crighton.'

As Max automatically followed him to the front door, the older man continued with obvious enjoyment, 'Oh, and by the way, perhaps I'd better warn you, I've had a word with the senior partner in your chambers, alerting him to certain facts I felt he ought to know. After all, a chambers like yours trades on its reputation, and anything that might damage that reputation has to be very swiftly and mercilessly dealt with, doesn't it...rather like anything that might threaten a man's marriage or his financial status.

'It's the mark of an intelligent man, I believe, to act quickly and decisively to protect what he values.'

Max said nothing. He didn't need to. He knew exactly what Robert Burton was saying to him. He had somehow or other persuaded Justine not to go ahead with her divorce because he had no intention of allowing her to profit financially from her marriage to him. Simpler and far more financially expeditious to remain married to her. But it was his remark about his *own* professional status that had alarmed Max the most, especially that comment he had made about speaking with the head of his chambers.

Although technically Max was his own boss and none of the other members had any kind of jurisdiction over his actions or his morals—in practice... Well, he would soon find out, since no doubt the subject would be raised at this afternoon's meeting, if it was going to be raised.

'Hell and damnation,' he muttered grimly as he consigned Justine to the past and the long list of his ex-lovers an hour later as he left his mews house *en route* to the old-fashioned set of chambers in the Inns of Court where the high status of their address more than compensated for the cramped office that Max occupied.

The senior partner's office was, quite naturally, the most luxurious: large, elegantly furnished, reeking of that unmistakable indefinable aura of old money, class and power, and Max could never walk into it without coveting it and everything that went with it. Already he had promised himself that one day it *would* be his.

3

‘Ah, Max, there you are....’

As Harold Cavendish, the senior partner, gave him his benign smile and waved him into a chair, Max stiffened warily when he realized that he was the last to join the meeting.

As the meeting followed its normal and predictable course, Max allowed himself to relax a little and mentally began to run over in his mind who would make the most suitable replacement in his bed.

When the meeting was over, Max got up to leave, then froze as the senior partner placed a restraining hand on his arm and told him quietly, ‘Er, no, Max. I’d like *you* to stay. There’s something we need to discuss.’

Harold Cavendish waited until the others had gone before beginning to speak. Max might not be very popular in chambers and Madeleine’s father might have had to put pressure on them to take Max on, but there was no doubt whatsoever about the effect he, and his brand of dark, smooth good looks, had on their female clientele. It wasn't just his own business that Max had increased while he had been with them, as Harold himself was keenly aware.

Max always reminded him of a particular breed of German dog, all sleek good looks and power on the outside, but inwardly possessed of an unreliably vicious streak that, when provoked, could be extremely dangerous. His wife had once told him wryly that it was the thought of harnessing and controlling all the sexual power and uncertainty that was Max that made women behave so foolishly over him.

'It's the knowledge that they're never quite totally in control of him that is so alluring,' she had told him. 'Max represents the dark and dangerously exciting side of sexual attraction.'

'Chap's a bounder,' he had objected gruffly. 'Look at the way he treats poor Madeleine.'

'Yes, I know,' his wife had agreed ruefully, 'and I'm afraid that that just makes him all the more potently alluring.'

Harold had shaken his head, not really understanding what she meant, and he was no closer to understanding now just why so many pretty women were foolish enough to get involved with Max.

Harold waited until Max had closed the door before telling him uncomfortably, 'Had a chat with Robert Burton. He, er...seemed to think there could be something unprofessional going on between you and his wife....'

Max said nothing.

'He's a very powerful man and we handle a lot of his friends' and contacts' work.'

Max still said nothing, and Harold found himself fighting against a sense of irritation with him that he wasn't doing the decent thing and making things easier for him.

'Fact is, old chap, that to put it bluntly, Burton isn't too happy about the way...'

'His wife's solicitor was instructing me with regard to her divorce,' Max interrupted him coolly. 'If Robert Burton chooses to misinterpret that...relationship...then...'

'Well, yes. Yes, of course,' Harold agreed hurriedly. 'But one has to think not just of one's own reputation, you know, but the reputation of chambers as a whole as well, and if it gets around that...well...if Burton should get it into his head to put the word about... The fact is, Max, that we've discussed the subject among ourselves and Jeremy tells us that you've no major work on at the moment, so we think…that is, we feel…it might be a good idea for you to take some extended leave, say a month or so…just until this unpleasantness blows over, and then…'

Max stared at him in disbelief.

'You're barring me from chambers,' he accused. 'You *can't* do that.'

'No. No…of course not,' Harold agreed hurriedly, 'no such thing…no such thing at all. Fact is, old chap, that all of us need to take a decent break from time to time, and young Maddy would probably appreciate the chance to see a bit more of you….'

Max looked coldly at him. It was on the tip of his tongue to tell him that he didn't give a damn about what Maddy would appreciate, but he managed to restrain himself.

Robert Burton had certainly managed to put the wind up Harold, he acknowledged bitterly. Pompous old bastard, who was he to tell Max what he could and couldn't do. Take some extended leave… They couldn't *make* him, of course, no, no way could they do that, but they *could* make life pretty unpleasant for him if he refused, Max admitted angrily. If they chose to do so, they could adopt tactics that ultimately could force him out of chambers, and once that became public knowledge, his chances of continuing to receive not just the fat briefs he had grown accustomed to getting, but also the status and accolades that went hand in hand with being a member of such a prestigious set of chambers, would diminish abruptly. There was no way, after the work he had put in, the sacrifices he had made to get where he was, that Max was *ever* going to allow himself to be downgraded or side-tracked to somewhere second rate.

As he listened to Harold's pompous meanderings, he told himself fiercely that when the day came when *he* took over as head of chambers, he would make *everyone* involved in this pay for what they were doing to him, especially that creep Jeremy Standish, the clerk-cum-office manager, whom Max knew perfectly well neither liked nor approved of him.

'So you can see, I'm sure, what I mean—' Harold was continuing to waffle uncomfortably '—and like I said, Maddy, I am sure, will...'

Max had had enough, and giving an impatient shrug, he stood up.

'A month...' Max began, but Harold, suddenly becoming courageous and mindful of his fellow members' urgings and the responsibility he owed them, insisted firmly, 'Two months, Max. That will give plenty of time for any potential unpleasantness to die down....'

Two months... Max gave him a hard stare, tempted to argue but sharply aware of how it would make him look if he lost.

God, but Justine had truly mucked this up, he fumed half an hour later back in his own small office. And if he had her here right now...he'd... Two *months...* Just what the hell was he going to do?

As he stared angrily out of his office window, there was a brief rap on the door and Jeremy Standish walked in.

'Maddy was on the phone while you were with Harold,' he told Max. 'She asked me to remind you that it's Leo's nativity play tomorrow afternoon and that your grandfather will be going....'

As Jeremy saw the murderous expression darkening Max's eyes he couldn't resist adding, mock innocently, 'I'm sure Maddy will be delighted when she knows that you're going to have a couple of months off. You must miss her and the children so much with them living in the country and you living in town....'

Leo's flaming nativity play, that was *all* he needed, but of course, if he didn't go, his

grandfather was bound to start asking awkward questions. Max still hadn't repaid the
loan he had cadged off him when he and
Maddy had got married—and, in fact, he had
no intention of repaying it. Max had witnessed
his grandfather's growing involvement with
his own son and already sensed that if he
wasn't careful, Leo might begin to usurp his
own so-far-unchallenged position as his
grandfather's favourite, and there was no way
Max was going to allow that to happen. He
was already beginning to think it had been a
mistake to allow Maddy to have so much contact with his grandfather and thus easy access
to his ear. Not that he had any fear that his
grandfather would pay any attention to anything she might choose to say. His grandfather
despised women and was an old-fashioned
chauvinist.

Two flaming months and not even the
chance of a fortnight or so in Aspen now to alleviate it. And of course, he would have to tell
Maddy, whether he wanted to or not. The last
thing he wanted was for her to ring the chambers and find out that he wasn't there—and
why. And, in fact, he would have to warn her
not to say anything to her parents, either. With
any luck he could keep the whole thing pretty

quiet. As his brain began to swing into action, Max started to make plans.

Perhaps it might be as well to remind Harold that any hint of his enforced 'holiday' getting out would reflect just as dangerously on the reputation of the rest of the partners as it would on him. Max might be under no illusion that Robert Burton's real intention in putting pressure on Harold was to humiliate *him*, but it would do no harm to overlook that and to point out that on the surface at least, he totally believed that Harold was acting simply out of concern for the chambers as a whole, and since he had no option but to accept the situation, what he needed to do now was to make everyone else believe that taking such a period of leave was his *own* choice. Perhaps he could even earn a few 'brownie' points with his grandfather and Maddy's family by making out that it *was* his wife and children that had motivated him, and living in Haslewich at his grandfather's expense would certainly save him money. And of course, he still had women friends in Chester with whom he could alleviate his undoubted boredom.

By the time he had cleared his desk, Max had almost managed to persuade himself that two months' leave was exactly what he wanted...almost...

'The bed's quite definitely William and Mary, and when I told him what it was really worth...' Guy Cooke broke off from his description of the furniture he had been asked to value to look keenly at his ex-business partner and to ask gently, 'Jenny, what is it, what's wrong? You haven't heard a word of what I've just said.'

'Oh, Guy, I'm sorry,' Jenny apologized immediately, giving him a small smile. 'There's nothing really wrong, it's just...'

'Jenny, I *know* when you're happy—and when you're not,' Guy reminded her dryly.

Jenny shook her head and admitted, 'It's Jack, our nephew. His school report this time is, well, not very good at all, and the headmaster has asked to see Jon about him.'

'What's the problem, do you know?' Guy asked her sympathetically.

'Well, we're not sure, but we think it could possibly be because of David. You know that Jack and Joss bunked off school to go and look for Jack's father....'

'Mmm... Chrissie mentioned it,' Guy acknowledged, referring to his wife, who was in a rather roundabout way, a member of the Crighton family.

'Both Jon and I have talked to Jack, and so has Olivia, but he seems to have this bee in his bonnet at the moment about David,' Jenny told him. 'It's perfectly natural that he should, of course; after all, unlike Olivia, he was still really very much a child when David disappeared and he couldn't totally take in the situation. But what's more worrying is that Louise seems to think that Jack is actually blaming himself in some way for David's disappearance.'

'Blaming himself...' Guy gave her a sharp look. 'Why on earth should he do that?'

Jenny shook her head. 'I don't know. We've both tried to talk to him about it, but he's at that age...' She gave a small sigh. 'We've all always been so close, and we thought he was happy living with us, but now we're both beginning to question whether or not we did the right thing and whether he might ultimately have been happier going to Brighton with Tania.'

'I shouldn't have any concerns about that,' Guy interrupted her firmly. '*I* certainly know who I'd prefer.'

Jenny gave him a wan smile. 'Tania *is* his

mother,' she reminded him. 'Even if Olivia says that in her opinion Jack has been far better off with us.'

'Olivia should know, she *is* Jack's sister.'

'Yes, I know, and we've been through the whole history of David's disappearance with Jack and explained to him about the…the problems that had arisen here with the business.'

'It can't have been easy for you,' Guy commented. 'I can still remember just what you and Jon went through at the time.'

'It was a shock, especially for Jon when he found out that his twin had been defrauding one of their clients. I know it's a dreadful thing to say, but if that client hadn't died when she did and Ruth hadn't been able to refund the money David had "borrowed" from her estate, I don't know what would have happened.

'Olivia, Jon and I have explained to Jack just what the situation was. While, legally, his father is free to return to this country if he should want to do so, there could be no question of him ever being able to practise in the business.

'I know it's an issue that we would have had to deal with at one stage, but I just wish that it hadn't manifested itself right now when Jack is working towards his A levels.'

'Mmm... I know that Joss is planning on going up to Oxford, but what is Jack hoping to do?'

'We had talked and thought he wanted to follow Jon into the practice. There's a very close bond between them, but just recently... I know all teenagers go through a turbulent period, but it seems lately that Jack really resents us both, but particularly Jon. His behaviour is hurting Jon, although he never says anything.'

'Mmm... I expect he's concerned that he might be rearing a second Max, although...' He stopped when he saw Jenny's expression and asked, '*Is* that what Jon thinks, Jen?'

'Not exactly, but he has said recently that he wonders if he's adequate father material. He blames himself for the fact that Max is as he is. He always has done, and I feel the same way— that we both failed him. We can't help wondering if there was *something* we could have done, something we neglected to do, some sign we missed or some...' She paused and shook her head. 'Jack is nowhere near being like Max, of course, but Jon is beginning to feel that somehow or other he must have failed him—Jack's become so abstracted, so withdrawn just recently, and of course you always worry that...about...'

'Drugs,' Guy supplied shrewdly for her.

'Well, one reads such things,' Jenny admitted, 'and although we're only a relatively quiet small country town, we're not that far from Manchester or…'

'I know what you're saying,' Guy agreed. Then he added quietly, 'I could put a few feelers out for you if you want me to….'

Guy's family, the Cookes, were involved in every aspect of Haslewich life, including some which were not strictly ethical or honourable.

There was a local story that the Cookes had once included in their number a member of the Gipsy band that had travelled through the area, and it was from this alliance that the family had inherited their strikingly dark tangled curls and good looks.

Jenny hesitated. The headmaster had recently alerted all the parents at the boys' school to the fact that drugs were being sold outside the school gates, despite the police's attempts to put a stop to it. She had no reason to suspect that either Joss or Jack were taking them, and she was pretty sure that Jack's recent change in behaviour and attitude was because of his confused emotions about his father.

'I wouldn't want Jack to think that we didn't

trust him,' she told Guy slowly. 'Jon's worried that Jack might feel that, as our nephew, he comes second place to Joss, which isn't the case at all. We love them both very dearly, although of course in different ways, and because Jon was himself always aware that in his father's eyes he could never compare to David, Jon is determined that Jack won't suffer in the way that he did.'

'It's a very difficult situation,' Guy acknowledged.

'Jon hates having to take anyone to task,' Jenny told him ruefully, 'but it is *so* important that Jack works hard and gets good grades when he sits his A's.'

'I saw Max driving into town earlier,' Guy told her.

Jenny forced a small smile.

'Oh, did you? Good. Maddy *will* be pleased. She was afraid that he might miss Leo's first performance in the play school Christmas play,' she told him with a smile.

She wasn't smiling ten minutes later, however, as she hurried back to her car, pitting her body against the cold of the sharp east wind. Maddy had confided in her only a few days ago that she was concerned about Leo's growing antagonism towards his father.

'Gramps thinks I'm overcoddling Leo, but I've tried to explain to him that it's because he doesn't see very much of Max and Max isn't...Max doesn't...'

Maddy's voice had trailed off, but she hadn't needed to explain. Jenny knew exactly what her eldest son was and what he wasn't. Joss spent more time with, and was far closer, to his small nephew than his father, and Jon, too, made sure that he gave his small grandson as much attention as he could.

Maddy wasn't there when Max arrived at Queensmead. She had gone out to do some shopping, taking both children with her. The rich scent of the greenery and fruit she had used to make the Christmas garlands that decorated the hallway and stairs, as well as the warmth of their seasonal colours against the mellow patina of the panelling, might have caused another man to stop and savour not just the seasonal spirit they evoked but also the quiet skill of the woman who had made them, but Max gave his wife's handiwork no more than a brief, cursory frown as he headed for the stairs. Before he could climb them, his grandfather's study door opened and the older man limped painfully into the hallway, his austere expression giving way to a warm smile as he saw his favourite grandchild.

'Max,' he exclaimed eagerly. 'You're back. Come and have a drink with me.'

Max watched the way his grandfather's hand trembled as he poured them both a Scotch. He was aging rapidly, his once-tall, ramrod-straight frame now spare and bent, his walk betraying the wariness of someone who had lost the security of being able to depend on his own physical strength.

'Maddy's gone out—shopping,' he told Max. 'Why on earth do women need to make such a fuss about Christmas? You'd think Maddy was going to be feeding an army from the way she's been carrying on. She hasn't even had time to change my library books for me this week,' he added with the petulant selfishness of the elderly. 'And she forgot to make my nightcap last night.

'Come over here,' he instructed Max abruptly. 'There's something I want to show you.'

Frowning, Max followed him, watching as he struggled with the lock on the drawer of his desk before removing a card, which he thrust in front of Max.

'It's from David,' he told Max tersely. 'It came yesterday. It's post-marked Jamaica...'

'Jamaica...' Max's frown deepened. The last they had heard of David was that he was somewhere in Spain, but that had been more than a year ago, and despite all his own father's attempts to do so, he had not been able to trace the whereabouts of his twin brother.

'I knew he wasn't in Spain, told Jon so, too, but he wouldn't listen,' he could hear his grandfather complaining.

'It's time he came home, Max. I want him home. This is where his place is. This is where he would be if that damned woman hadn't driven him away.'

It was no secret to Max that his grandfather blamed Tania, nicknamed Tiggy, David's estranged wife, for his son's disappearance, claiming to anyone who would listen that it had been Tania's unstable temperament and the eating disorder she suffered from, along with her dangerous mood swings and her extravagant life-style, that had prompted David's near fatal heart attack and then caused him to disappear.

Max frowned as he studied the postcard his grandfather had handed him, not really paying much attention to what the older man was saying. After all, he had heard it all before, and if it had not been second nature to him to keep on his grandfather's good side, he would have lost no time in cynically pointing out that there were far easier ways of removing an unwanted wife from one's life than to flee the country.

Even so, he couldn't resist saying jibingly, 'Well, Uncle David has nothing to fear from Tiggy now that she's got a new man in her life.'

'Exactly,' his grandfather pounced. 'I want David found, Max. I want him found and I want him to come home before…' He stopped, wincing as he started to massage his aching hip.

'Dad's already made several attempts to trace him,' Max pointed out uninterestedly, 'and…'

'Using detective agencies. Pah…useless… Jon should fly out to Jamaica himself, and if he had any real brotherly love for David… But then, of course, he's always been jealous of David and I…

'I'd go myself if it wasn't for this damned hip,' he told Max angrily. 'Damned if I wouldn't. I know David…he's my son…my flesh…my blood.…'

Listening to him, Max forbore to point out

that so was his own father, but then Ben most
certainly did not know Jon, and what he knew
of David was only what he had allowed himself to know…what he wanted to believe David to be rather than what he actually was.

Jamaica… Max dropped the card onto the
table, where it lay face up, white sands gleaming under an impossibly blue sky and an even
bluer sea… Jamaica…

His body suddenly stiffened.

'If you really want someone to go and look
for Uncle David, I suppose I could fly out there
and do a bit of checking up, look around…' he
began, pseudo-hesitantly.

'You!'

The delight in the old man's voice might
have touched the heart of another man, but
Max refused to allow anything, anyone, to
touch his, and he simply, instead, gave him a
calculated smile.

'But how can you?' his grandfather protested shakily. 'Your work…'

Max shrugged carelessly.

'As it happens, things are pretty slack at the
moment, and I had been thinking of taking a
few weeks' leave. I may as well spend some of
it in Jamaica as here under Maddy's feet….'

'You mean you *really* would go, Max?'

Max watched dispassionately as his grandfather fought to control his emotions, coming over to him and grasping his shoulders as he blinked rapidly and told him huskily, 'I *knew* I could rely on *you*, Max. You're your uncle David all over again. He *wants* to come home, I know he does. Once he knows that that unhinged woman isn't going to make a nuisance of herself... My God, just let her try. She's already caused enough damage. When I think...'

'It's going to be an expensive trip,' Max warned him, ignoring his comments about Tiggy. 'And...'

'That doesn't matter,' his grandfather quickly assured him.

'Jamaica's a fair-sized island, and there's no saying just whereabouts David might be,' Max pointed out—or even if he would still be there, Max acknowledged, but he kept that thought to himself. A few weeks in Jamaica at his grandfather's expense was exactly what he needed right now. Smiling to himself, he mentally thanked Harold. Who knew, he might even be able to pick up some potential new clients while he was out there.

Finding David was, of course, another matter entirely and not one he was inclined to give any serious thought to. After all, if his uncle genuinely wanted to return home, there was absolutely nothing to stop him from doing so.

Silently he studied his grandfather. Did he really honestly believe what he was saying; that the *only* reason David had left—*disappeared*—was because his marriage had broken down? Well, if so, it was no business of his to enlighten him, but the old man really must be losing his grip.

'Max, you don't *know* how much this means to me, my boy,' he heard Ben telling him gruffly. 'I should have *known* I could rely on *you*. Your father...' He stopped and shook his head. 'It's always been a disappointment to me that Jon doesn't...that he isn't...he doesn't know how *lucky* he's been to *have* a brother like David,' he finished heavily. 'I lost my twin brother...'

Max looked impatiently at his watch.

'Look, Gramps,' he interrupted, cutting across the old man's all-too-familiar reminiscences, 'if I'm going to Jamaica, I should make a few phone calls. It's not going to be easy getting a flight to the Caribbean at such short notice at this time of the year. Half of Belgravia and Sloane Square will be flying out there on the first flights out of Heathrow after the New

Year, and then I'll have to get myself sorted out with a hotel.'

Given the choice, Max would have infinitely preferred to ignore the Christmas and New Year celebrations at Haslewich completely, of course, and taken the first flight he could to the Caribbean, but he knew that not even Maddy would wear that one.

'Yes. Yes, of course,' his grandfather agreed.

'And… I think we should keep this thing just between the two of us for now,' Max told his grandfather smoothly. 'As you've said, Dad doesn't seem to be too keen on having David home and…'

'Yes. Yes, you're right,' his grandfather conceded.

Max smiled confidently at him. The old boy was amazingly easy to manipulate once you knew which buttons to press. The one marked 'David' was *always* a dead cert. Contemptuously, Max wondered why his own father didn't press it a little bit more often. There was no way that he, Max, would allow the old man to patronize him and put him down, comparing him unfavourably to others the way Ben did with Jon. No way at all, and it irritated Max that Jon *should* do so. After all, his father could be stiff-necked and stubborn enough

when it suited him, and Max already knew
that the news that he was going to Jamaica to
look for David would not be received well in
his parents' household—for a variety of reasons.

The last thing his father would want was for
David to be found and encouraged to come
home. Not because, as Ben seemed so delud-
edly to believe, Jon was jealous of his twin.
Max knew that Jon wouldn't welcome the
complications and hassles that would arise
with having David and all the potential problems surrounding his fraudulent behaviour
back on his doorstep.

In his father's shoes, Max knew that *he*
would have lost no time at all in informing Ben
of just what his precious son had done. But
Jon, to Max's disgust, had gone to inordinate
lengths to protect his father from discovering
the truth about his favourite.

David *wouldn't* come back to Haslewich, of
course, and Max knew full well that it was extremely unlikely that he would even be able to
find him—not that he intended to try very
hard! A leisurely month or so relaxing in the
sun was more the kind of thing he had in
mind. He would pay some local agency to

make a few general inquiries, of course, just to keep Gramps happy.

He would wait until after Christmas to break the news to Maddy that he was going to Jamaica. That way, there was no risk of him coming under family pressure or disapproval and no risk either of his father or anyone else bending Ben's ear to try to make him change his mind.

'Oh, Maddy, he looks so sweet.'

Maddy turned to give Jenny a rueful, watery smile before they both turned back towards the stage where Leo was giving his first public performance in the play school nativity play as one of the 'shepherds.'

The sturdy house-tame lamb, born late in the year and abandoned by her mother to be hand-reared in the kitchen of a local farm, decided that it was time she had some attention and playfully butted Leo.

Manfully he grabbed hold of her collar, commanding, with the same intonation he had heard his aunt Olivia using to the pretty golden retriever puppy that was the latest addition to her household, 'Sit...'

Even Ben, seated at the other side of Jenny, had given an appreciative bark of laughter, and as Jenny told Maddy mirthfully later when the audience had stopped laughing, Leo had most definitely stolen the show.

Max, on Maddy's other side, gave his son a dispassionate, contemptuous look. The child irritated him. Surely he realized that sheep did not 'sit.'

Leo was beginning to annoy Max. The boy had actually dared to stand in the doorway to Max and Maddy's bedroom the last time Max had come home, glaring belligerently at him and refusing to allow Max to enter.

'Make him move,' he had told Maddy softly, without breaking eye contact with Leo, 'because if *you* don't...'

When the parents went backstage to collect their offspring, it was Jon whom Leo ran excitedly to once the play was over, flinging himself into his grandfather's arms and then burrowing his face against Jon's neck as Jon swung him up off the floor.

There was something about one's grandchildren that made them so infinitely special and precious, Jon acknowledged as he kissed the little boy and ruffled his hair.

Jon had no way of explaining to himself why it was so easy for him to love Leo, when it had been so hard for him to love Max. Leo was

Max's son; you couldn't look at him without knowing that. Physically he looked exactly as Max had looked at the same age, but temperamentally, emotionally...

It made Jon's heart ache with compassion for Leo and anger against Max, to see the way Max treated his son. It was no wonder that Leo now refused to go near him. Maddy was very loyal and never criticized Max, but Jon had seen the pain in her eyes as she watched Max ignoring Leo, turning his back on him and deliberately showing the child how little he cared about him.

Initially, when Leo had been born, Jon had forced himself to stand back, to remind himself that he was Leo's grandfather and not his father, but then he had watched Joss playing with him, seen the bond growing between uncle and child, seen the way Max was threatening to damage his son emotionally by rejecting him, and he had made himself a vow that for as long as Leo needed him in his life, he was going to be there for him.

Jon knew already, without knowing how he knew, that it would be Leo who one day would take his place in the family business, that Leo, like him, would be a Crighton who wanted to stay close to the place that had bred him, that Leo would be *his* kind of Crighton, just as Jack had also been showing signs of wanting to come into the family firm.

Jack... Jon started to frown slightly as he thought about his nephew. He had believed that Jack was happy with them, that he had accepted his father's disappearance, but these last few months... Jack's headmaster had warned them that if Jack's work did not improve, there was no way he was going to get the A level grades he needed to go on to university. Jon had discussed the subject with Jack, but far from being concerned, Jack had merely told him truculently that he didn't care—that he'd changed his mind, that he didn't *want* to be a solicitor after all.

'Then what do you want to be?' Jon had asked him exasperatedly. It would be some years down the line before Jack could possibly join the family practice so could not relieve the pressure both he and Olivia were experiencing currently with so many new cases coming into the Haslewich office. Olivia had joined Jon a few years before and now they were considering taking on a third partner because they were both having to work a lot of extra hours. But that particular route, bringing in someone from outside the family, hadn't appealed to either of them. And as if work wasn't enough of a worry, Jon and Jenny were both concerned about Maddy and how she and the two children were being affected by the fact that Max spent so little time with them.

'She's such a lovely girl. She deserves so much better,' Jenny had protested the last time they had discussed their son's marriage. 'I feel so helpless to do anything, though. Every time I try to raise the subject, she fobs me off. She's happy here in Haslewich, she says she likes looking after Gramps. She loves Queensmead, and there's no doubt that she's turned it into a proper home, but she's living the kind of life that's more suited to some Victorian great-aunt than a young woman, and I'm afraid... It's so unfair, Jon, she's got such a lot to give. I *know* it's a dreadful thing to say, but I really wish that she could meet someone else, someone who would value her and love her....'

That was as close as either of them had come to acknowledging that Max did not love his wife, but then, why discuss something that was so painfully obvious to everyone who witnessed it.

If Maddy did ever decide to leave Max and make a new life for herself somewhere else, he would lose the special closeness he had with

Leo, Jon acknowledged, and he would hate that.

'I love you, Jon,' Leo whispered tremulously to him now, as though he had picked up on his grandfather's thoughts.

Jon hugged him. Just very occasionally, when he was feeling especially emotional, Leo referred to him as 'Jon.' The rest of the time he called him Grampy.

On the other side of the room, where he had been deliberately flirting with the nursery class's pretty young teacher, Max suddenly frowned as he watched the interplay between his son and his father.

What was Jon doing holding Leo like that, as though he was *his* child, and Leo, what was *Leo* doing looking at Jon as though... Ignoring the pretty teacher's mock shy response to his sexual innuendo, Max strode across the room, firmly taking hold of Leo and swinging him down to the floor as he commanded curtly, 'Leo, stop acting like a baby.'

The combination of being wrenched away from Jon and the frightening presence of his father caused Leo to tense and scream protestingly in Max's hold.

'Go away, I don't like you,' he told Max

loudly, causing one or two nearby parents to stare.

Max looked coldly at his son. *No one* was allowed to tell Max that they didn't like him.

'It's time Leo went home,' Max instructed Maddy coldly over his shoulder. 'He's behaving badly.'

Maddy shook her head urgently at Leo. There was to be a celebration tea for the children served in the hall just as soon as she and the other hard-working helpers had got everything ready, and Maddy knew how much Leo had been looking forward to this treat. He had talked of it for days, and only yesterday he and Maddy had made special little cakes for the party while he practised the three short sentences he had to say in the play.

Maddy's heart ached for him as she saw the expression in his eyes as he watched his father.

Another mother, another *woman*, would no doubt have coaxed and protested 'Max... no...you know how much he's been looking forward to the party,' but Maddy knew that anything she might try to say or do to alleviate the situation would only make things worse. She could see from Max's expression that there was no way he was going to back down, and she knew, too, that there was something

in Max that would give him pleasure in denying his child his enjoyment. She had no idea
what it was that had warped Max's character
so badly and made him the man he was, nor,
she suspected, did anyone else. He could not
have had better or more loving parents...but
Jenny had intimated to her that Max had always been a difficult child...some children
were.

'Take him away, Maddy,' Max reiterated acidly.

Heavy-hearted, Maddy started to reach for
her son, but before she could take him, Joss
suddenly appeared, coming between her and
Max, sweeping Leo up into his arms and toss-
ing him playfully in the air before calmly
walking away with him still in his arms, apparently unaware of the fact that Max was
commanding him to stop.

'Oh, Max, how lovely to see you. Maddy
wasn't sure you were going to make it....'

As she heard the purring voice of the town's
most predatory divorcée, Maddy heaved a
thankful sigh of relief, quickly making her
own escape. Barbara would, no doubt, keep
Max engaged in conversation for as long as she
could.

In the room that had been set on one side for the party, Joss was playing with Leo.

Between them, Joss and Jon were supplying Leo with all the right kind of male role modelling any mother could want for her son, all the right kind of male values, so why, why, did she yearn for Max to pick up his son and look at him with that same look of love and pride she could see in Jon's eyes when he held his grandson?

'Max will never be able to love anyone else until he learns to love and accept himself,' Ruth had once told her, but for once Maddy had felt that the wise family matriarch had been wrong. Max *did* love himself. Max would always love *himself*—and never love any one else?

Quickly, Maddy went and picked up Emma, holding her tightly in her arms while she watched Leo playing with two of his small classmates.

Ten minutes later, when she walked back into the other room, Max had gone, and so, too, had Barbara Severn.

4

![arrow decoration]

Max waited until the rest of the family had dispersed after the Christmas celebrations before breaking the news to Maddy of his impending trip to Jamaica.

'You're doing what? But your father has tried to find David.'

She paused in the act of picking up the children's discarded toys to push her hair out of her eyes and stare slightly myopically at Max. She had put her glasses down somewhere and now she couldn't find them, and without them it was hard for her to read Max's expression properly.

'Correction,' Max informed her laconically. 'What my father has done is to put in motion some half-hearted inquiries via a couple of low-key investigation companies. What Gramps wants *me* to do is to fly out to Jamaica to do some rather more muscular investigating.'

'But Jamaica,' Maddy protested. 'I thought

David was supposed to be in Spain. What makes Gramps think that he's in Jamaica?'

'David sent him a card. He showed it to me and it's in David's handwriting, all right.'

'But I don't understand,' Maddy protested. 'You're always saying how busy you are, how impossible it is for you to take time off....'

'It's January. January can sometimes be relatively quiet, and it just so happens that I don't have any ongoing cases in hand. What are you trying to say, Mad?' he taunted her softly.

'Surely you don't think that I'm *deliberately* avoiding spending time with *you*...not when you're *such* a wonderful, stimulating and exciting...partner....'

Maddy's face became suffused with uncomfortable colour. She didn't need Max underlining for her just how dull and boring he found her.

'Does your...does your father know?' she asked him huskily.

'Not so far as I know. Why should he? It isn't really any of his business, is it?' he asked her coolly. 'Although no doubt it soon will be. *You* won't be losing any time running to my parents to tell them, will you, Maddy?'

'David is your father's brother,' Maddy reminded him quietly, swallowing hard on the pain lodging in her throat. 'Your father is also concerned about the effect David's absence is having on Gramps...and on Jack, too.'

'So, no doubt he'll be delighted to hear that I'm going to try and find our missing black sheep, won't he,' Max mocked her.

'Grow up, Maddy,' he advised her grimly. 'If you're looking to my parents to put a veto on my going, you're wasting your time. They don't have any more power to control my life than you do.'

'If that's true, then why have you waited until now to mention the fact that you're going?' Maddy responded with unaccustomed sharpness.

Max gave a slow, cruel smile.

'Oh, very good, very quick... I didn't say anything, my dear wife, because Gramps is bankrolling the trip and I didn't want my father getting any ideas about trying to persuade him to change his mind. Now it's too late, my flight is booked and so is the hotel.'

'Oh, Max,' Maddy whispered, closing her eyes against the tears she could feel burning the back of her lids. She didn't know what hurt her most, Max's obvious contempt for her or the fact that he could so callously and so openly admit to using his grandfather's desperate wish to see his son again to fund what both she and Max knew was going to be an abortive trip. She doubted that Max would make even the smallest attempt to find David.

'Oh, Max,' she whispered again under her breath as she heard him leaving the room.

Angrily Jack skimmed flat stones across the dull surface of Queensmead's small lake, gritting his teeth against hot, bitter tears. He was a boy…a man almost…and men didn't cry, not even when…

He had come over to Queensmead to see Maddy, but she had been out when he had arrived, and as he walked past his grandfather's library he had noticed that the door was open and that the old man was lying asleep in his chair.

With no particular purpose in mind he had walked into the room. While he wasn't afraid of his grandfather, Jack couldn't honestly say that he particularly liked him.

'He's still hurting because of Uncle David,' Joss had once told him wisely when Jack had complained that their grandfather never seemed to have much time for them. 'He's afraid of letting himself love us….'

'He loves Max,' Jack had pointed out.

'He loves Max because Max is the nearest thing he's got to David, and he loves David because David is the first-born of his twin sons, like the brother he himself lost....'

'What did you think of my father?' Jack had asked his cousin quietly.

Joss hadn't answered him for a while, and when he had, he hadn't been quite able to look Jack in the eyes as he told him, 'I can't remember all that much about him. He was always working and...'

'I'll bet you're glad that he wasn't *your* father, aren't you?' Jack had demanded bitterly, abandoning the pretence of wanting or needing to know Joss's opinion.

'He's my uncle,' Joss had reminded Jack quietly, trying to pretend not to understand. 'I share his blood, his genes, almost as much as you do, Jack. It's the same for me as it is for you.'

'No, it's not,' Jack had retorted savagely. 'It's not the same for you. For a start, Grandfather doesn't...he doesn't like me, Joss. I can see it in his eyes when he looks at me. He blames me because of Dad.'

'No, he doesn't,' Joss had objected. 'How can he? We all know the reason why Uncle David...'

He had stopped there, and Jack hadn't continued to argue with him. What was the point?

He had lost count of the number of times he had gone over that final row between his parents, that furious, pressured, trapped sentence his father had flung at his mother before they had left for the party to celebrate David and Jon's fiftieth birthday.

'For God's sake, Tiggy, will you *listen*,' his father had shouted furiously. 'Bloody kids, I never realized they were so expensive!'

'David, don't be ridiculous,' Tiggy had snapped back. 'Jack has to have a new school uniform. He's completely outgrown his old one. You're just going to *have* to find the money from somewhere...he *can't* go to school otherwise.'

They had still been arguing when Jack had crept past them to go to his own room.

His parents. Why did they have to be the way they were?

Why couldn't they be like other people's parents, or even better, like his uncle Jon and aunt Jenny?

Just thinking about his aunt and uncle made him feel both better and worse. Just knowing they were there in his life made him feel safe, and yet, at the same time, he experienced guilt for needing to have them there to make him feel safe...guilt and disloyalty.

A duck squawked protestingly and took flight from the lake, momentarily bringing Jack's thoughts back to the present.

As he had walked into the library he must have disturbed his grandfather, who had suddenly woken up, glaring belligerently as he saw Jack.

'Oh, it's you, is it?' he had muttered. 'My God, with that mother of yours, it's no wonder David doesn't want to come home.' He had reached up and picked up a postcard that was lying on his desk, his fingers trembling as he touched it. '*This* is what your father is reduced to because of her,' Ben had told him bitterly. 'Living like some native in a place...'

His mother's fault—and his? Was *that* what Ben was trying to say?

Instinctively Jack had picked up the postcard his grandfather had flung down, his eyes blurring as he tried to focus on his father's handwriting—handwriting he couldn't really recognize or relate to, and even though he brushed his thumb over the brief message, as though hoping to somehow or other absorb something of the man who had written it, something of the man who was his father, he

could feel absolutely nothing, just an intensi-
fying of the deep-rooted sense of pain and anger he always felt when he thought of him.

What kind of man *was* his father, what kind
of man would he himself become, what kind
of a father? Not one like Jon.

Savagely Jack flung another flat stone skim-
ming over the dull, still water. His uncle Jon
would never walk out on his family, his children. His uncle Jon. Grimly he remembered
how at Christmas when they had all exchanged their gifts to one another, his uncle
had reached for him, hugging him warmly,
hugging him before he had turned to Joss, but
Jack had seen the look in his eyes when he *did*
hug Joss, had seen it and known that it was the
look of a father for a dearly loved child. His
uncle Jon loved him, housed him, cared for
him out of a sense of duty and responsibility,
out of his general and characteristic love for all
of mankind, but he loved Joss very differently.
He loved Joss as a man loves his son. What
was it he, Jack, had done that had caused that
lack of love from his father? There were so
many questions he needed to ask him, so
much he needed to know.

In walking away from him, disappearing,
his father had cheated him of the right to ask

those questions, and Jack felt that he couldn't get on with his life, couldn't move forward until they were answered.

He knew how concerned his aunt and uncle were about his school work, but how could he explain to them, how could he tell them how alienated he suddenly felt from them, how afraid and alone?

His grandfather was fond of repeating stories about Jack's own father's teenage years, the sportsman he had been, the scholar, and hinted at, but never openly declared, his sexual skills and exploits. His father, according to his grandfather, had been a man to admire and emulate, but to Jack he was little more than a flat cardboard figure without flesh and meaning, a vague shadow, a dim memory, someone with whom he had no sense of shared history or shared blood, someone who had fathered him but who had then walked away.

Jack reached for another pebble. It had started to rain, a thin, fine, penetrating drizzle, and he didn't have a coat, but Jack didn't care, just as he didn't care that by rights he ought to be at home studying. Why *should* he care? Who cared for him? Not his father... No, never him.

'Maddy, have you got five minutes to spare?'

Maddy smiled briefly at her mother-in-law as Jenny popped her head around the kitchen door. It was eleven o'clock in the morning and she had just settled Gramps down with a cup of coffee and some of her home-made biscuits. Leo had gone for a walk with Joss, his chest swelling with pride when Joss had gravely invited him to go with him, and she had driven over to Olivia's earlier in the morning to drop Emma off there to play with Amelia and Alex.

As for Max's whereabouts! Maddy's smile faltered. He had gone out immediately after breakfast, saying that he needed to go into Chester to finalize the details of his trip to Jamaica.

'I've come to ask you a favour,' Jenny began, sitting down opposite Maddy at the kitchen table as she accepted her offer of a coffee.

'I know how busy you are with Gramps and the children, but with Ruth deciding to spend the next six months in America with her family and all the extra work we're going to have with the Mums and Babes home now that we've finally got the go-ahead on our new property, I was wondering, well hoping, that I could persuade *you* to take on a more formal role with the charity. You've been wonderful at helping out with the fund-raising and taking a lot of the paperwork off Ruth's and my shoulders, but what I'd like to ask you is if you would consider taking over Ruth's role as the charity's treasurer.'

Maddy stared at her.

'You want *me* to do that, but…'

'Please don't say no,' Jenny begged her. 'Ruth and I talked the whole thing over before she went away, and we had hoped to get an opportunity to talk to you together, but what with the wedding and Christmas… Ruth and I are both in agreement about this, Maddy. You'd be perfect for the job. You're a whiz with figures, and when it comes to organizational flair…'

Jenny shook her head and laughed.

'Your talents are wasted on us, Maddy, you should be heading some multimillion-pound organization.'

Maddy stared at her and blushed, her glance not quite meeting her mother-in-law's as she told her quietly, 'It's very flattering of you to think of me, Jenny…and to go to so much trouble to boost my ego,' she added wryly, 'but flattering though…'

'I'm not *flattering* you, Maddy,' Jenny interrupted her firmly. 'What I've said is no less than the truth. Jon was commenting only the other day that he'd give anything to have an office manager with your skills. You have a very special gift, my dear,' she told her daughter-in-law gently, 'and I don't just mean your gift with people. Joss complained the other week that maths is supposed to be one of his strengths, and yet you are far quicker mathematically than he is himself....'

Maddy gave a small, self-conscious shrug. 'It's just one of those odd quirks,' she protested uncomfortably. 'I...'

'Maddy, I could shake you,' Jenny told her mock angrily.

'You're always putting yourself down, but let me tell you, if you think that I'm asking you to take Ruth's place as the charity's treasurer and secretary out of some kind of misguided altruism, you couldn't be more wrong. I...the charity desperately needs you and your skills. Our accountants have already warned me that I *must* find someone to take over Ruth's role, and Ruth herself has hinted that she would like you to take over from her permanently if you can be persuaded to do so.'

'But the charity *is* Ruth,' Maddy pointed out.

'Of course,' Jenny agreed. 'It was Ruth's experience of being an unmarried mother and having to part with her baby that led to her establishing our first mother and baby home, and as you know I had my own reasons for wanting to become involved....'

Gravely Maddy nodded her head. Harry, Jenny's first baby, had died shortly after his birth. To lose a child would, Maddy knew, be the ultimate tragedy. She loved her two with a fierce maternal love that made even the direst and most miserable times of her marriage worthwhile because it was her marriage that had given them life. But these were emotions too close to her heart for her ever to be able to discuss them with anyone, even someone as sympathetic as Jenny.

In truth she could think of no cause she would rather be involved in than Ruth and Jenny's mother and baby homes, and it was true that she did have a quiet, calm way of establishing order out of chaos. But if she made such a commitment, she would want...

Jenny watched the expressions chasing one another over her daughter-in-law's face and saw the quiet, despairing sadness shadowing her eyes, and she immediately knew its cause.

'Has Max gone back to London?' she asked Maddy.

'No...no, he hasn't...'

Refusing to look at her, Maddy got up and collected their empty coffee cups.

'Maddy, what is it? What's wrong?' Jenny asked her insistently.

'Nothing...nothing's wrong,' Maddy fibbed.

'It's Max, isn't it?' Jenny guessed. 'What...'

'No, not really,' Maddy denied, and then admitted, 'Well yes, it is...but it's not...he's going to Jamaica to look for David.'

Jenny stared at her. Of all the things she had expected to hear, this had quite definitely not been one of them. An affair—not the first for Max and very likely not the last—an admission that her marriage had not turned out the way she had hoped, those she had fully expected and been prepared for, but this...

'He's doing what? But... How? Why? He can't... What about his work...?' Jenny asked, thoroughly bewildered.

'Apparently it's all arranged,' Maddy told her quietly.

'Gramps has asked him to go and since...since Max is having a quiet period at work at the moment, he decided, he felt... He knows how much Gramps is missing David, and Max seems to think that it shouldn't be too difficult to track him down if he is in Jamaica....'

Jenny started to frown, her shock giving way to a mixture of anger and unease. Max would *never* agree to put himself out to such an extent simply out of concern for his grandfather. Jenny felt her heart start to sink. *What* was Max up to? She knew all about the card that Ben had received from David, post-marked Kingston, but *anyone* could have posted that for him, and even if he had actually been on the island, David could be anywhere by now.

Max knew as well as they all did that there was nothing to stop David from making proper contact with his family if he wished to do so. It was cruel of him to encourage Ben in his false hopes, his false beliefs that David was a victim of unkind circumstances, isolated from his family by fate instead of by his own choice. There was no point in suggesting to Maddy that *she* might try to prevail upon Max not to go. As Max's mother, Jenny knew perfectly well that Max listened to no one, heeded no one, *cared* for no one, other than himself.

She could still vividly remember finding Max in the graveyard one afternoon, the plants she had so carefully tended around Harry's grave all ruthlessly ripped out of the earth, their petals crushed and dying. When she had finally managed to fight back her tears to ask Max why he had destroyed them, he had simply shrugged his shoulders.

'They aren't doing any good,' he told her callously. 'He...' He had aimed a kick in the direction of Harry's headstone. 'He's dead, anyway.'

'I just feel that I can't relate to him at all,' Jenny had told Jon through her anguished tears later.

'Why...*why* do something like that...something so...so senseless and destructive? He knows how much Harry's grave means to me.'

'Perhaps that's why he did it,' Jon had suggested. 'Perhaps he feels jealous.'

'Of Harry?' Jenny had protested. 'How *could* he? He never even knew... Where have I gone wrong, Jon?' she had asked her husband in despair. 'We wanted him so much and yet now...'

Grimly she had closed her eyes. How could she say even to Jon that she didn't love her own child, and, anyway, it wasn't true. She *did* love him, but the things he did, the way he was, no, those she could not love.

'Leo is starting to become very...' Maddy

paused and swallowed. 'He's very difficult when Max is around and I... I feel that Leo needs Max to be here at home for him...to spend more time with him, but Max...'

'Oh, Maddy,' Jenny sympathized sadly. 'I'm so sorry. I'm so very sorry.'

Maddy gave her a wan smile.

'Can I think about the Mums and Babes thing and let you know?'

'Just as long as you say yes,' Jenny conceded. 'We really do need you, Maddy.'

'You're looking very pensive,' Jon commented to his wife as he walked into the sitting room and saw her standing, staring through the window, obviously deep in thought. 'Did you see Maddy...?'

'Mmm...' Jenny agreed.

'So what's wrong? Has she refused to help you by taking Ruth's place?'

'No. She did say she needed time to think about it, but I believe I'll be able to persuade her to agree.'

'So, what's wrong, and don't tell me nothing because...'

Jenny shook her head, interrupting him. 'It's not Maddy, it's Max. Maddy was in a bit of a state when I got there, and it turns out that

Max is planning to fly out to Jamaica to look for David.'

'He's *what?*'

'Yes, I know,' Jenny acknowledged wryly, correctly reading her husband's expression. 'I was as stunned as you. I mean, Max has *never* shown the remotest interest in David's whereabouts, and I doubt very much... According to Maddy, he's doing it to please Gramps, who, by the way, is apparently underwriting the whole trip.' Jenny looked across at her husband and recognized his concern.

'According to Maddy, Max is flying out to Kingston the day after tomorrow and...' She stopped, frowning, asking Jon, 'What was that? I thought I heard someone outside the door.'

Jon crossed the room and fully opened the sitting room door, which he had left slightly ajar.

'There's no one there,' he told Jenny. 'It was probably one of the cats.'

'Jon, what are we going to do about this?'

'I suspect there isn't anything we *can* do other than register our disapproval,' Jon told her quietly. 'You know Max.'

'He can't possibly believe he's going to find

David. You've had professionals searching for him.'

'In Europe and South America,' Jon agreed, 'but until dad got this latest card, I had no idea that David might be in the Caribbean.'

'We still don't know that he is. He could easily have got someone else to post the card or have even been there and moved on,' Jenny reminded him tiredly. 'I hate to say it, but I just can't see Max going to the trouble of travelling all that way just to please Ben.'

'Mmm…'

'Maddy didn't want to say anything, but I could sense that she was very upset about the whole thing. I feel so guilty about her sometimes, Jon. If she was our daughter, the last thing we'd be doing is to allow her to remain in such a destructive marriage. She deserves more, better….'

'Maddy isn't as weak as Max seems to think. She's got some very special strengths, and my guess is, although I have to admit she's never confided as much in me, she has her own reasons for wanting to stay in her marriage.'

'The children, you mean…'

When Jon remained silent, she looked at him and then begged worriedly, 'Oh, Jon, you're surely not suggesting that poor Maddy has some impossible, old-fashioned romantic fantasy that Max will change, that he's going to...'

'Fall in love with her? No, I don't believe she thinks that,' Jon agreed, 'but like Saul, who was also the victim of a broken marriage before he met Tullah, providing a secure family background for her children is very important to Maddy, and maybe she has decided that marriage to Max with all its drawbacks, when balanced out against the security of the extended family network the children have living here, balances out reasonably acceptably for her.'

Jenny shook her head.

'Jon, Maddy is still a young woman. She's...' She paused and then looked directly at her husband as she reminded him, 'A woman's late twenties and thirties are supposed to be the most highly sexual and productive of her life. Maddy needs...'

'A man?' Jon supplied for her.

'I was going to say "love,"' Jenny corrected him dryly, shaking her head at the look he was giving her.

'Mmm... Well, Maddy and Max and their matrimonial troubles aren't our only problem at the moment, are they,' Jon commented.

'What are we going to do about Jack?'

'I don't know,' Jenny sighed. 'He seemed so happy with us, but just lately… I hate to pry, but I've actually asked Joss if he… They've always been so close, but while they haven't fallen out, they're tending to spend more and more time apart these days. All Joss can say is that Jack talks a lot about his father and that he seems very angry with David.'

'With good reason, and it might be David he's angry with, but it's *us* he's taking his anger out on. When I had to talk to him about his school work, he was very quick to point out to me that I'm not his father and that, technically, I don't have any parental rights over him.'

'Oh, Jon,' Jenny murmured, going over to her husband and giving him a loving hug. She knew just how much Jack's comment would have hurt him.

Her husband was, in many ways, a rather shy man, cautious about showing his emotions, due, in the main, to the rejection he had suffered at his own father's hands, but there had seemed to be a rapport between him and Jack. Joss, their youngest child, loved his father dearly, but then Joss loved *everyone* and was loved by everyone in return, and so it had been with Jack, with whom Jon had started to build a tentative relationship of shared mutual trust and shared mutual, if never verbally expressed, awareness of their vulnerability.

'He's a teenager,' she reminded Jon now, in Jack's defence, 'and they all tend to go through a difficult stage. Look at the problems we had with Louise while she was in the throes of her crush on Saul.'

'Don't remind me,' Jon groaned with a rueful smile. 'But Jack's different,' he added quietly. 'He's...he's very dear to me, Jen, very special.... I feel, in many ways, that he's been entrusted to me so that I can make good the deficits in my own parenting.'

'I know,' Jenny told him softly. 'And I think that deep down inside, Jack knows it, too, but at this moment... Once he matures, he will realize and appreciate just how much you love him, Jon....'

Maddy turned her car in through the gates to Queensmead after paying a visit to Olivia, fiercely blinking away the evidence of the tears that had been threatening her all day.

As she dropped the car down a gear to avoid the pot-holes the winter rain had left in the driveway—Max had complained furiously about the state of the drive and the damage it could potentially do to his expensive new car—Maddy bit worriedly at the corner of her mouth, a habit she had developed as a small child and one she had never entirely grown out of. It often left her mouth with a soft bee-stung look about it that had made Max tell her tauntingly once, when he had not visited Queensmead for almost six weeks, that if he hadn't known better he might have thought she had been enjoying the attentions of a lover.

There was one aspect of Max's trip to Jamaica that, as yet, no one other than her seemed to have picked up on, and she devoutly hoped that they would not.

She knew enough about her husband's business to acknowledge that the months of January and February could often be quite slow, but for him to claim that he had no work pending and that he could take what amounted to at least two months off, indicated to Maddy that there could be some other and rather more sinister reason for Max's absence from his chambers.

She stopped the car and turned to smile at her children.

Max was not popular with the other members of the chambers, she already knew that, but there was also no question about the fact that he was a highly skilled and very successful divorce barrister who acquired, by reputation, the very cream of the country's divorce cases.

Maddy was by no means lacking in intelligence. She had also trained in law, although she had never practised, because she had chosen to bring up her children. Despite what Max and to some degree her own family chose to think, she was very much afraid that Max's decision to take a couple of months' leave was not as voluntary as he wanted others to believe.

Maddy knew that both she and the children were secure enough, financially—she had her trust fund. But it was not her *financial* future that was causing her to feel such concern, it was…

'Maddy, where the hell have you been?'

She tensed as Max suddenly materialized beside the car, wrenching open the driver's door as he glared angrily at her.

'I've got to go out this evening, and the old man's complaining again that you haven't changed his library books. There's all my packing to be done as well.'

'I've got Gramps' new library books with me,' Maddy told him pacifically as she reached into the back of the car for the children while Max stood and watched, without making any attempt to give her assistance.

It would never have occurred to her to ask for his help, and, anyway, Leo, now that he had caught sight of his father, was already stiffening in her arms, his body tense with rejection and fear.

It worried her that Leo was so antagonistic towards his father, but he was too young yet for her to be able to explain to him that Max's indifference towards him, which she suspected was the cause of Leo's feelings, had nothing to do with Leo himself and was simply the way that Max felt towards anyone whom he considered unimportant or not worthy of his time or attention.

She had realized very early on in her marriage how little she meant to Max, and had long ago stopped being hurt by his lack of love and respect for her, or so she told herself. Emma had been conceived without any of the emotions she herself had once considered essential between two people who were creating a new life.

Maddy smiled painfully to herself as she lifted her small daughter out of the car. Thankfully, Emma herself had no notion and never would have if she could help it, of the empty, banal, cynically selfish act that had led to her procreation.

'Why don't you go to a prostitute?' Maddy had hissed tearfully at Max when he had walked into their bedroom late one night, deliberately waking her up by slamming the door and then proceeding to switch on the lights and yank back the bedclothes. She had been wearing a night-dress, a habit she had developed during the long nights she had spent alone. Max had smiled cruelly at her as he dropped onto the bed beside her, naked and plainly ready for sex.

'Don't bother taking it off,' he had advised her tauntingly. 'I don't want to look at you. Anyway,' he had said as he pushed her night-dress aside, ignoring the tense hostility of her motionless body and the pain in her eyes, 'why should I *pay* someone else when I've got you here. After all, one—' he had then proceeded to use a phrase that had seared Maddy's emotions, sickening and humiliating her as he concluded '—is much the same as any other and gives the same degree of release.'

'If that's all you want, you should...' Maddy had shot back only to stop, her face flushing with mortification as she saw the white glint of his teeth as he laughed at her.

'I should what? Go and take care of myself in the bathroom like some adolescent...? Oh, no...' he had advised her calmly, his hands touching her, arousing her physically, even though emotionally she hated herself for being so responsive to him. As he entered her, Maddy wondered why he was with her. Was the reason he was with her now, the reason he *needed* her, because whomever he had been with, whomever he had been *expecting* to spend the night with had, for some reason or another, turned him down? It had been out of that, out of his usage of her body to assuage the physical desire he had felt for another woman, that she had conceived their second child.

That time, when Max had tightened his lips and looked calculatingly at her as he told her he did not want a second child any more than he had wanted a first, she had ignored the way she was shaking with nerves inside and had told him quietly, 'Perhaps you should have thought of the consequences before having sex with me, although I should imagine it would be rather more embarrassing for you if the woman whom you had expected to have sex with that night was standing here instead of me, telling you that she'd conceived your child....'

Max, of course, hadn't been in the least bit fazed nor repentant. He had simply shrugged his shoulders and told her dismissively, 'With her, the situation wouldn't have arisen because *she* would have taken good care to make sure there was no...problem. You see, unlike you, my dear, she enjoys sex, and she knows how to make sure her partner enjoys it as well.'

In some ways her daughter was even more precious to her because she knew that she had been conceived only by chance, Maddy acknowledged as she kissed Emma's plump face before shepherding both children towards the house.

5

'My mother was here yesterday. What did she want?'

Maddy carefully finished ironing the shirt in front of her before answering Max's sharp-voiced question.

'She came to ask me if I would take over from Ruth on the Mums and Babes charity committee,' she informed him quietly as she smoothed the shirt and added it to the pile she had already ironed.

Max had bought himself what looked like an entire new wardrobe of leisure clothes for his trip to Jamaica, and, of course, he had insisted that they all needed to be washed and ironed before he left.

His flight was in the morning, and Maddy knew that, in many ways, it would be a relief to see him go. Leo had been fractious and upset at breakfast time this morning, not wanting to go to play school, clinging to her and crying when she had had to leave him.

'What? My God, she's trawling the bottom of the pond if she's reduced to asking you, isn't she?' Max derided insultingly.

Maddy didn't say anything. What was the point? She knew from past experience that any attempt to defend herself would result in an ignominious defeat, with her fleeing the battlefield, wretchedly unhappy and in tears, while Max revelled in his ability to verbally destroy her.

Shedding tears over Max and his behaviour was, as Maddy had long ago discovered, a waste of time and energy, just as loving him had laid waste to her emotions, devastating her self-esteem and her sense of herself, her pride and her self-respect.

In the early days of their relationship, Max had enjoyed manipulating Maddy's emotions. She unsuspectingly believed that he genuinely wasn't aware of how much his verbal cruelty hurt her, and willingly allowed him to soothe the pain of the wounds he had himself inflicted with the balm of his love-making.

These days, that shy, tremulous responsiveness to him in bed, that eagerness to lose herself in his arms, to give herself over completely to his physical possession, had changed to a stiff-bodied, protective reluctance.

Not that Max minded her lack of desire to have sex with him. Why should he? She was, after all, the one who was losing out, not him. He, after all, always had a lover he could take to bed, a lover who was always far, far more attractive and far, far more adventurous in bed than Maddy could ever be. Or at least he had until recently!

Already Max's body was beginning to ache, to miss the pleasure, not just of the physical release that sex gave him, but more importantly, of knowing that there was someone in his life over whom he was in control, a woman, the kind of woman that other men wanted, whom he could make want him.

His glance flicked over his wife in dispassionate assessment. Maddy was a fool to herself in some ways; there *were* men who found her particular type of soft, femininely curved body highly desirable, even if he himself preferred the lean, longer-limbed, model-girl, head-turning type of woman, and if she wasn't so humble and eager to please, if she made a bit more of an effort with herself...

Frowning, Max turned away. It wasn't like him to waste his time thinking about his wife. She *was* his wife, and while he might deride and taunt her for her plainness and lack of sexual allure, there were, as he had discovered, certain valuable compensations in having a woman like Maddy as one's wife. For one thing, it left him free to concentrate on pursuing his own sexual adventures without having to worry about what Maddy might be up to behind his back. With any luck, his present unwanted faithfulness to his marital vows would soon be over. Max had no doubt that he would very quickly find just the kind of woman he most liked. Jamaica could well prove to be very fertile ground for producing a congenial bed mate—or two—for him.

His frown deepened slightly. Irritatingly, this afternoon, when he had gone to Chester, he had bumped into Luke Crighton, who had, it seemed, already heard about Max's trip to Jamaica and the purpose for it, and, in typical Luke fashion, had immediately commented that he doubted very much that Max would have any success in finding David. And more than that, he had actually implied that Max was perfectly well aware of this fact and that he was using his grandfather's obsession with his son to get himself a free holiday.

'Interesting that you should be able to take so much time off,' Luke had commented dryly. 'Very few barristers of my acquaintance, including myself, are in a position to give themselves so much leave.'

'It all depends on whether or not one has specialized in a particular type of case,' Max had retaliated, 'and, of course, on generating a decent income...'

'Or having a rich wife,' Luke had countered.

Max had pretended he hadn't heard him. There had always been a certain amount of rivalry between them, and Max was well aware of the fact that Luke did not particularly like him.

'Your grandfather wants to talk to you before you go,' Maddy reminded Max quietly now.

His grandfather's deification of David was, in Max's opinion, totally pathetic. *He* would never allow himself to become so emotionally involved with or dependent upon another human being.

Of all human emotions, love was, in Max's opinion, the most overrated as well as the most capricious. Look at the way people glorified mother love. Mother love. His mother had *not* loved him, and neither had his father. He had simply been a child they had conceived, produced as a replacement for the baby they had lost, a substitute for their precious Harry.

As a child he had heard his grandfather saying as much to his mother.

'Max will help take the place of the boy you lost. If you ask me, you brooded too much after losing him. You should have had another child sooner and not waited so long....'

'No one can ever take Harry's place,' he had heard his mother saying with unfamiliar sharpness to his grandfather.

He certainly hadn't. Nor had he been enough for his parents. He could still remember all the fuss there had been when the twins had been born, and they had only been girls. His mother had fussed over them far more than she ever had over him. He knew it.

And as for Joss...

And then there was Jack. He could never imagine himself getting emotional over a child the way his father did over Jack, and he wasn't even his own son.

Leo and Emma bored him, and it irritated him to see the way his father fussed over them both, especially Leo, picking him up, hugging him, showing him the affection Max could never remember him showing him.

'What's that he's got?' he derided now as he caught sight of Leo clutching the battered old teddy bear he'd had since babyhood.

'He's too old to be playing with baby stuff,' he told Maddy, ignoring the anxious look she was giving Leo. 'You're turning him into a real mummy's boy. It's time he started to grow up.'

Maddy bit her lip as Max walked out of the room. She had been trying for several months to gently coax Leo to part with his baby comfort toy and had, to some extent, begun to be successful.

'Don't worry about it,' Leo's play school teacher had comforted her, 'boys *do* tend to be much more clingy at this age than girls. The best thing to do is just to ignore it.'

'I'm afraid that the other children will tease him,' Maddy had confessed.

'I'll keep an eye out for anything like that,' his teacher had promised her. She added gently, 'He isn't the only child who still needs the comfort of a favourite toy from time to time, so try not to worry.'

Noticeably, though, Leo was much more babyish and clingy with her whenever Max was at home, and Max himself, of course, didn't help the situation by drawing attention to it.

Once she'd got the children in bed, she would have to do Max's packing, and then Maddy promised herself she'd have an early night.

Having Max around drained her. It wasn't so much his demands for things like clean clothes and her services of cook-cum-valet that were so exhausting, as the fraught emotional climate he always seemed to create whenever he was at home.

She would be glad when he had actually gone. She bent down to unplug the iron.

Maddy tensed her body under the bed-clothes as the bedroom door opened and she saw Max's outline framed in the light from the landing.

As he switched on the bedroom light and shut the door, she quickly closed her eyes, listening as he walked cat-footed towards their bathroom.

When she heard the shower running she opened them again.

Max's flight was due to leave at ten, which meant he'd be leaving the house around seven. She glanced at her alarm clock. It was just gone midnight, which meant... She glanced towards the closed bathroom door. In another seven hours... Only another seven hours. Quietly she turned onto her side, the side facing towards the bathroom door but away from the centre of the bed, her body well over onto her own side of the large king-sized bed.

Once, in the early days of their marriage when she had annoyed him in some way, Max had come to bed late, waking her from the exhausted sleep she had fallen into, having waited up for him to return home until well after midnight, to tell her unmercifully that he wanted her to move onto her own side of their bed so that her body didn't come into contact with his while they slept.

Mortified, she had done as he had requested, hot, silent tears seeping soundlessly into her pillow as she lay there battling with his rejection, the first of many, many silent tears she had shed.

The bathroom door opened. She could hear Max padding round to his own side of the bed in the darkness after he had switched off the bedroom light.

The mattress dipped as he got in, a rush of cool air touching her skin as he lifted the duvet.

Automatically she was prenaturally aware of him, of his every movement and breath. In her mind's eye she could visualize his naked body, lean and superbly muscled. Physically Max had an almost animal-like quality about him, a pantherish grace that, when she had first seen him undress, had made her catch her breath in silent, helpless awe, her senses drunk on the sheer physical beauty of him...on that and on her love.

His skin tanned well, and the soft hair that shadowed the male shaping of his body was dark and silky, just begging to be touched, stroked. Maddy had been a virgin when Max had first taken her to bed.

'Maddy... I know you're awake....'

Instantly she stiffened. Max's hand was on her upper arm.

She could feel his breath against her hair. She was facing away from him. They hadn't had sex for more than three months, and, in fact, she could probably have counted on the fingers of both her hands the number of occasions on which they had had sex since Emma's birth, and not need to include her thumbs.

Painfully she noted her own mental use of the words *had sex* rather than the softer and far more evocative *making love*. Making love...that was something she and Max never did, even if she had once stupidly thought...

She caught her bottom lip between her teeth as she felt Max's fingertips stroke along her arm with just enough sensual deliberateness to make the tiny hairs growing there stand on edge and, even more humiliatingly, her nipples start to peak.

It was a physical reaction to the experienced way he was touching her, she knew, for despite all the insults that Max had thrown at her, despite all his assertions to the contrary, Maddy knew that her body had been intensely responsive to him.... Had been. She caught her breath on a small, sharp sob as he bent his head and started to gently caress the curve of her shoulder with his mouth. She could feel the softness of his hair against her skin and against her body; his body felt cool and sleekly hard.

His teeth nipped sharply at her skin; he was close enough to her ear now to whisper tauntingly in it, 'Don't you want me, Maddy?'

"No. No, I don't..." How she longed to be able to scream the words at him. Her. Gentle, quiet, docile, obedient Maddy. But she knew she couldn't. For one thing, she might wake the children, and for another...

His hand was cupping her breast, playing with the hard peak of her nipple.

She could hear, feel, the satisfaction in the small, soft male laugh he gave as he kissed her throat, and her whole body started to shudder.

Her spine started to arch in sensual longing as he played with her breast, cupping it in his hand, teasing the nipple.

The first time he had touched her like this, he had laughed at the way she had responded to him, totally unable to control the intensity of her reaction to his touch. Now she was older...wiser...and stronger? She winced as she felt the need, the longing flood through her. It had always been like this with him. Their marriage was an emotional desert, a complete sham, but she had never once, either before she had met him or, even more dismayingly, since, experienced anything like the desire he could arouse within her, for any other man. It was as though he possessed some potent spell, some magical quality that enabled him to conjure up within her a hidden well of sexuality that no one else was able to touch. She hated feeling like this...needing him like this...hated it...and hated herself, too, for betraying it.

As he felt her familiar frantic response to his touch, Max smiled secretly to himself. To Maddy he might claim that she was not as responsive, not as desirable, not as able to arouse him as other and more alluringly attractive women, but while it was true that she was not so sexually experienced, not so sexually knowing, he knew perfectly well that his wife's innocent attempts to control the enticing intensity of her sensuality was almost as erotic and appealing to him as her body's physical, quivering pleasure and longing at being touched.

Maddy was quite simply so sensually sensitive, so acutely responsive, that Max knew now that if he was to touch her intimately, gently caress her clitoris or play with it for a few seconds with the firmer touch of his tongue, she would orgasm almost immediately.

He knew it, but he had no intention of giving her that pleasure, no intention whatsoever. Her body had changed subtly since he had first known her; taking care of two energetic children and a demanding elderly man had started to fine down the soft plumpness she had had when they had first met, so that when he touched her Max was immediately conscious of the smallness of her waist as it curved inwards beneath the soft warmth of her breasts and the feminine curve of her hips.

Her belly, small and slightly rounded, quivered beneath his touch. Max smiled in the darkness.

Maddy lay mutely beneath him as Max

turned her over and entered her. She knew better than to protest or to resist. This way at least it would all be over quickly. Fighting against what she knew to be the inevitable only prolonged the ignomy she had learned to fear.

It would be over soon, and if she closed her eyes and tried to concentrate, perhaps this time…

Maddy waited until Max was asleep beside her, sliding furtively out of the bed and heading for the bathroom. Lying on his side and awake, Max watched her.

It appealed to the cruel, dark streak pervading his nature to picture Maddy alone and tearful in the bathroom, forced to relieve the tension of the sexual desire he had aroused inside her, by herself.

Dry-mouthed, her heart pounding, Maddy shuddered in self-disgust as the final pulse of her orgasm died away. It seemed incredible to her now that she had once been foolish enough to believe that Max loved her.

'But how could you do the things…what you did to me…' she had whispered to him in dismay when he had finally revealed to her that he had absolutely no love for her whatsoever.

'I closed my eyes and thought about your trust fund,' he had taunted her.

'But you were so...you...you wanted me,' Maddy had protested awkwardly, blushing a little at her own forwardness.

'No... I've never wanted *you*,' Max had told her cruelly. 'I'm a very good actor, my dear. I just pretended that I wanted you. No man worthy of the name could ever want *you*,' he had added with gentle sadism. 'It simply isn't possible.'

And as she looked into his eyes, Maddy had known that he meant what he said. She had literally been sick with shock, reliving over and over again the way he had touched her, the intimate things he had done.

The sex he had given her then had been very different from what there was now, she acknowledged as she crept back into bed.

Despite her orgasm, her breasts still ached in unsatisfied arousal. She couldn't understand why he still had the power to affect her like this and didn't want to analyze what that response said about her as a woman. She had never been sexually adventurous, and according to Max, she had certainly never been sexually satisfying to him as a man. Emotionally, she certainly no longer loved him, had never surely loved him. How could *anyone* love Max as he was? No, what she had loved was the image he had so obligingly and manipulatively provided for her. So why, why, why did she still react to him like this?

On the edge of sleep, Max luxuriated in the pleasure of his own sexual satisfaction. One of the pluses of having sex with Maddy was that he didn't have to use a condom. With anyone else, he was meticulous and thorough about protecting himself from any risk of contracting any kind of sexually transmitted infection.

A scare as a teenager, which had had his then GP clinically outlining the dangers of what he was inviting, had made him sharply aware long before it had become a serious issue, of the wisdom of not taking any kind of risks with his sexual health.

'You were a long time in the bathroom,' he taunted Maddy, enjoying the shocked tension he could sense gripping her body as she realized that he wasn't asleep. 'What were you doing?'

When she didn't reply, he added in a soft, unkind voice, 'My mother really must be a fool if she thinks you could step into Ruth's shoes. Are you sure you didn't misunderstand her, Maddy? Perhaps she was asking you to *clean* the office, not take charge of it. After all, that's much more your line, isn't it. Cooking, cleaning, looking after old men and young children.'

Blinking fiercely into the darkness, Maddy swallowed hard against the agonized lump of wretchedness in her throat and silently made herself a promise. Tomorrow morning she was going to telephone her mother-in-law and tell her that she had thought it over and that she was willing to take over from Ruth.

The enormity of the decision she had made kept her awake long after Max had fallen into a deep sleep. She must be mad. She couldn't possibly do it. But Jenny had said she could. Maybe Jenny had just been feeling sorry for her, pretending that she thought she could. Jenny... Tiredly her eyes closed.

Several miles away in Jenny and Jon's home, someone else was finding it difficult to get to sleep.

Nervously Jack felt beneath his pillow, his fingers tightening on the sharp shape of his passport. Beneath it in a plastic folder was the ticket he had bought with the money he had withdrawn from his building society account—and the currency.

From Maddy he had found out the name of the hotel where Max was going to be staying. He still felt guilty about the underhanded way he had lured her into giving him that information. He had always liked Maddy. She had been kind to him. But he didn't like Max. It had been an extra piece of luck that the flight left at just the right time in the morning for him to leave the house just as though he was going to school.

He would have to leave his bike at the airport and hope that it didn't get stolen before someone could pick it up, and then no doubt there would be a hefty parking fine to pay in order to do so, but Jack knew that once the truth about what he had done and where he was had been discovered, he would have far greater sins to atone for than the mere loss of his bike.

He closed his eyes against the sudden rush of tears that threatened him as he recalled the look in his uncle Jon's eyes on New Year's Eve, which they had celebrated at home with Jenny cooking a family dinner for everyone.

He had been so tempted then to tell him everything, but somehow he had managed to stop himself.

Only one person could provide him with the

answers to the questions he wanted to ask, and that one person was his father, and if his uncle Jon really cared about him he would have known and understood that instead of... He could feel the tight, hard ball of anger-cum-resentment that had been growing inside him ever since the previous year, filling him with sick misery.

His uncle Jon had known then how important it was to him to find his father, to see him, talk to him...ask him...but Jon had told him with a slow shake of his head that he doubted that his father would ever be found.

'I rather think it will be up to him to find us, rather than the other way around, Jack,' he had told the boy gently.

'You mean he doesn't *want* to be found,' Jack had pressed him angrily.

'I suspect not,' Jon had agreed. 'Certainly my attempts to find him have come to a dead end.'

But he had been lying, he must have been, because here was Max, Jon's son, flying out to Jamaica and making no secret of the fact that he expected to return with his father.... His uncle Jon must have known where his father was all the time. Jack felt the tears burn against his eyelids as he fought to suppress them. The plastic cover of his passport felt sticky with the nervous perspiration off his hand.

He had to go, everything was planned. Max was travelling first class, and he was travelling economy—even that had virtually emptied his account—so there was no danger of Max spotting him until after their plane had landed in Jamaica; he certainly intended to make sure that Max didn't do so. And once they were there...

Jack's stomach churned with apprehension and dread, but it was too late to change his mind now.

His father... What was he doing now? Did he ever think about *him?* He could feel his fear turning to the sickening mixture of anger and helplessness that had become so familiar to him over recent months. His father... Joss didn't know how lucky he was...or how much he, Jack, envied him. He looked across to the bed where his cousin lay sleeping. They still shared a room, despite the fact that now that Louise and Katie had both left home they could each have had their own.

Jack's thoughts shifted away from his cousin. He knew how hurt Joss would be that he hadn't confided in him. Would his uncle allow him back...want him back after the way he would have deceived him, or would he decide that he was far too like his father, far too inclined to behave dishonestly, to permit him to do as they had both planned and follow him into the family practice?

Jack wanted to follow in his uncle's footsteps, but first he had to be sure that he was worthy of doing so...that he wasn't somehow tainted by being his father's son. Tiredly Jack blinked his gritty eyelids.

The enormity of the task he had set himself loomed menacingly over him, and he could feel his resolve start to weaken. He could still change his mind. There was still time. No one knew...but no...no...he couldn't do that; couldn't go on with his life until he knew...until he was sure. He could feel the hot blur of tears burning the backs of his eyes. Fiercely he gritted his teeth. He wasn't going to cry, only kids cried and *he* wasn't a kid any more. In less than two years he would be eighteen and officially an adult.

6

The children had been dropped off at their play school groups, Gramps was in the library with the *Times* and his post, the kitchen was immaculately clean and Max was, no doubt, already winging his way towards the Caribbean. In short, Maddy recognized as she glanced nervously towards the telephone, there was now nothing stopping her from ringing her mother-in-law and informing her that she had decided to agree to her suggestion that she take over from Aunt Ruth. Nothing. No reason. No excuse not to do as she had promised herself so fiercely she would do last night.

Then, in the dark depths of her despair, she had felt a self-loathing for the way she was physically unable to stop herself from responding to Max, from yes, hateful though it was to admit it, from physically wanting Max. What was left of her pride and self-respect had insisted that she must...must find a way out of the private pit of self-destruction her marriage had become.

Two young children, an old man and an even older house might keep her physically occupied, but they did nothing to keep her mentally busy, to stop her thinking, dwelling on the running sore, the emotional misery, her marriage had become. The work Jenny was offering her, though, would certainly do that.

'You've always been good with figures,' Jenny had told her, and yes, it was true, she had a neat, tidy, orderly brain, the kind of brain that positively enjoyed producing order out of chaos. But she was still afraid, afraid that the task she was offering to take on would prove too much for her and that to make a public statement that she thought she could do it would only result in her ultimate ignominy and the humiliation of having to admit that she had been wrong.

But then, how much ignominy, how much public humiliation was there left to endure when she suspected that Max's infidelities were no secret to his family. No one ever referred to them, of course. Tullah and Olivia were kindness itself whenever the three of them got together for their regular weekly meetings—as mothers of young children they had more in common than merely being related by marriage to one another, but while when they talked about their children and their domestic problems, they talked as equals; when it came to the more intimate areas of their marriages, Maddy was suffocatingly aware of the way in which Tullah and Olivia exchanged brief glances before tactfully disengaging from any conversation that may have underlined the differences between their relationships with their husbands and Maddy's with hers.

For there was no doubt about it, their relationships were different from hers. Saul, Tullah's husband, was quite obviously and publicly very ardently and passionately in love with his wife, and Caspar, Olivia's American husband, equally devoted to her.

Maddy loved their company, their warmth, their shared friendship, but oh, how she wished that there was someone in her life whom she could turn to and talk openly to about her real feelings, her despair and pain over the emptiness of her marriage, her guilt over the way it must be affecting her children, and all the other complex and destructive emotions that she suffered.

Quickly she reached for the telephone.

Jenny answered after the fourth ring.

'Jenny, it's me, Maddy....' She took a deep breath. 'If you really meant it about me taking over from Aunt Ruth, then I'll...I'll do it....'

There was a small pause and then Jenny responded, 'You will? Oh Maddy! That's wonderful!'

Underneath the slight surprise she could hear in her mother-in-law's warm voice, Maddy could also quite clearly discern her very genuine relief and pleasure. Suddenly her own spirits started to lift, and Maddy began to experience a sensation, a feeling that had been denied her for so long that it took her quite some time to recognize just what it was.

After she had put the phone down, having promised Jenny that she would accompany her on a visit to the site of what was to be a third block of low-rent apartments for single mothers, followed by a meeting with the contractors to review their progress, Maddy sank shakily into one of her kitchen chairs to savour the extraordinary and unfamiliar adrenalin boosting mixture of excitement, pride and exhilaration flooding her body.

The strength of it was such that it practically made her feel giddy. She had done it...she had *done* it and she was committed now. It was too late to change her mind.

There were things she had to do, plans she had to make. Tullah owed her baby-sitting favours, and she knew that the other woman would be at home this afternoon. She hurried to the telephone.

'You're doing what? Maddy, that's *wonderful*,' Tullah responded excitedly when Maddy told her, explaining to her why she needed her help at such short notice in having Leo and Emma for a couple of hours.

'We're meeting the contractors at four, and Jenny said it could be sixish before we're finished. That would mean you giving my two their tea.'

'No problem. After all, you've done it often enough for me,' Tullah responded promptly and truthfully.

'Look, why don't you come back with me when you pick Emma up from play group. We could have some lunch together and that would still leave you with enough time to go home and get changed before you meet Jenny.'

'I'm not really sure I'm up to this,' Maddy confessed to Tullah a couple of hours later as she stood in Tullah's kitchen sipping the tea Tullah had just made them.

'Of *course* you are. Jenny obviously thinks so, otherwise she wouldn't have asked you to take the job on. Still—' Tullah paused, her head on one side as she surveyed Maddy thoughtfully '—in my experience a new job often calls for a change of image....'

'A change of image...' Maddy looked uncertainly at her. 'I don't think...'

'Trust me, I'm a career girl,' Tullah reminded her with a grin. 'I know.'

Maddy couldn't dispute what Tullah was saying.

Before her marriage to Saul, she had been totally career-orientated and very successfully so.

Even so...

'I'm not really the sort of person...that is...'

Maddy's voice trailed away miserably as she tried to find the words to express to Tullah her own awareness of how impossible it was to do anything with her plain features, her hair that never seemed to hold a style, and her body, which just didn't seem to be the right kind of body for the sort of power dressing that Tullah could carry off so superbly.

'Leave everything to me,' Tullah instructed

her firmly. To Maddy's confusion, she added, 'I've been itching to get to work on you for ages.'

Shortly after Maddy had left, Tullah had rung Olivia to give her the news. 'Now that Jenny's persuaded Maddy to take over from Ruth, it gives us the ideal opportunity to bring her out of herself. With the right hairstyle and clothes—'

'It's going to take more than a haircut and some new clothes to repair the damage to Maddy's sense of self-worth that Max has inflicted, Tullah,' Olivia interrupted her cousin-by-marriage quietly.

'Yes, I know that,' Tullah agreed. 'But a little bit of confidence in herself and the way she looks, the ability to reflect to other people just how beautiful she is on the inside—and we all know that she is—*they* could be the stitches that will hold that wound together and give it the opportunity to heal,' Tullah insisted.

Olivia gave a rueful sigh. 'I hear what you're saying,' she acknowledged, 'and for Maddy's sake I wish it might be true—'

'It could be,' Tullah broke in.

'All right, what exactly have you got in mind?'

'Well, if you could offer to take charge of

Leo and Emma and my four, I could take Maddy shopping, get her to the hairdressers...'

'Mmm... I don't see any problem with that,' Olivia murmured.

It still touched her heart to hear Tullah referring to Saul's three children from his first marriage, along with the one they had had together, as 'her four.' Never had any stepchildren had such a devoted and genuinely loving surrogate mother, Olivia was sure of it. Olivia had always had a special spot for her cousin Saul, and she couldn't have been happier for him, for them both, when he had fallen in love with Tullah, her friend.

'Mmm...well, it won't be easy persuading Maddy to spend a day shopping in Chester,' Olivia warned Tullah.

'We won't be going to Chester,' Tullah told her sweetly.

Olivia frowned as she stared into the receiver. Haslewich was a very pretty, bustling small country town, but she doubted that Tullah would be able to find the kind of 'new look' she was talking about giving Maddy in any of its clothes shops. And then the penny dropped.

'If you're planning to persuade her to go to *Manchester...*' she guessed.

'Not Manchester, London,' Tullah informed her, laughing as she heard the choking sound that Olivia made on the other end of the line.

'We can stay overnight in Max's mews place. In fact, we could stay a couple of nights. It will take at least a couple of days to get through everything—shopping, the hairdressers, and, of course, we'll have to visit one of the large toy stores to bring all the little ones back something.'

'Maddy will never agree,' Olivia told her, gasping a little at the audacity of her friend's plans.

'Maddy will agree. Jenny and I are going to insist that she does,' Tullah argued. 'Remember *you* said she'd never agree to take Ruth's place.'

'Mmm...' Olivia acknowledged ruefully.

'Oh, I can't wait to see Max's face when he comes back from Jamaica and sees...'

'It doesn't matter how much you change her outward appearance, Tullah,' Olivia warned her gently, 'you can't change what's inside her—and that applies to Max as well as to Maddy.

'Max likes hurting people. He enjoys it.

You'll never change that or Maddy's vulnerability to him, not even with the most expensive hairstyle and clothes that London can provide.'

As the taxi set him down outside Max's hotel, Jack blinked in the brilliant light of the Caribbean sunshine. He had deliberately hung back at the airport, the last to pick up his luggage from the carousel, keeping a nervous eye out for Max, but as a first-class passenger—at his grandfather's expense, of course—Max had cleared the airport well ahead of his younger cousin.

After the cold January dampness of home, the heat of the Caribbean struck Jack like a physical force, but the perspiration drenching him as he stood outside the exclusive resort complex where Max was staying wasn't just caused by the strength of the sun.

He had it all carefully planned. Nothing could go wrong. He had checked and rechecked over and over again; rehearsed the scene that now lay in front of him until he was convinced that he was totally prepared for any argument Max could possibly put to him, and just to make sure... Reaching into his inside pocket, Jack withdrew his passport. Taking a deep breath as he removed it, he opened it and ripped out the inside pages before wrenching the whole thing apart down the length of its spine. Once he was sure that there was no way it could be repaired, he stuffed the small pieces back into his jacket pocket.

There. Now there was no way Max could send him back.

Taking a deep breath, he turned towards the hotel. It had come as a slight shock to him to discover that the hotel where Max was staying was not as he had anticipated, in Kingston itself, but on its own in a secluded area of the island where it could be reached only by car via a long drive, whose entrance was guarded by men wearing immaculate uniforms and very serious-looking guns.

By the gates and here outside the main building of the complex, large notices were posted, warning visitors not to stray outside the perimeter fence unless they were with a group, and most especially not wearing or carrying anything of material value.

Here inside the complex, though, that warning plainly did not apply, from what Jack could see at least, and his heart sank as he recognized how impossible it was going to be for him to afford to stay here. What was Max doing at a resort complex, anyway? Jack would have thought that the kind of inquiries that Max needed to make in order to find his father could surely far more easily be made if Max was centred in Kingston.

A little reluctantly he entered the foyer.

Max had just finished having a shower when the telephone rang. He picked up the receiver, studying the reflection of his naked body in the mirror opposite him while he listened to the receptionist telling him that there was someone in reception asking for him. As he thanked her, Max's eyebrow lifted in an amused gesture.

That was quick! He hadn't expected the stunning redheaded air stewardess, to whom he had slipped his hotel phone number at the end of the flight, to get in touch with him so quickly.

Not that he was complaining. She had passed on to him the information that she would be having a two-day stopover in Jamaica before flying home, which meant that by the time she left he should, given the potential of the female guests he had already assessed strolling through the foyer of the hotel, have found someone to take her place.

Not that Max intended to spend all his time on the island looking for sex. He had heard that it possessed several good golf courses.

He was determined to go home with a better handicap. Luke still had an advantage over him in that department. Smug bastard. It would be good to invite him to play and then casually drop the information that he was now playing off six to Luke's seven as against his present ten.

With a month or so to work on his game, there was no reason why he shouldn't get it down that far. One way or another...

As to his mission to find David... He dropped the towel and reached for his clean clothes. He had taken the precaution before leaving home of arming himself with the addresses of a couple of private detective agencies in Kingston. A few phone calls home to his grandfather, laying a series of hopeful trails that would, of course, ultimately peter out, would keep the old man quiet, and when, ultimately, he had to return without any concrete news of David's whereabouts...

Max gave a small shrug. The old man must know that there was no real chance of David reappearing until he himself chose to do so.

Zipping up the cool off-white linen trousers

he had just pulled on, Max once again studied his reflection in the mirror. Not for him the garish 'leisure wear' he had seen sported by some of the other male guests. His short-sleeved shirt, like his trousers, was plain—and expensive—his feet bare in the cream canvas deck shoes he had put on. He looked like every right-thinking woman's dream of how a man should look—and he knew it.

Smiling to himself, he opened his bedroom door.

His heart in his mouth, Jack watched as Max walked out of the lift and towards him. He hadn't seen him as yet and when he did…

'Hello, Max…'

'Jack! What the hell's going on? What are *you* doing here?'

As he saw the fury burning in his cousin's eyes, Jack licked his overdry lips. Fear and tension crawled viciously through his stomach like maggots. He had never been a particularly good traveller, and now, suddenly, he felt acutely sick.

'I've come to help you find my father. It's my right,' Jack announced shakily, forcing himself to remember the words he had prepared so carefully.

'Your *right*. Don't give me that, you little...'

Jack winced as Max reached out and fastened hard fingers around his upper arm, tightening them on his wrist, too, until Jack actually thought it might break as he jerked him towards him.

'I don't know what the hell you think you're doing here, Jack, but...'

'I've just told you. I've come to find my father.'

'Your father... Your father doesn't *want* to be found...he isn't *going* to be found. Your *father*...'

Angrily, Max gave him a brutal shake.

God, but this was the last thing he needed. It was going to ruin all his plans. There was no way he was going to have a stupid little boy like Jack...

'Give me your passport, Jack,' he demanded savagely. 'You aren't staying here. I'm putting you on the first plane back home and then I'm going to ring my father and...'

'You can't. I don't have... I've lost my passport,' Jack told him.

The look Max gave him in the silence that followed made him literally shiver with fear.

'You've...done...what?' Max demanded slowly, spacing out the words with careful menace. 'I think you're lying to me, Jack,' he continued equally softly. 'In fact, I do hope that you *are* lying, because if you aren't... Have you any idea what they do to illegal immigrants over here...unauthorized visitors?'

'I... I'm not unauthorized. I *had* my passport...I...I just don't have it now.' Swallowing hard, Jack forced himself to meet the look in Max's eyes.

Max was, after all, only his cousin. That was all. Max had no real authority over him. Anyway, it was *his* father Max was here to find. His father, not Max's. He had more right to be here than Max. Much more right.

'I think we'd better continue this conversation in private,' Max was telling him coldly. 'Come with me.

'If you're telling me the truth and you really don't have your passport, then you're in big, big trouble,' Max told Jack gently. 'Real trouble, Jack. The kind of trouble that will probably result in you spending your time over here in prison, because, let's make no mistake about it, that's exactly where the authorities are going to put you once they learn that you're here without your passport, and you do realize that it's my duty to inform them of that fact, don't you...'

'The British consul...' Jack began bravely, but inwardly he was sick with fear. This was worse, much worse than he had imagined. He had known that Max would be furious, of course, and that he would attempt to send him home. But that Max might confront him with the threat of having him sent to prison had never once occurred to him, and now he was beginning to panic, all his carefully rehearsed arguments deserting him as he fought to control his fear. Despite the air-conditioning in the foyer, his body was bathed in sweat; he felt clammy, nauseous, his head ached and he was desperately, desperately afraid that he might actually start to cry.

'The British consul nothing... Do you know what they really think of young idiots like you? They don't give a damn, Jack. And you...'

'They'll let me ring home, though, and speak to Uncle Jon....'

Max looked at him, and Jack knew that he had hit a nerve, scored a point somehow against all the odds. It threw him a little that Max of all people could be stopped by the threat of his own father, when Uncle Jon was, as everyone knew, one of the kindest, gentlest men there was. But instinctively Jack knew that he had found the way to make Max back off, and thankfully he clung on to it.

'They'll let me speak to him and...'

Max was thinking fast. Oh, yes, they would let Jack speak to him, and it would be typical of his father that the first thing he'd do would be to get on a plane and come out here to sort out the mess Jack had made, in person, and once he did...

His father was no fool. One look at this place would immediately convince him that the last thing Max intended to do was to search for David. His father's opinion of him was of complete indifference to Max, he couldn't care less what he thought, but what he *did* about it was a different matter. And if he went home and managed to convince Max's grandfather that the only thing Max was doing in Jamaica was getting a free holiday at the old man's expense, then that holiday would very quickly be over with.

Max couldn't have his father coming rushing over here to Jack's rescue, but the last thing he wanted was to have the wretched youth here, cramping his style. It would be impossible, of course, for Jack to afford to stay here in the same hotel—and equally impossible to send him home, until a replacement passport had been obtained for him.

'Come with me,' Max instructed his cousin, heading back towards the lift. He would have to ring home himself and tell his father what had happened, reassure him Jack was okay and get him to send out some money to cover Jack's expenses, and then he would have to find some cheap boarding house where Jack could stay until a replacement passport could be organized for him.

Cursing him under his breath, Max pushed him into the lift, ignoring Jack's wince of pain as his youthfully bony shoulder banged against the metal door frame.

It was quite late in the evening when Jenny actually stepped into her kitchen, rather later than she had intended to be home, but after the meeting with the contractors who were working on the new house, which she and Ruth had recently acquired for conversion into their third lot of single-parent flatlets, Jenny had been so thrilled and impressed by the way that Maddy had handled herself during the meeting that she had insisted on taking her to the town's pretty and well-patronized wine bar, so that they could discuss the meeting over a sandwich and a cappuccino.

'That was quick of you to spot the mistake the plumbing contractor had made with his costing,' Jenny had applauded her daughter-in-law. 'You really are going to be an asset to us Maddy. You're going to need to get to know the trust's accountant. I'll set up a meeting with him for you.'

The trust, which had originally been run informally by Ruth and herself from their individual homes, now boasted a small office in Haslewich, which was, in fact, one room in the building that the family legal practice occupied and which Jon had been talked into parting with.

'Who are the accountants, by the way?' Maddy had asked her.

'A firm in Chester,' Jenny had responded. 'Luke recommended them. Griff Owen, who deals with our accounts, is an old friend of his. They were at school together.'

'Griff Owen. He must be Welsh,' Maddy had commented.

'Yes, he is,' Jenny had agreed, adding, 'I'll give him a ring and fix up a meeting with him for you. When...'

'I'd prefer it if you could leave it for a little

while,' Maddy had confessed. 'I'd really like to have as much financial information about the charity as I can at my fingertips before I meet him.'

They had parted on mutually happy terms half an hour later, Maddy to drive over to Tullah's to pick up Leo and Emma and Jenny to come home to make her own family's tea.

'I'm sorry I'm late,' she apologized to Jon as she walked into the kitchen, going up to him to give him a loving kiss before asking, 'Where are the boys?'

'Joss has cycled over to see Caspar. Apparently there was something he wanted to talk to him about. He said not to worry about any supper for him.'

'Maddy was wonderful this afternoon. I really saw another side to her. I always knew she had it in her, of course. No one could handle Gramps the way she does and not...'

Jenny broke off, her happiness dying from her eyes as she felt Jon's tension.

'What is it, Jon? What's wrong?' she asked him uncertainly.

'I've just had a phone call from Max.'

'From Max...but why...what...?'

'Jack's with him.'

'Jack!' Jenny gave him bewildered look. 'But

he can't be,' she protested. 'Max is in Jamaica and...'

'So, apparently, is Jack!'

'How? Why? Have you...have you spoken to him?'

'Yes,' Jon confirmed heavily. 'Apparently he drew the money out of his building society account to pay for his ticket and...'

'It's because Max is out there to look for David, isn't it,' Jenny guessed.

'Yes,' Jon agreed. 'Jack seems to think that if anyone has the right to seek out David, then that person should be him.'

'He *is* David's son,' Jenny agreed. 'But to have done such a thing and behind our backs... What does Max intend to do, put him on the first flight home?'

'I'm afraid it isn't going to be quite as easy as that,' Jon told her. He added quietly, 'For a start, Jack has apparently either lost or destroyed his passport, which makes it impossible for him to leave the country until it can be replaced. And for another...' He looked briefly away from Jenny, and when he looked back at her she could see his troubled expression and it made her heart sink.

'Jack says that so long as Max stays out there, then so will he.'

Jenny looked concerned.

'But he can't *do* that. What about his school work...his studies? Jon, you've got to make him come home.'

'I can't,' Jon told her.

'But he isn't eighteen yet,' Jenny protested. 'He's still under age.'

'He is still under age,' Jon agreed, 'but *I* have no legal guardianship over him. Tiggy and David are still his parents. Tiggy is holidaying in Australia with her new husband, and David is, of course, unreachable! And to be honest with you, Jenny, I'm reluctant to push Jack too far in case he...well, Jamaica isn't the place I'd want to have him living rough in, and if he took it into his head to...'

'To disappear,' Jenny filled in for him, her throat suddenly going painfully dry. Jack might not actually be her son, her child, but she loved him as though he were, and the thought of him being alone and in need, in danger, filled her with the most acute sense of maternal despair.

'I know,' Jon sighed, reading her mind as she looked up at him and then leaned her head against his shoulder.

'So, what is going to happen? What have you...?'

'Well, Max was talking about installing him in some kind of cheap lodgings in Kingston until he could get him sorted out with a new passport, but I wasn't happy with that idea. I had a word with the hotel manager, who confirmed that Max had a twin-bedded room, so I managed to arrange, for the time being, for Jack to stay there with Max.'

'Max agreed to that?' Jenny asked her husband in surprise.

'Not at first,' Jon agreed grimly. 'However, I had to persuade him—and remind him—of the fact that it is his grandfather who is footing the bill. Of course, we'll pay Jack's costs. I just wish...' He paused and shook his head. 'I just wish Jack had discussed...talked...told us...' He stopped and then gave a reluctant laugh as he commented ruefully, 'I'd have given anything to see Max's face when Jack presented himself to him.'

Husband and wife exchanged a mutually understanding look.

'Mmm...having Jack along with him will quite definitely cramp his style,' Jenny agreed quietly.

Maddy smiled as she bent down to kiss Leo's sleeping face as she tucked his duvet in around him.

He had been on edge in the car coming home from Tullah's, asking her anxiously, 'Will... Is Daddy going to be there when we get back?'

Gently Maddy had reassured him, wondering sadly as she did so how many children of his age asked that question in the hope of getting a negative answer rather than a positive one.

Oh, but she had enjoyed herself this afternoon with Jenny.

The terrible attack of butterflies she had suffered before the meeting with the contractors had disappeared once she had found herself getting involved in Jenny's discussions with them.

Like Ruth and Jenny, Maddy felt acutely sympathetic to the plight of young girls and women struggling to provide a secure and stable home for their small children, and she fully supported the aims of the small charity, originally set up by Ruth, to provide good-quality, low-rental accommodation for such single mothers.

Two houses had already been bought and converted with the money donated to the charity. Each flat possessed its own small kitchen and bathroom, and all of them had access to the child-safe gardens, which Ruth and Jenny had insisted were a mandatory feature of the properties they acquired.

Day-to-day management of the flats, the collection of rents, repairs to the properties and their allocation to tenants were also all handled by the charity, which, in effect, meant that they were dealt with by Jenny and Ruth, when she was in the country, with the aid of the two women who both worked part-time in the office.

Until her late-life marriage, Ruth had taken the leading role in the charity's business affairs, and as Jenny had explained ruefully to Maddy, she herself had done her best, but she simply did not have Ruth's aptitude for finance and figures.

'You obviously have the same sort of gift,' she had told Maddy, who had shrugged modestly and protested that being able to have a reasonably good mathematical brain was hardly a 'gift.'

'Oh, but it is,' Jenny had assured her. 'You don't know what a relief it is to me to be able to hand over all that side of things to you, Maddy.'

In point of fact, there was rather more to the job she had agreed to take on than Maddy had first realized, but to her astonishment, instead of feeling daunted by this knowledge, what she actually felt was a very definite sense of elation.

What *was* daunting her, though, was Tullah's determination to give her a new image. She smiled a little sadly to herself. It wasn't that she didn't doubt the advantages of improving on the way she looked. What she did doubt was the possibility; the plausibility of anyone actually being able to do so.

When she had been a teenager, her mother, emerging briefly from her own world, had taken an appalled look at her round-faced, chubby daughter, dressed in her school uniform, and quickly reckoned up in her head that Maddy was fast approaching eighteen but looked in actual fact far more like a fourteen-year-old. She had promptly booked Maddy into a health farm for a fortnight, telling her that she needed to lose weight and, in her own words, 'learn to do the best she could with her looks.'

Maddy had hated every moment of it. The other inmates at the appallingly expensive health hydro had been almost exclusively middle-aged women with whom Maddy, shy and insecure, had had virtually nothing in common.

The eight pounds she had lost during her enforced stay had quickly been put back on, plus some more once she was back at school, and the make-up lessons she had endured had only reinforced what her mother had already told her—that she was hopelessly plain and that she could never hope to attract a man simply by being herself.

And yet, knowing that, she had still allowed herself to believe that Max had fallen in love with her.

How easily she had been persuaded to delude herself, but in doing so, she had cheated her children of their right to have a father who loved them, and that hurt her far more than knowing that Max did not love her—nor ever would.

It was funny how when he was not there she was able to be perfectly analytical about him and their relationship, their marriage, and yet she knew perfectly well that if he were to walk in through the door now and touch her...

She closed her eyes.

She was not going to think about that or about him!

7

Two weeks later Maddy paused before the glass window front of one of Chester's most exclusive shops, surreptitiously studying her reflection, torn between nervousness and elation. She was on her way to her first meeting with the charity's accountant, Griff Owen. She was wearing a subtly understated and unbelievably expensive softly tailored suit in a totally impractical shade of vanilla, which did wildly, improbably flattering things to the colour of her skin and the shape of her body. However, despite Tullah's attempts to persuade her otherwise, she had refused to allow her to unfasten anything more than the first top button of the matching silk shirt she was wearing underneath it.

'But you should, you've got the most wonderfully feminine curves,' Tullah had protested, ignoring the wry smile Maddy had given her as she had looked pointedly at Tullah's own softly feminine and full breasts.

'No, I can't wear it like that,' she had protested when Tullah had tried to coax her. 'It's…it's far too…'

'Dangerous,' Tullah had suggested softly.

'It's just not me,' Maddy had informed her primly, putting a protective hand to the neck of her shirt.

However, it was not so much her new clothes that had suddenly made Maddy walk tall and pause every now and again to stare in wide-eyed disbelief and a certain amount of awed pleasure at her own reflection in the shop windows—a hitherto unknown pursuit and indulgence—as the new haircut Tullah had coaxed her into having. Well, not so much coaxed, Maddy conceded, remembering how Tullah had virtually frog-marched her into the exclusive London salon where she had booked an appointment for her, using goodness knew what means to persuade the busy stylist to make room for her, and then stood guard over her in the salon to prevent her from leaving while she and the stylist had discussed what kind of cut would best suit Maddy's delicate, fine-boned features.

A happy glow suffused Maddy's face as she remembered the complimentary and unbelievably flattering description the stylist had made of her face; *her* plain, round, dull face. Only it wasn't round or dull any more, and as for being plain... Whether because of the soft feathered cut the stylist had given her, combined with the magic he had wrought with high and low lights, or because of the additional weight she had undoubtedly lost over the last few months, Maddy didn't know. All she did know was that she had returned from her trip to London with her appearance so dramatically changed that even now, three days later, she still had to pinch herself just to make sure that this stylish, slender, pretty, *happy*-looking woman she could see looking back at her with wide-eyed awe and delight, actually was herself.

'Pretty Mummy,' Emma had lisped, while Leo, her darling, precious Leo, had flung himself into her arms after her return from London and held on to her as though he never wanted to let her go again.

It had been fun shopping with Tullah, at least it had been once the ordeal of the visit to the hairdresser was over. What had not been quite so much fun, however, had been the accidental discovery in the mews house of several items of another woman's underwear.

Maddy was no fool. She knew that Max

wasn't faithful to her. The underwear had been ruthlessly stuffed in a rubbish sack, along with the bedding she had stripped from Max's bed before remaking it for her own use.

It had been amusing to note her parents' reaction to her changed appearance the night she and Tullah had had dinner with them. Her mother had asked briefly about Leo and Emma, but her main topic of conversation during the evening had been Maddy's father's probable appointment as the next Lord Chief Justice. A cool, chaste kiss on the cheek from her mother at the end of the evening and an awkward embrace from her father had reinforced Maddy's conviction that she had done the best possible thing she could for her children's emotional welfare in ensuring that they grew up in Haslewich, surrounded by the love of their paternal grandparents and the rest of Max's family.

She might not have given them the kind of *father* they deserved, but she certainly intended to do the best she could to remedy that deficit by making sure that they learned, at second hand, through Max's siblings and cousins and their marriages, just how a loving family household worked.

But for once, it wasn't her children who

were the main priority in Maddy's thoughts as she made her way through Chester's busy medieval streets to the offices occupied by the charity's accountants.

Every evening for the last ten days, once the children were safely in bed and Gramps dozing in front of the television, she had shut herself in the kitchen and carefully immersed herself in the financial workings and background of the charity, absorbing as she did not just its history and its make-up but every nuance of how its systems worked and where its strengths and weaknesses—from a financial point of view—lay. And what she had discovered was that, despite the money Ruth herself had put into the charity and the heroic money-raising endeavours of Ruth and Jenny plus Tullah, Olivia and Guy Cooke and his wife, Chrissie, along with several others, the charity was operating on a veritable shoe-string.

The rents charged to the single mothers, who were the charity's tenants, nowhere near covered the expense of maintaining the buildings, and soon, with another set of flats to finance once the new conversion had been completed...

If the charity was to operate comfortably, then it was going to need more funds, a safer operating margin. Ideally, Maddy would have liked to see a situation where money could be invested to bring in an income to cover, not just any shortfall in the small rental income, but also allow for any unexpected expenses.

The cause was a good one, no one could doubt that, and the townspeople supported it generously, but it was a sad fact that they were never going to be able to meet the increasing demand for accommodation from the often very young mothers, who either found their way to the charity's offices by themselves or increasingly were directed there by the local social services.

'Time was when a girl in trouble was taken in and cared for by her own family,' Guy Cooke's aunt Libby, who worked in the charity's office, had commented to Maddy when she had gone in to collect some funds. 'There's many a child of my generation who was brought up to think its grandmother was his or her mum. That's the way things were. Now, of course, it's all different.

'People just don't have the same family network to fall back on any more.'

Maddy had agreed gently.

'Very often a girl's mother is having to go out to work herself, and modern houses aren't built to accommodate several growing generations.'

'*Tell* me about it,' Libby Cooke had groaned wryly.

'I've just had my eldest, Mark, come home from university.

'He's got his degree but no job as yet, and now he's talking about having his girlfriend move in with us....' She rolled her eyes.

Maddy liked Chrissie Cooke, Guy's wife, to whom she had been introduced by Jenny. Jenny and Guy had, at one time, run a small antique shop together. Jenny had sold her share of the business to Guy when she had become more involved with the charity, and he had gone on to develop and expand it to include the organization and management of a justly nationally admired antiques fair, which was held in the stable yard and grounds of Lord Astlegh's home at Fitzburgh Place.

Guy, whom Maddy had also met and liked, had an extremely shrewd business brain as well as a sharply perceptive mind.

He and Chrissie were in the process of having a new house built on some land that Guy had acquired close to Lord Astlegh's estate, and they were presently living with one of

Guy's sisters and her husband while they waited for their new property to be completed.

Maddy, who had been shown the plans by an excited Chrissie, had marvelled enviously over them with her. The house had been specifically designed for family living—Chrissie and Guy were planning, as they both joked, to have a full clutch of children.

While the inside of the house was going to be thoroughly modern, the construction of the building and the materials used were strictly traditional.

'The look we're aiming for is that of a very pretty Georgian rectory,' Guy had explained to Maddy with a wide grin.

'Very Jane Austen,' Chrissie had supplemented.

Recollecting Queensmead's collection of odd-sized rooms and warren of connecting passages, as well as the problems she was having in coaxing a local builder to agree that converting a couple of the smaller bedrooms into *en suite* bathrooms and dressing rooms for some of the bedrooms wasn't the near Herculean task she and the builder both knew it to be, Maddy could only look on in quiet envy.

'But Queensmead has its gardens and its grounds and that wonderful ballroom,' Chrissie had protested when she had voiced her thoughts.

Maddy had smiled. The last time the ballroom had been used had been for Ruth's twenty-first, and she very much wanted to redesign certain parts of the garden, but of course Queensmead wasn't actually hers.

But today wasn't the day to be thinking about her personal problems, she reminded herself firmly, as the large clock facing down into one of Chester's main streets reminded her that if she didn't hurry she was going to be late for her appointment.

Jenny had told her very little about the man she was going to see other than that he had recently joined the partnership and that he was, apparently, an old school friend of Luke's.

Luke had apparently recommended that they switch the charity's accounts to Griff Owen when their original accountant in Haslewich had announced that he planned to retire.

Maddy's step quickened, nervous butterflies fluttering wings of tension in her stomach.

The office was situated in a row of renovated and extremely smart terraced houses on the periphery of the small city and overlooking the river.

An immaculate but very approachable receptionist took Maddy's name with a pleasant smile and invited her to take a seat.

Obediently Maddy did so, picking up a copy of *Cheshire Life* more as a barrier to hide behind than because she wanted something to read. She hadn't missed the admiring glance the receptionist had given her clothes, which had boosted her confidence, but not enough to completely stop her from feeling apprehensive.

What if the accountant treated her the way that Max did? What if he patronized her and made her feel small and insignificant?

What if…what if…

Quickly she opened the magazine she was holding so defensively.

Upstairs in Griff Owen's office—traditionally furnished with a highly polished partners' desk and appropriately heavy-duty leather-upholstered chairs chosen to harmonize with the design of the elegant Georgian room, with its carefully renovated plasterwork and fireplace—the modern technology that he favoured for efficient management of his business were all housed, out of sight, in another room. This office was used strictly for interviews and for when he needed time on his own to think. Griff Owen frowned as he placed the charity's file on the desk.

The accounts, while perfectly in order—meticulously so, in fact—showed to him certain glaring missed opportunities for making the charity's money work more efficiently for it than it already did, but Luke had warned him that Ruth, who effectively was the charity, had very strong views about the manner in which her pet project was run.

'Ruth is very much a people person,' Luke had informed him, warning him that when the charity had been considering making a switch from their previous accountants to him, 'she won't take very kindly to anyone treating the charity as if money were everything.'

The accountancy practice that Griff had been head-hunted to manage had been lacking in a certain thrusting vigour before he had taken over its management, due in the main to the fact that two of the other five partners were, in Griff's opinion, at a stage in their lives when the golf course held more allure than the practice. The other three, being their sons, were not really in a position to be as brutally honest with their fathers as he intended to be.

When it came to dealing with the older brigade of their client base, the retired colonels and the nervous elderly widows, Messrs. Joyce and Baring Senior were perfect, ideal role models of what such clients expected and wanted their accountants to be, but when it came to their other business, the business that brought in real money… Griff's frown deepened.

He and Luke were close-enough old friends for him to have been able to confide his doubts about joining the practice before he had done so, but as Luke had pointed out, heading the practice would give him the free hand he had not had in his previous job, and besides, he had private reasons for taking a step back out of the fast-moving career track he had been on.

The charity's business as such was normally something he would have handed to one of the seniors to deal with, but as Luke had quite rightly told him, nearly all of the charity's long-time supporters were involved in the top echelons of local thriving, thrusting businesses. Luke's cousin Saul, for instance, had persuaded his employers, the huge multinational Aarlston-Becker, to not just make a generous one-off donation to the charity, but also, in effect, to 'sponsor' several of the flatlets. Interestingly Griff had also learned from Luke that it had been Maddy Crighton's suggestion that had prompted Saul to put the proposal to Aarlston in the first place.

Maddy Crighton. It had been what Luke had *not* said about his cousin Max's wife, rather than what he *had* said about her, that was making Griff wonder about the wisdom of getting involved in a business relationship with her.

He had gone round to see Luke when he and Bobbie had returned from spending Christmas in America and it had been Bobbie who had championed the other woman to him, saying in that fascinatingly alluring American accent of hers, 'Poor Maddy is a marvel. How on earth she puts up with Max I shall never know.'

Luke had raised one eyebrow and remarked quietly, 'I don't think that Griff is interested in Max and Maddy's marital problems, my love.'

A woman trapped in an unhappy marriage and who made no attempt to free herself from it was, in Griff's experience, a very dangerously dependent, clinging-vine type of woman who was looking for a 'prince' to come riding along to her rescue. Such women often had an unfortunate tendency to attach themselves to the professional males in their lives, convincing themselves that their professional nurturing cloaked a desire to nurture them on a much deeper and more intimate level. Doctors were often the victims of this undesirable fixation, and so he had discovered were solicitors...and accountants!

While there was no permanent partner sharing his life at the moment, Griff had had two serious long-term relationships, the second of which had ended two years earlier. He and the woman concerned had accepted that since Griff did not want to commit himself to marriage and family and she did, it was best that they went their separate ways. Which was not to say that he had not, as she had overemotionally claimed at the time, cared very deeply about her—he had—and now, at thirty-six, he was wary of getting involved at that kind of level with anyone else.

He had several good women friends, some of whom were ex-lovers, and others, the wives of friends who, in other circumstances, could have been lovers.

Most of the women who knew him described Griff as madly attractive and sexy, and maddeningly self-sufficient. To his male friends he was, quite simply, a good and steadfast friend, the kind of friend who kept his most private thoughts and his most private emotions safely to himself.

Griff could hear footsteps approaching his office door. Collecting himself, he went to open it.

Jenny had told Maddy that Griff Owen was a man of Luke's generation rather than her father-in-law's, but what she had not prepared her for was the stunning effect of his six-foot-odd frame and his thick, rich dark copper hair brushed back from a face that could have been modelled from the tomb of some medieval warrior prince.

Knowing he was Welsh from his name, she had somehow mentally visualized a much shorter and stockier man, dark-haired and Celtic. This man was virtually as tall as Max, his body, from the way he moved, whip-cord lean and muscular, his face… She risked a second nervous look at the strong, almost cruel lines of his face; the nose that spoke of a lineage that went back to the days when Wales was the birthplace of a race of men born to lead others; the tight aristocratic line of his jaw; and most of all, that almost shockingly sexual, rich, thick hair that for some reason had her fingers curling into protestingly protective small fists as she fought against their instinctive urge to reach out and touch it.

Touch it... Touch him... Blindly Maddy tried to step backwards out of the room, to step backwards from him and from...

But it was already too late, already he was reaching towards her, placing a guiding hand, its fingers lean and long and very, very male, on her arm, urging her, *drawing* her, forwards into the room.

'Mrs Crighton... Griff Owen...'

Dumbly Maddy allowed her hand to rest limply in his as he shook it.

'Please come and sit down.'

Dazed, Maddy let herself be led, not towards the desk but instead to a chair set to one side of the elegant Adam-style fireplace.

As she sat down, Griff Owen took the chair opposite her, calmly placing a file of papers on the table between them—or at least his demeanour appeared calm to Maddy.

Playing for time, Griff focused on the file and then on his own hand splayed firmly across it, fingertips pressed to the paper with enough pressure to turn them white beneath his nails.

In the heartbeat of time during which he had opened the office door and seen Maddy standing there, the elegant, stylishness of her clothes and her hair giving off one message while the desperate anxiety in her eyes gave off another, Griff had been struck; felled by a blow to the heart the French refer to as *coup de foudre*. With one glance, one brief, all-encompassing look, Maddy's features had become totally engraved on his heart; he ached, yearned to hold her, to protect and cherish her. With that one glance he had, in short, become the prince who would ride into her life and rescue her from the prison of her unfulfilling marriage, her unworthy husband.

To say that Griff recognized all these complex emotions and sensations immediately and totally, however, was to slightly exaggerate the truth. He was still, after all, a man, and as such not proxy to divine and God-like awareness and understanding. What he did, however, recognize was that he felt the oddest, strongest and most dangerous upsurge of protective male emotion towards Maddy that he had ever experienced in his life, and, typically, he reacted to it, *against* it, by frowning sternly at her and adopting towards her a crisp and very distancing business-like tone of voice as he asked her formally how well she was acquainted with the financial affairs of the charity.

A little to her own surprise, Maddy discovered that his formidable, not to say unfriendly, manner, instead of increasing her nervousness, actually put her on her mettle somewhat, calling forth from her a responsive coolness of voice and demeanour as she calmly ran through her understanding of the way the charity's finances worked.

Griff was impressed and rather taken aback. Her shy, hesitant manner masked a brain that was obviously far sharper than he had imagined.

'I haven't done any in-depth work on the matter as yet,' he announced, not quite truthfully, 'but it occurs to me that if the charity is to establish the kind of sound financial base it needs, much better use must be made of the income it receives.'

'I agree,' Maddy concurred, and then further confounded him by informing him crisply, 'However, what I feel we are desperately in need of is a way of drawing more voluntary finance into the charity.'

'You mean through collections, car boot sales, that kind of thing,' Griff ventured.

'They do bring in *some* income,' Maddy

agreed. 'But what we need if we are going to be able to fulfil Ruth's hopes of expanding, to provide more flatlets and larger flats to accommodate our mothers as their children grow older, is to establish some regular form of funding or outside help that we can rely on as a regular form of income. I'm thinking here of increasing the support we get from local industry and perhaps of getting some kind of government aid as well. Although, of course, we would have to be extremely careful on that front in order to ensure that the charity maintains full and complete control of its own affairs. Through Saul Crighton's good offices, we've already managed to persuade Aarlston-Becker to sponsor some of our flatlets, and what I'd like to be able to do is to use that as a springboard from which we can launch an appeal to local businesses to persuade them to follow suit. If we can upgrade Aarlston-Becker's sponsorship from a few flatlets to a complete house of them, then so much the better, but to do that, of course, we'd have to find a way of establishing a competitive rivalry between Aarlston and another large company, along with some sort of inducement to whichever of them helps us the most—perhaps naming the house after the company and, of course, ensuring that they get as much good publicity as we can get for them for helping us....'

'You've obviously got a very good understanding...a very good instinct...for people management' was all that Griff could say as he privately marvelled at her grasp, not just of the charity's financial situation but also of the best usage of the social assets it possessed.

'Not really,' Maddy returned, for once looking him in the eyes with confidence. A small, rueful smile curled her mouth as she told him, 'I'm a mother of two young children. That very quickly teaches you what natural competition is all about.'

She laughed, obviously expecting him to share her amusement, but Griff had to look away from her.

Maddy's smile died. What on earth had she said to produce that immediate and betraying tension in him? Was it perhaps because she had brought the issue of her motherhood into a business discussion?

Uncertainly she looked down at her hands. When she and Jenny had discussed how she would handle this meeting, Jenny had simply said to her, 'Just be yourself, Maddy. That will be more than enough.' And Maddy had drawn confidence, not just from Jenny's gentle words but also from the combined urging and praise of Olivia and Tullah. Now, immediately, she was full of uncertainty and self-consciousness and a totally unexpected and unfamiliar surge of protective anger. Why should this man, who was, after all, paid for his professional service to the charity, look away from her in dismissal simply because she had made a comment that brought her status as a full-time mother and with it, no doubt in his eyes, her lack of credibility in the career professional stakes into the ball park.

For reasons she couldn't begin to understand, where Max's contempt for what he considered to be her lowly status as a mother reduced her to a bundle of self-defensive misery, this man's brought such a startlingly strong surge of virtuous anger that the force of it caused her eyes to widen and her lips to part on a small, soft sound of surprise.

His attention caught by the sound of her sharply expelled breath, Griff turned his head to look at her. Immediately his gaze was drawn to her mouth. Her teeth were small and white, neatly and evenly spaced like a young girls', but her lips...

Griff could feel himself starting to perspire

inside the crisp coolness of his shirt. Her lips just looked so incredibly soft and...

'Have you made any plans for lunch?'

Maddy's eyes widened even further. Whatever she had expected him to say, it was not that.

'No. No, I haven't,' she responded truthfully. 'I... I was going to buy a sandwich and...'

'I... I'd like to take this issue of getting other companies to follow Aarlston-Becker's example and sponsor flats a bit further,' Griff told her. Did his voice sound as gruff and raw with emotion to her as it did to him? Did it betray to her as it did to him just how much she had thrown him off guard...? Had she...? Quickly he reminded himself that he was an accountant and she was representing a client.

'The hotel opposite does an excellent business lunch.'

'I...' Maddy hesitated, searching frantically for some excuse to turn him down, without wanting to examine too closely just why she felt such a panicky and wholly personal surge of need to do so.

'I...'

When was the last time an attractive man

had taken her out to eat? When was the last time…?

This was *business*, she reminded herself sternly, at the same time as an unexpectedly rebellious little voice inside her was arguing that her suit, and her hair, deserved to be shown off and appreciated, if nothing else.

'I… I'd like that,' she heard herself accepting weakly, while her head pounded in frantic anxiety at what she had done.

'Good.'

As he turned his head to smile at her, Griff momentarily forgot the stern reminder he had just given himself about his professional role. Maddy, totally unprepared for the effect of this lazy, teasing, reassuring and, at the same time, somehow dizzying and oh, so flattering, sexy male, with the predatory curl to his mouth, felt as though she had just jumped out of an aeroplane and gone into free fall.

The effect, at once so exhilarating and so terrifying, was enough to make her forget everything but the feeling that soared through her veins, and somehow or other she discovered she was on her feet and allowing Griff to guide her towards the office door without having any real idea of how she had come to move out of her chair.

Later, she could never remember what they had said to each other as they walked towards the hotel's restaurant. Something banal and commonplace about the city and the weather no doubt, but as soon as they got to the door she suddenly froze.

She couldn't do this. She was a married woman. A married woman with two children...a married woman to whom things like this simply didn't happen.

Shocked by her own thoughts, she swallowed hard. What was the matter with her? *Nothing* was happening. She was having lunch with the charity's accountant, that was all.... A simple business interaction that took place between hundreds of thousands of other people every working day without them behaving as though...as if...

The doorman opened the doors, and Griff reached forward to place his hand politely and protectively beneath her elbow.

Helplessly, Maddy closed her eyes. Now she knew just what all those Victorian writers had meant when they had described how their heroines had been brought close to swooning point by the ardency of their lover's touch on their hand.

Her whole body suddenly felt as though it

was pulsing with the most embarrassing intensity of sexual awareness. It wasn't lust. She didn't, as she had once heard a friend claim, suddenly yearn for Griff to rip off her knickers and push her up against a convenient wall, so hotly intense was her desire to have sex with him. No, this was a different kind of sexual awareness. Not so much a sharp, urgent need, as a long, slow pulse of dawning awakening to the reality that Max was not, after all, the only man she could be physically responsive to.

Through their lunch, while he was discussing with Maddy in a logical and businesslike manner the problems she was likely to face in persuading businessmen to take on board the kind of long-term sponsorship she had in mind, Griff, at a deeper and far more intimately personal level, was totally absorbed in drinking in everything about her. The way she spoke; the soft liquidity of her eyes, especially when she was emotionally involved in what she was discussing; the extraordinary softness of her voice; the deep perceptiveness and awareness of her understanding; the colour and texture of her skin; the line of her nose, her jaw, her body; the shape of her mouth. Griff had never experienced anything like he was experiencing now with Maddy...for Maddy...

Did she, he wondered, realize how often she spoke of her children and how little of her husband? Griff's only knowledge of the man was what he had learned second-hand from Luke, who had been grimly dismissive and contemptuous of the other man, while acknowledging that he could be a formidable adversary.

It was gone three o'clock when Maddy shook her head and laughingly refused a third cup of coffee.

'I must go,' she protested. 'The…'

'I know…the children,' Griff said, completing her thought.

Maddy flushed a little and smiled. The two glasses of good wine she had had with their meal were still having their effect.

She very rarely touched alcohol and certainly not normally during the daytime.

Griff, she noticed, had shaken his head over a second glass, explaining to her, 'I have to drive out of the city to see some other clients later, Sue and Lewis Ericson. I don't know if you know them. Like you, they were introductions from Luke. They're friends of his.'

'Yes… I think I know who you mean,' Maddy had responded, her forehead crinkling in a way that had made Griff yearn to reach across the table and smooth away her tiny frown lines with his lips.

'Don't they hold Gilbert and Sullivan open-air operettas in their garden during the summer?'

'That's them,' Griff had confirmed. 'They're both avid Gilbert and Sullivan fans—that's how they met, apparently. It might be worth your while to have a word with them. I know that, apart from covering the costs of holding the operettas with the fee money, they also like to make a donation to local causes. Of course, they're more Chester-based than Haslewich, but still...'

'I'll talk to Luke about it and see if he'll put in a good word for us,' Maddy had responded eagerly.

'I could mention it to Luke if you like,' Griff offered. 'I'm having dinner with him and Bobbie this evening.' He paused and looked at her. 'In fact...'

'I... I really must go,' Maddy interrupted him, her voice suddenly a little tremulous as she hurried to deflect the invitation she suspected he was about to give her. Not because she wouldn't have enjoyed both receiving it and accepting it, she acknowledged shakily as he immediately responded to her tension by signalling to the waiter that they were ready to leave, but because she knew she would accept.

To be with a man and to be aware of his interest in her, his desire for her, was a totally new experience for Maddy, and yet somehow, she discovered that it was astonishingly easy for her to recognize that the signs were there: that ardent, caressing look in Griff's eyes whenever he looked at her came from genuine emotion and wasn't being manufactured to cloak some ulterior purpose.

After all, what possible ulterior motive could Griff have in pretending an emotional interest in her he did not really feel?

He was an extraordinarily attractive man, too attractive, her senses warned her as they reminded her that Max, too, was a very attractive man. Attractive, handsome, sexy men attracted women, as Maddy knew to her cost with Max, but then, of course, fair-mindedness forced her to acknowledge that it was up to the man whether or not he responded to them.

'Your eyes are like the sky,' Griff whispered huskily to her as they left the hotel. 'Clear and sunny one moment and then clouded the next. They're clouded now. Clouded and just a little bit sad.'

Looking down into her startled face as she

turned towards him, he reached for her hand, holding it tenderly within both of his own. As she stood facing him, a most extraordinary sensation of warmth and security wrapped itself around her like a gentle, protective cloak.

'No,' Griff told her hoarsely as he looked from her mouth to her nervously darkened eyes. 'You needn't worry, I'm not going to kiss you, not here, not now. But one day I shall, Maddy, and when I do...'

As she listened to him, Maddy could literally feel her knees starting to buckle as the bittersweet tide of exhilaration and shock swept through her.

Griff lifted one of his hands from hers, raised his index finger to his own lips, and then reached out and gently placed it against hers.

In her shock, Maddy allowed her lips to part. Not, she comforted herself later, with any deliberate intention of enticing Griff to slip his finger between them, and certainly not so that he could caress the moist softness just inside her bottom lip in a way that made her instinctively and betrayingly take a step closer towards him.

The instant she realized what she was doing, she flushed self-consciously and stepped back, but not before she had seen the hot, hunting look of sensually driven satisfaction that burned in Griff's eyes.

A little to her bemusement, he insisted on escorting her to her car, causing her to tease him laughingly, 'I see you've heard about my notorious lack of any sense of direction from Luke and Bobbie. Just because the first time I drove to their house I took a wrong turning and nearly ended up in Wales!'

'They haven't said a word,' Griff reassured her huskily. 'If I had my way you'd never get lost again, Maddy, because I'd be there beside you, everywhere you are....'

It made her face colour up a second time, but this time not in self-consciousness.

With Max she had experienced the unwelcome awareness of her body responding with frantic, almost feral need and desire to a man whom her brain did not like and whose treatment of her had frozen her emotions way past the point where they could easily be revived. She had despaired of herself, asking herself what kind of woman she was that she should demean herself by allowing Max time and time again to reduce her to a pulp of aching physical need when she knew that once the sex was over he would walk away from her in contempt. With Griff, she suddenly realized in a glorious sunburst of freeing joy that here was a man she could like and love and want. And it wasn't until she had said goodbye and driven several miles out of the city that she came back down to earth with a spine-jarring bump as she remembered that she wasn't *free* to feel those emotions or that desire.

'So, how did you get on in Chester?'

Maddy wondered guiltily if it was possible for Jenny to sense from the very quality of her silence over the telephone wire just how conscience-stricken her question had made her.

'I... I... He was very...kind. He suggested that we think about getting the Ericsons involved in some fund-raising.

'They're those friends of Luke's who have the Gilbert and Sullivan operettas in the summer....'

She was speaking too fast, betraying too much, Maddy recognized dizzily, but she couldn't help it. She felt both elated and ashamed, excited and afraid. When the telephone had rung she had been standing in the kitchen nursing a mug of cold coffee while staring dreamily into space, and just for a second before she had rushed to answer it and heard Jenny's voice, she had actually wondered if her caller might be Griff.

'Oh, yes, I think I know who you mean,' Jenny was agreeing, her own voice so calm and placid, so normal that Maddy felt confused. How could her mother-in-law not have picked up on and recognized just how much her own life had changed? Couldn't she *hear* the emotion in her, Maddy's, voice…sense it, in the ether, the very air. Maddy felt as though her feelings, her guilt, were written in huge, burning brands of fire across her face, and yet she knew that given the chance to relive events she would not have changed a single thing.

She was still thinking about Griff two hours later as she bathed the children and put them to bed. Tullah had rung to ask how she had got on and so, too, had Olivia. Scarlet-cheeked, she had responded as carelessly as she could that her meeting with Griff had gone fine, thankful that they could not actually see her expression.

She couldn't wait to go to bed, to lie there in the private darkness and relive every heart-stopping second of her time with Griff, savouring each look, each touch, hugging the secret knowledge of them to her.

It wasn't like when she had met and fallen in love with Max; this was different. This was more of a response of her poor, starved, deprived senses to the knowledge that she was wanted, desired. Instinctively she knew that had her marriage to Max been happy and fulfilling, had he loved her, then Griff would have been nothing more than an extremely attractive man whom she might have flirted very lightly with simply because she was a woman.

Her marriage was neither happy nor fulfilling, though, and she sensed that Griff was aware of her loneliness and unhappiness, even though he had not referred to them.

She had no thought in her head of the future, of any consequences, she was far too bedazzled and euphoric for that kind of logic.

She had had today…she would have tomorrow, and that was enough.

'What's got into Griff?' Luke asked his wife in amusement as he followed her into the kitchen with the dishes from the first course of their meal. 'It's like he's on another planet.'

'Or in love,' Bobbie whispered excitedly. 'Do you think he's met someone at last? Oh, Luke…'

'Griff in love…' Luke cut across her excitement, shaking his head. 'No, Griff isn't the type to let himself go emotionally. He's far too self-contained. He likes to be in control.'

'So do you,' Bobbie pointed out mischievously, 'but you fell in love with me.'

'Mmm...' Luke agreed, pausing to reach out and take her in his arms, slowly kissing her until she pushed him away, pink-cheeked.

'Luke, Griff will wonder what on earth we're doing.'

'Mmm... I'll blame you and tell him there was a crisis in the kitchen.' Luke was nuzzling just behind her ear, one hand tenderly placed across her still-flat stomach, and Bobbie could feel herself starting to melt.

'Stop trying to distract me,' she demanded. 'I'll bet you ten dollars that I'm right and that Griff is in love.'

'Ten dollars,' Luke teased her. 'Dollars aren't legal tender in this country, and anyway, you'd lose. I know Griff. He...he would never allow himself to fall in love.'

'Falling in love isn't something you can control,' Bobbie objected as Luke picked up two of the serving dishes she had just filled with rice and vegetables.

Maybe it wasn't, Luke acknowledged inwardly as he carried the food into the dining room, telling Griff urbanely as he set the dishes down, 'Sorry about the delay, a small crisis in the kitchen.'

'Mmm… You're still wearing it round your mouth,' Griff told him dryly, grinning as Luke automatically touched his fingers to his mouth and grimaced as they came away stained soft pink with Bobbie's lipstick.

'Don't mind me,' Griff assured him. 'I'm just envious, that's all.'

'Envious?' Luke queried. 'I thought marriage and commitment were a definite no-no so far as you're concerned.'

'Mmm… Well they do have certain advantages.'

Luke would have questioned him further, but Bobbie had come in with the rest of the food and she started to ask Griff how his meeting had gone with Maddy, whom she knew had been coming in to Chester to see him.

'I had hoped that she might be able to join us for dinner, but she couldn't make it,' she added, unaware of the effect she was having on Griff, who had bent his head over the food to study it with immense interest the moment he had heard Maddy's name mentioned.

'She felt she had to be there for the children and Gramps this evening, although I know that Jenny would have been happy to stand in for her for one night out. That's Maddy all over, though, she is just so conscientious.'

'Well, they say that opposites attract,' Luke intervened curtly, 'and "conscientious" is the last way I would ever describe Max.'

Bobbie gave him a fond look. She knew that Luke would never forgive Max for coming on so strongly to her the first time she had met the family, despite the fact that he had been married to Maddy.

'Poor little tyke,' he had commented angrily the last time they had visited Queensmead for a family gathering. 'Anyone can see that Leo is terrified of his father.'

'It must be difficult for them with Max having to spend so much time away in London,' Bobbie had palliated.

'*Having* to,' Luke had drawled, and wisely Bobbie had not pursued the argument.

Now, though, thinking of Maddy, she asked Griff eagerly, 'Do you think you'll be able to do anything to help the charity? We were all really pleased when Maddy agreed to take over from my grandmother on the committee. She thinks she's not up to the work, but we all know that she is.'

'She certainly has a very sound grasp of the

charity's finances,' Griff agreed, deliberately trying to keep any emotion out of his voice.

He succeeded so well that Bobbie gave him a confused look, but Griff was continuing in a more hearty tone, 'Which reminds me, I did tell her that I would have a word with you, Luke, about the possibility of getting the Ericsons involved in holding a fundraiser for them.'

'The Ericsons... You mean one of their Gilbert and Sullivan nights? Oh, that would be wonderful,' Bobbie enthused immediately.

'Oh, why on earth haven't we thought of doing something like that before?' she asked Luke excitedly. 'I know that Sue Ericson would be thrilled to have an excuse to put on an extra show.

'As you know, Ruth, my grandmother, originally set up the charity,' Bobbie told Griff as she turned towards him. 'And I suppose we've all rather left it to her to suggest ways and means of funding it, because it is so very much her brainchild....'

'I've also discussed with Maddy, Mrs Crighton, the possibility of getting further outside sponsorship of either individual flatlets or possibly an entire house on a corporate basis.

She's made a start in that direction via the sponsorship obtained from Aarlston-Becker.'

'Yes, that was a wonderful idea of Maddy's,' Bobbie cut in enthusiastically. 'Gran was thrilled to bits with it, and it was Maddy who was insistent that it was made clear that the charity retained full and total control over the usage and tenancy of the flatlets they sponsored. She really is brilliant at that kind of thing. I just wish…'

Bobbie caught her husband's warning eye and checked herself. She'd almost let slip before details of Maddy's private life, and it wouldn't do to discuss this with Griff no matter how close a friend he might be of theirs.

Luke, knowing full well Griff's views on people who stayed in relationships that weren't good for them, expected to hear Griff commenting in that slightly brusque way he sometimes had that if Maddy wasn't happy in her marriage, then it was up to her to get herself out of it, but instead, rather to his astonishment, he simply said unexpectedly gently, 'No, it can't be very easy for her, although I imagine she's far too loyal to say a great deal.'

He didn't say anything more, but something about the tone of his voice and the look in his eyes alerted all Bobbie's feminine intuition.

First thing in the morning she promised herself *she* was going to have a *long* chat with Maddy.

'Thanks for this evening.' Griff leaned forward to kiss Bobbie fondly as she and Luke accompanied him to the front door to say good night.

Luke had handed on his apartment in Chester to his brother following his marriage to Bobbie, and the couple now lived in a pretty renovated farmhouse on the Haslewich side of the city.

As he turned to leave, Griff espied the new Mercedes parked in the drive and teased Luke, 'You must be earning plenty of "refreshers",' he said, referring to the sums of money counsel were paid by clients for the time they had to spend waiting in court for a case to be heard.

'*Earned* is the right word,' Luke countered. Then, straight-faced, he added *sotto voce*, 'Really, the seats in some of those courts are so damned uncomfortable.'

Griff laughed as he walked towards his own car and unlocked the door.

Bobbie waited until she and Luke were inside the house before she pounced on him, demanding eagerly, 'Did you *see* the look on

Griff's face when he talked about Maddy? I think he's fallen for her.'

'What?' Luke shook his head and laughed. 'No way! Maddy just isn't Griff's type. He's a man who shies away from any kind of emotional involvement or dependency. The thought of a woman who needs the kind of gentle handling and emotional input that Maddy needs would be enough to make him run a mile….'

Still shaking his head, Luke smiled down at her as he slipped his arm around her waist and lowered his mouth to kiss her.

The telephone's ringing brought Maddy out of a confused dream. Sleepily she reached for the receiver and murmured, 'Hello.'

'Maddy, it's me, Griff.'

Instantly she was totally awake, sitting up in bed, dragging the covers up around her breasts, even though she knew it was impossible for Griff to see them, her face flushed with excitement and pleasure, her toes curling wantonly against the mattress.

'I've just got back from having dinner with Luke and Bobbie. I felt so envious of Luke, knowing that he was going to be spending the night holding the woman he loves in his arms. I just wish…'

Maddy was shaking so much she almost dropped the receiver.

'Oh, God, Maddy, I can't believe this is happening to me,' she heard Griff groan. 'Tell me that you feel it, too…that I haven't completely gone off my head. Oh, Maddy…'

'Griff,' she began, intending to protest that he shouldn't be speaking to her so, that she was married…a mother…and that it was impossible for him to love her, plain, dull, boring Maddy.

But her heart was beating frantically fast, and in the dim light of the moonlit bedroom she could see her own reflection in the dressing table mirror. Perhaps it was a trick of the moonlight, but her eyes seemed to be gleaming with a soft, intoxicating shine and her skin looked mysteriously pale, her new hairstyle emphasizing the rounded curve of her cheekbone. She looked, she recognized with a heart-thudding surge of excitement, like a woman who was eagerly awaiting her lover—a lover she knew wanted her just as much as she wanted him.

'Yes,' she heard Griff encouraging her rawly.

'Just…Griff…' she told him simply, but her mouth was curving into a smile, and the free hand she had raised towards the receiver was suddenly and betrayingly stroking the cream plastic, her fingers sliding down over the wire to entangle slowly with the coils.

'I… I'll ring you tomorrow,' Griff promised her. 'Dream about me…please.'

Ten minutes after he had rung off, Maddy was still sitting up in bed staring giddily into space, hugging the secret of her new-found love tightly to her.

Griff couldn't sleep. He could almost feel the adrenalin surging through his veins, smell the scent of his own hormones, his own arousal on his skin.

Ruefully, he walked over to his bedroom window.

The way he was behaving was crazy and he knew it. Maddy was wrong in every possible way a woman could be wrong for him, and on top of that, she was married. She was…

He threw back his head, closing his eyes, the Adam's apple in his throat moving against the tautness of his skin as he swallowed hard on the emotions gutting him.

Maddy was Maddy. It was as simple as that.

She was Maddy and he loved her, would always love her. In his mind's eye he could still see her, her small-boned body, those huge, wary eyes, her face, her hair. He groaned and opened his eyes.

Oh, God, if she was only here with him right now. It raised the goose-flesh on his arms, and with it their covering of soft male hair, just to think of all the ways he wanted to make love with her, of all the ways he wanted to show her how he...

He imagined kissing her, parting the soft shyness of her lips, exploring them with his tongue before probing beyond their sensual barrier to the moist sweetness of her mouth. She would protest and be slightly shocked, but in her eyes, as she opened them, he would see how much she shared his feelings, his love.

As he held her and kissed her, she would reach out and touch him, a little hesitantly at first, her face flushing that delicious shade of soft pink it went when she felt shy and uncertain. But then, once she knew—and he would make sure that she did know, just how much he wanted her to touch him—her confidence would grow and the fingers she slid exploratively over his skin and into his hair would tremble just a little bit, betraying her passion

for him. He would take hold of one of her
hands and lift her fingers to his mouth, gently
kissing them, sucking on them....

Griff groaned. His whole body ached with
the pulsing heat of his need.

Inside his head his thoughts ran wild. In his
imagination, Maddy was totally naked as he
was himself, her skin shimmering like pale silk
in the moonlight on his bed. Her body would
be soft and womanly, all gentle curves, just
made for the touch of a man's hands. When he
touched her she would watch him, dark-eyed.
Her body trembling every now and again with
tiny little shudders of sensual pleasure.

Griff made a low sound of male urgency
deep in his throat.

8

Max laughed as Jack's shot went wide of the fairway and bounced off into the rough, and then he jeered, 'Your father would never recognize you from your golfing, Jack. He played off nine. You're more like my father,' he told him mockingly.

Jack had had enough. Hot and furiously angry, he flung down his club and told Max bitterly, 'I thought we were supposed to be *looking* for my father and not playing golf.'

'You heard what the investigation agent we went to visit said, Jack,' Max countered smoothly. 'Jamaica has its own way of life, its own rules. Out here if a man wants to keep himself private, if you know what I mean, well man, then that's his business.'

'You haven't done anything to try to find my father. If you want my opinion, I don't think you ever intended to try to find him,' Jack stormed. 'In fact, I think...'

Max moved so quickly that Jack was taken

completely off guard when he grasped hold of his upper arm in a grip so painful that it made Jack wince and cry out in protest, his eyes shocked as he looked into his cousin's face and saw the venom there.

'If I were you, I shouldn't waste your time *thinking,* Jack. You don't have the genes for it,' Max told him brutally. 'Look at your mother.'

White-faced, Jack stared at him. Although he would never have been able to admit it, he wished desperately that he had not come out to Jamaica, and not just because of Max. He was missing his aunt and uncle very much, and Joss even more so. Every morning when he opened his eyes and realized that the person occupying the other single bed opposite his own was not Joss but Joss's elder brother, he wished passionately that he was back home in England with his family. His eyes filled with youthful tears as he yanked his arm out of Max's loosening grip.

His *father* was his family, supposedly, that was why he had come out here in the first place, but it was the kind of wise love in his uncle Jon's eyes that he yearned for, the understanding warmth of his aunt Jenny's maternal care, the camaraderie he shared with Joss, his friends, his hobbies...his home.

Inwardly he was filled with panic at the thought of actually meeting his father, even if outwardly that fear and dread found expression in his frustrated anger against Max because he was doing so little to merit them being here.

Apart from one visit to the small, privately run bureau in the centre of Kingston, so far as Jack could tell, Max had done nothing to instigate any real search for his father.

They had been in Jamaica for several weeks, and so far the majority of Max's time was spent either beside the pool or on the private golf course within walking distance of their hotel complex.

Now Jack had had enough. Ignoring Max, he picked up his discarded club and walked quickly back down the fairway. Angry tears filled his eyes. He had never particularly liked Max, but now he felt as though he hated him, and it was obvious to see the contempt in which Max held him. That remark he had goadingly made about his mother...

Jack stopped walking and closed his eyes. Even now no matter how hard he tried to lock them away, to banish them from his mind, there were times when the memories, the images of his mother, returned to haunt him. His mother, pretty, slim, laughing, flirting, always dressed so beautifully, her hair silky, her face...her scent...

Jack felt his stomach lurch, his mind filled with another image of his mother, her hair sticky and matted with food, her body swollen and distorted by her gorging...binging. The nauseating stench of sickness heavy on the air and on her person, her sobbed pleas to him to say nothing, to help her conceal what she had done.

That had been in the days before Olivia, his sister, had returned home to discover what was going on. Days, weeks, months, years. How many, Jack did not know. He only knew that they had seemed to go on forever, filled with a mixture of conflicting emotions. Love and pity for his mother. Shame for her weakness, anger against her and against his father, who did nothing to stop her, who had to be protected from what she was doing. How swiftly, how frighteningly all those memories came back to him now.

Jack opened his eyes and turned his head. Just along the beach from the golf course he could see the hotel complex, and suddenly he longed for the solitude and privacy of the hotel bedroom. It would take him only a few minutes to reach the hotel if he took a short cut along the beach instead of waiting by the clubhouse for the tourist bus. He could hand in the golf club he was still carrying later.

Strictly speaking he shouldn't do it, and not just because of the hired club—there were warnings posted all over the hotel and golf course telling guests not to take the risk of walking outside the perimeter fences that separated the hotel and its environs from the public beach.

Thefts from tourists who were foolish enough to ignore these warnings were apparently quite commonplace. The gangs of youths who roamed the public beaches obviously saw rich tourists as their legitimate prey.

Jack grimaced to himself. He was scarcely likely to interest them. He was certainly not rich, neither was he carrying an expensive camera or wearing designer clothes, items that had been mentioned as specifically being of interest to the youthful thieves.

It was a problem that the authorities were doing their best to tackle, but Jack shrugged mentally, he was scarcely likely to be attacked in broad daylight.

Max frowned and glanced down the fairway. It had amused him at first when Jack had

stormed off, more especially because Max had
seen the telltale glint of moisture in his eyes,
but Jack had still not reappeared, and the last
thing that Max wanted was for the boy to take
it into his head to ring home and pour out any
grievances into his parents' ears. Having him
hanging around was an irritation Max could
well have done without, but he had noted just
how many attractive and quite patently
wealthy women had approached him, using
the excuse of asking if Jack was his son.

He was supposed to be meeting one of them
later. He frowned. Again he felt no guilt about
the way he had upset Jack by deliberately nee-
dling the younger man about his mother, but
Jack had stalked off with one of the golf clubs
for which he, Max, had had to pay out an inordinate sum of money in a covering deposit,
which doubtless would not be returned to him
without a complete set of golf clubs.

Irritably he replaced his own club in his bag
and set out after Jack. He couldn't have got
very far. He had only been gone a matter of
minutes.

Max walked down the fairway, fully expecting to see Jack heading back to the clubhouse,
but instead, there was no sign of him.

Absently Max turned to look out to sea. Eleanor Smythson—his date for tonight—had mentioned that her husband's private yacht was moored at one of the island's most exclusive marinas.

As Max looked back, his attention was suddenly caught by a lone figure walking along the public beach towards the hotel, his shoulders hunched, head down. There was no mistaking the thin, gawky frame of his young cousin.

Grimly Max cupped his hands together and called after him, but either Jack could not hear or wasn't going to acknowledge that he could.

What the hell was the young fool playing at, Max wondered wrathfully, just as Jack disappeared when the bay curved sharply round, a tumble of brushwood and palm trees obscuring Max's view of him.

Angrily he set off after him.

Jack's first intimation of danger came as he crossed the small jutting post of land where the coast curved so sharply that the area of beach he was on could be seen neither from the golf course nor the hotel grounds. The four men, three of them black and one of them white, rose up out of the brushwood where they had obviously been lying in wait, so quietly and so quickly that Jack had no time to do anything other than draw a quick breath of shock before they were upon him.

They smelt of drugs and the pomade they used on their 'Rasta'-styled hair, their eyes frighteningly blank of any kind of humanity as one of them reached savagely for his watch, ripping it off Jack's arm so that it caught his skin and then flinging it away in disgust.

'It ain't no Rolex, man,' he told his companions as one of them grabbed Jack's wrist, even more painfully than Max had taken hold of his arm earlier, and demanded aggressively, 'Your money, man, where is it? We kill you unless you tell us...'

Even though he was still holding the club, Jack's own instincts and upbringing he had received from his uncle Jon prevented him from raising it to ward them off. The thought of striking another human being with it, even in self-defence, was as alien to him as what was happening.

He tried to protest that he had no money, but all he got for his pains was a sickeningly painful knee thrust into his groin before he was thrown to the ground.

'Perhaps we kill him, anyway. White pig,'

he heard one of them suggesting as they ripped off the jacket Jack was wearing, the one who was holding him down laughing at him as he tried to reason with them.

Max saw them before they saw him, every atavistic instinct he had ever possessed rising up inside him like flood water under ice. Max, too, had been raised by Jon Crighton, scholarly, gentle, wise Jon, who had, to his own anguish, failed to implant any one of those single virtues in his eldest son.

Max was a chancer, a winner, a man who met all of life's challenges head on, and for some reason, as he looked at his young cousin being set upon and systematically kicked and beaten by his attackers, by some mental act of legerdemain that Max didn't bother to try to understand, the body of his cousin lying on the sand suddenly became transformed into that of his own small son, so that it was Leo's small, dark-haired vulnerability that was under attack. Leo's tiny body that was lying there motionless, *his* cries of pain the only sound Max could hear as the drug-crazed gang gleefully took turns to kick Jack.

The club that Jack had been unable to use in his own defence had been flung contemptuously to one side by his attackers. Spying it,

Max made soft-footedly for it, but just as he reached it one of the quartet spun round and saw him.

Grinning hugely, the youth reached into his waistband and removed a long, sharp-bladed knife, at the same time jumping forward to place one foot on the shaft of the club as he waved the knife with taunting insolence in front of Max's unprotected body.

'You want it,' he gibed, indicating the club, 'come and get it, then, man.'

Like Jack, Max was immediately aware of the fact that the man was high on drugs, and one of the quartet, despite the racist taunts they were throwing at him as they cheered on their companion, was quite definitely of mixed blood if not completely white, Max decided, even if like the others he was sporting long Rasta ringlets.

Keeping his eyes fixed on his opponent's face, Max made a grab for the club, wincing as the knife slashed down on his unprotected fingers. He saw the sun glinting on the knife as his attacker wielded it again and felt the sharp blade slicing down across his chest and then his arm, his torso, his leg. As blood started to stain the sand, Max suddenly knew that the man in front of him intended to kill him, that he would actively enjoy killing him.

'Maddy looks very happy these days,' Jon commented with a smile as he watched his daughter-in-law drive off with her two children. He and Jenny had been looking after them for her while she took his father to hospital for a check-up. Jon had offered to accompany the elderly man, but Maddy had shaken her head, explaining gently, 'He hates other men seeing him vulnerable. He's terribly sensitive about the fact that he isn't able to be as active as he'd like, and that makes him feel cross and out of sorts with everyone.'

'You're a saint, Maddy,' Jon had told her ruefully, but she had shaken her head a second time, used to hearing her family call her this, and corrected him mischievously, 'Only sometimes...'

'Yes, she does,' Jenny agreed quietly now, in response to his comment about their daughter-in-law, so quietly that Jon turned his gaze away from the departing car to his wife's face.

'Something wrong?' he asked her intuitively.

'Yes and no,' Jenny told him. 'Maddy *is* looking much happier, and of course, I'm pleased about that, but...' She paused and then told him unhappily, 'From something Bobbie said the other day, I think Maddy may have become involved with Griff Owen.'

'Griff Owen, the accountant?' Jon queried. Then he added, frowning, 'What exactly do you mean by "involved," Jenny...?'

'Well, I don't think they're actually having an affair—not yet—but Bobbie seems to be convinced that Griff has fallen for Maddy. Apparently Griff is a regular dinner guest of theirs—as you know, he and Luke are old friends—and it seems that Griff has been hinting very pointedly to her about inviting Maddy as well.'

She saw Jon's raised eyebrows and added a little defensively, 'He talks about her a lot as well, Bobbie says, and you can see for yourself how much she's bloomed recently, how happy she is.' She gave her husband a troubled look.

'I want her to be happy, of course I do, but... She's so vulnerable, Jon, and I'm so afraid for her. After the way Max has treated her, to have another man, even if he seems a personable, caring man...'

'Have you said anything about any of this to Maddy herself?' Jon asked her quietly.

Jenny shook her head.

'No. How can I? After all, Max...'

Jon walked up to her and took her in his arms, smiling lovingly at her.

'I understand what you're trying to say,' he agreed. 'But Max has never been a good husband to her, even if he *is* our son. Maddy deserves to be happy, Jen, and the children deserve to grow up in a happy, loving home. If another man can give Maddy the love she and they need and she returns it, then it really isn't for us to try to interfere.'

'No, never, not *that*,' Jenny protested, making a small anguished sound against his chest. 'It's just that I'm worried *for* her, Jon. After all, what do we know about this man? He might hurt her just as much.'

'Ah, so it's those maternal feelings of yours that are causing the problems, is it? I should have guessed,' Jon teased her. 'If that's really what's bothering you, I imagine it would be a simple enough matter to organize things so that we can get to know him a little better, especially since Luke and Bobbie already number him among their friends.'

'I so much wish that things could have been different,' Jenny sighed, 'and that Max...'

'Max is a fool,' Jon told her gruffly, pausing to drop a tender kiss on the top of her head, 'and no one deserves to be happy more than Maddy....'

'Mummy, is Uncle Griff coming round tonight?' Leo asked Maddy eagerly as she drove home.

In the privacy of the car Maddy blushed pinkly.

'Er, no... I don't think so,' she told him huskily, unable to stop the delicious glow of pleasure that just thinking about Griff, just *hearing* his name, gave her, and yet, at the same time, feeling so absurdly guilty *because* of the way she felt. The way she felt... Not the way she had acted. As yet, she and Griff had done nothing.... As yet she and Griff were not lovers...as yet!

Tonight she was having dinner with him in Chester. She was going to drop the children off with Bobbie and Luke beforehand, and the plan was that she would then return to spend the night with them.

It had been Griff who had introduced himself to the children, arriving unexpectedly one afternoon just after she had picked them up from play school.

Maddy had held her breath a little as she introduced them to one another, especially when she watched Leo. Leo, who was so wary of his own father, and yet who, to her amazement and joy, seemed to have taken immediately to Griff.

'I think you've got Griff well and truly smitten,' Bobbie had teased her earlier in the week. Maddy had tried to deny any understanding of what she meant, of course, and had, naturally, failed!

Remarkably, perhaps, as she prepared for her dinner date with Griff later that evening with all the anticipation and excitement of any woman preparing to meet the man she loved, the very last thing that Maddy felt was any sense of guilt about Max. Perhaps that was because she didn't really feel married, she decided judiciously as she examined this lack of remorse for what she was doing. After all, she and Max had no shared history of ever having loved each other or having been intimate in the only real sense of the word that mattered.

Yes, they had had sex, but they had never been close, never been emotionally intimate, never shared their thoughts, their hopes, their joys or their pains.

Of course, she had been a little wary with Griff at first, a little reserved, flattered by his attention but unable to take his attentions too seriously. He was, after all, a handsome, successful man, while she—

But four nights ago when he had kissed her properly for the first time, all that had changed. Feeling his body tremble slightly with the force of his emotions, seeing the blind, aching need in his eyes, she had known when he told her that his feelings for her were feelings he had never, ever had for another woman, she had known that he was genuine, that implausible though it was, he *did* love her.

As yet she hadn't thought about the future. There simply hadn't been the time, or the need. It was enough, so much *more* than she had ever envisaged having, that there was this, that there was now.

But she had still held back from making the ultimate physical commitment to him, from crossing the Rubicon, which she knew for her would cut her off from her marriage and Max forever. Once she had committed herself that way to Griff there would be, could be, no going back.

And Griff seemed to know just how she felt. He hadn't pressed her, hadn't rushed or demanded. But she could feel his frustration and his need in the fierce passion of his kisses, and she knew that soon…

Soon, but not tonight. Tonight they were simply meeting to talk, to be together, and after—

'Get dressed up,' he had exhorted her tenderly over the telephone. 'Tonight we're celebrating.'

'Celebrating what?' Maddy had demanded, laughing.

'Celebrating life,' Griff had responded sombrely, 'life and love and you…'

She had had to buy a new dress—there was nothing in her wardrobe, the wardrobe of the old, cowed Maddy, that was remotely suitable for 'celebrating'. When she and Tullah had gone shopping, they had concentrated on businesslike daytime clothes. And besides, without knowing quite how it had happened, she recognized that she had recently shed, along with her old image, the remaining plumpness that was the legacy of her pregnancies and the unhappiness caused by her marriage.

She had found the dress she wanted in a smart little shop in Chester, very simple, very plain, and despite the fact that the slinky jersey covered her from throat to knee, also very, very sexy.

To feel so good about herself was a totally new experience for Maddy, and she smiled at her reflection as she fastened small gold studs into her ears, humming under her breath as she hurried downstairs.

Tomorrow Luke and Bobbie were taking her and Griff out to meet with the Ericsons. Maddy had already compiled a list of would-be invitees to the charity operetta and also another shorter one of the local companies she intended to approach to ask for sponsorship of new flatlets.

It was a matter of a few short weeks since Max had announced that he was going to Jamaica, but already that event felt as though it belonged to another life, the edges of those memories already dimming and fading.

This afternoon, when she had called to pick up the children, her father-in-law had told her smilingly, 'It's good to see you looking so happy, Maddy.'

And she had responded truthfully, 'It's good to *be* so happy.'

That was it, a final mist of scent and she was ready. Leo looked at her with interest as she checked to see that they had everything they needed, telling her seriously, 'I like you when you smile a lot, Mummy.'

Leo had become a different child since Griff had entered their lives. Suddenly her face was grave. For her own sake she could bear the pain of her relationship with Griff not fulfilling all its promises, but she knew she could not bear it for her children and especially for Leo, who already was growing close to Griff, quite obviously finding in him the role model, the father figure, the *father* he had never been allowed to find in Max.

Predictably, the only person who had struck a note of discord about Griff's visits had been her grandfather-in-law.

Always fiercely partisan where Max was concerned, Ben had demanded grittily of Griff on his first visit, why a man who was plainly in his mid-thirties did not have a wife and children of his own.

'Perhaps because I've never met the right woman,' Griff had responded calmly, refusing to rise to the older man's bait.

Leo was looking forward to their visit to Chester, not least because Griff had promised to take him for a trip on the river.

Having checked that Ben had everything he needed, Maddy loaded children and possessions into the car and turned on the engine.

'If Leo...'

'Don't worry, they'll be fine, and yes, I know

you'll be at the Grosvenor and that we can get in touch with you there,' Bobbie laughed, soothing Maddy's maternal anxieties.

'What time did you say that Griff was picking you up?'

'About eight-thirty,' Maddy told her.

'Well, it's not eight yet, so there's plenty of time for you to have a glass of wine before he gets here. It will calm your nerves…your maternal nerves,' Bobbie teased her as Maddy paused to give both her children a final goodnight kiss before following her hostess downstairs.

Griff frowned as he studied his reflection in the mirror. It was too early to leave to collect Maddy yet. He could do with a drink but he was driving. So much hinged upon the outcome of this evening.

'Dinner…to celebrate…' he had told Maddy, and he had meant it, but what he had not told her…what he still had to tell her…

He closed his eyes, mentally picturing her, conjuring up her vision so exactly, so intensely that he could almost hear the soft sound of her laughter, smell the scent of her skin, hear her breathing. His heart muscles constricted in a spasm of hard male longing. If she was here with him now...if she was here with him now, they would never make it as far as the restaurant. He doubted that they would make it even as far as his bedroom door, never mind his bed. He gave a low, frustrated groan. But tonight wasn't about gently dispelling her very natural inhibitions and doubts, about convincing her that in his arms, his bed, his love, she would only find joy and happiness. Tonight was about...

He closed his eyes, arching his throat, and then opened them again. He had known even before he had met them just how much her children meant to Maddy, just how loved and important they were, and he had mentally prepared himself for their rejection and even, it had to be admitted, to feel a small degree of resentment towards them, especially towards Leo, who, he had guessed from everything that had been said about how close he was to his mother and everything that had not been said, was going to be a difficult, spoiled and rather wilful little boy.

What he had not prepared himself for was the overwhelming surge of longing he had felt when he had first seen the three of them together, Maddy and her two children...her son, her daughter...

Hers…but not his.

And what had struck him immediately about Leo was not the hostility he had expected but instead, his acute vulnerability.

He had wanted to cry for Leo that afternoon, to cry for him and all his little-boy pain, for the fear, the hesitation, the nervousness he had seen in his eyes, and he had wanted to cry for himself as well.

Instead he had set himself the task of gently winning Leo's trust. Maddy would never come to him without her children. She was the kind of woman who would always put their happiness above her own.

Already he could see her anxiety about the bond that was being established between Leo and himself; her fears that somehow Leo could be hurt. Well, tonight he would do his best to reassure her that her children, her son, would never be hurt by him, because her children, her daughter, her son, would be the only children that he would ever have. Unlike Max he would never be able to give her a child of their own! His own!

He had found out purely by chance. His girlfriend, a girl he had met at university and whom he had expected to marry once they were both established in their chosen careers, had mentioned in conversation that her sister, who was older than her, had recently announced her engagement.

'We're all pleased, of course, but Mum and Dad want them to go for genetic counselling. There's a history of cystic fibrosis in our family, and although neither of us has been affected, any children that we have could contract the condition if our partner carries a corresponding gene.' She had pulled a wry face.

'I suppose really we ought to do the same thing. Perhaps if we all go together we'll get a special rate,' she had joked, and Griff, his mind more on the holiday they were planning to take walking in the Pyrenees, had agreed. At twenty-one he had still been rather callow and given to youthful demonstrations of overt masculinity. In short, he had, ridiculously he now knew, assumed that the fact that he was a strongly built young man with a healthy body and an even healthier sex drive meant that he could stand back and look with slightly disdainful amusement at other people's vulnerability and potential weaknesses. He hadn't tested positive for the cystic fibrosis gene, but on their return from France he had found a letter waiting for him asking him to call and see his doctor.

'I've got what?' he had demanded in bewilderment after the doctor had asked him to sit down. The physician paced his small office several times before breaking the news to him that he was the carrier of a recessive gene that, if passed on to his children, would mean that they would be born with Huntington's chorea.

'You don't *have* anything,' the doctor had explained patiently. 'You are simply a carrier for the gene. It is your children, should you have them, who could be the ones to suffer.'

That had been more than a decade ago, before counselling had become the accepted practice it was now, and he had been left to find his own way of dealing with the blow that fate had dealt him. Both his parents were dead, having been killed in a rail accident, and his elderly grandmother, who had brought him up, had died the previous year.

The first thing he had done had been to break off his relationship with his then girlfriend—he knew how important children were to her because they had discussed it. The second had been to arrange to have a vasectomy.

Since then, he had steered clear of the kind of emotional involvement that might potentially lead towards marriage and children. His ex had since married and produced the family she had told him she wanted, and he was not prepared to put himself or anyone else through the heartache he had suffered over that break-up.

There were, of course, women who did not want children, he knew that, but call it old-fashioned and chauvinist of him if you like, he knew instinctively that they were not *his* kind of women.

And so he had decided that permanent commitment and love were not for him.

And then he had met Maddy. Maddy with whom he had fallen helplessly in love the moment he set eyes on her. Maddy, who already had two children... Maddy, who he knew intuitively would want to have his child.

Sweat started to break out on his forehead.

Tonight he had to tell her that that would be impossible and why.

He glanced at his watch. It was time for him to leave.

9

It was just by the merest chance that they hadn't both been murdered. The police and the surgeon had told Jack that as he lay in numbed shock while the nurse re-dressed his head wound, and he tried not to wince as the pain shot through his battered and bruised body.

A sportsman running along the beach, a local hero well known to all the inhabitants, had disturbed the gang, their respect for him causing them to disperse silently into the undergrowth, leaving him to raise the alarm.

Jack had still been unconscious when they arrived at the hospital, felled by the blow to his head. And Max...

'My cousin. How is my cousin?' Jack asked anxiously.

Ever since he had come round he had been asking about Max.

He had seen him trying to reach for the club he himself had discarded as he lay prone on the ground, held down by one of the gang, and he had seen, too, the bright blood oozing from the knife cuts on Max's body, but it had been after that that he had been clubbed into unconsciousness, and since his recovery here in hospital, all his attempts to find out what had happened to Max had been frustrated by questions either about his own health from the medical staff, or questions about what had happened by the police inspector who had come to talk to him.

'My cousin...' Jack repeated in a louder voice as the surgeon, having assured himself that the head wound he had just inspected was to his satisfaction, smiled at the nurse and started to turn away.

Jack saw the look the three people standing round his bed exchanged. His heart started to thud ominously, his muscles turning to water.

'Something's wrong.... What is it? Tell me. Tell me!' he shouted hoarsely.

Once again the three people standing round his bed exchanged looks, and then unexpectedly it was the policeman who spoke first, asking him, 'Your cousin... That would be Mr Max Crighton?'

'Yes. Yes, that's right. I'm Jack Crighton and Max is my cousin.'

'And you were both staying at the Paradise

Beach Hotel,' the policeman pressed, ignoring Jack's obvious anxiety.

'Yes. Yes, we were…'

'Since the gang who attacked you had removed your cousin's personal possessions from his…body…and you were unconscious, it took us some time to discover your identities, and, in fact, we were only able to confirm these a short time ago. I…'

'Max's *body*,' Jack interrupted him sharply, his face abruptly losing its colour. 'Does that mean…'

'Your cousin is alive…just,' the surgeon told him grimly, guessing what he was thinking. 'He's in intensive care, and I'm afraid it will be some time before we can assess the extent of his injuries. If he survives…if…' The surgeon paused and shook his head.

'He's lost a great deal of blood—that we can replace. The other damage…' He paused. 'I suspect that we shall have to remove his spleen. The beating he received means that…' He paused again. 'And then he had a very serious leg wound.'

'Can I…can I see him?' Jack croaked, his eyes suddenly filling with tears.

'No. You are still not strong enough yourself

yet to be moved. You both have family at home in England?'

'Yes,' Jack answered hollowly.

'Then I think it is advisable that they are told what has happened. Your cousin...'

'Max isn't going to die, is he?' Jack demanded in panic, but to his shock, instead of reassuring him, the surgeon shook his head.

'It's too soon yet to say. For the moment he is alive. If you would like us to get in touch with your family...'

Shaken, Jack nodded his head. He couldn't trust himself to speak to either his uncle Jon or his aunt Jenny. He had never felt more frightened in all his life. No, not even when his mother had been ill and his father had disappeared, and not even when he had been attacked and felt the blows raining down on his unprotected body. If only his uncle Jon was here with him now. *He* would know what to do. He would. To his own chagrin Jack suddenly started to cry.

'He's in shock still,' he heard the surgeon telling the policeman as they both moved away from the bed. 'Have you any idea who...'

'Not yet, but whoever it is, they could find themselves facing a murder charge if we ever do get them. These tourists, *when* will they learn? What are the man's real chances of survival?' Jack heard him asking the surgeon, but they had moved out of earshot before he could hear the surgeon's reply.

Jon and Jenny were in the kitchen discussing whether or not they could manage to fit a summer holiday into their busy schedules, and if so, where they should go, when the telephone rang.

Jon took the call, both his expression and the tone of his voice alerting Jenny to the fact that something dreadful had happened.

'There's been an accident…in Jamaica,' Jon announced hollowly when he replaced the receiver.

'Jack,' Jenny breathed immediately. 'What's happened to him…what's wrong…is he…?'

'No, not Jack, although apparently he's been hurt as well. It's Max.'

'Max!' Jenny stared in disbelief at her husband. Somehow one always thought of Max as being invincible. Not so much superhuman, she acknowledged as shock wrapped its cocooning, distancing protection around her, as *in*human…. She started to shudder. Dear God, what was she thinking? Max was her own child, her son.

'What…what's happened?' she asked Jon, surprised to discover that the reason she was finding it so hard to say the words was because she was trembling so badly. Somehow one never equated Max with anything that might damage or harm him. Max was always the one who harmed others. Max was…

'I don't really know. It seems that Max and Jack were attacked on the beach. Both of them were badly beaten up, but Max… They want me to go out there. They seem to think…' Jon couldn't go on. He had been too shocked, too held in the thrall of disbelief, to ask any questions, simply listening while the hospital's representative advised him that Max was seriously ill in intensive care and that the surgeon felt…

'I'll have to get on to the airport, see about a flight.'

Jon felt as though he was trying to walk through deep water…thick mud…a vast force that couldn't be seen but which impeded his progress. While his brain screamed at him to hurry, hurry, hurry before it was too late, his actions, his voice, all seemed to have slowed down to a crippling crawl.

244   *Penny Jordan*

'Yes... Yes...' Jenny whispered, her voice cracking as she protested, 'Oh, Jon, this can't be happening. Max...' Suddenly she felt dreadfully cold, hugging her arms around her body as she fought the need to start rocking herself to and fro, to start keening her grief. Once before she had suffered the loss of a child, felt the pain, the sense of helpless hopelessness, of failure; it was a pain that once experienced could never fully be forgotten.

'Maddy. Maddy will have to be told,' she reminded Jon as he reached for the telephone. 'She and the children were going to spend the weekend with Luke and Bobbie.'

Fiercely Jenny pressed her hand to her trembling lips before whispering brokenly, 'Oh, Jon...'

'Maddy, there's something I need to talk to you about...something I need to tell you.'

Obediently Maddy stopped looking longingly at the ballroom dance floor where other couples were already dancing and reminded herself sternly that she was a grown woman and not a teenager. The fact that she had whiled away nearly a full hour this afternoon fantazising about how it would feel to be held in Griff's arms, held close to his body, while they drifted together over the Grosvenor's dance floor, their steps, their minds and their hearts in perfect time with one another, was a lapse of maturity rather than a reason for her to feel envious of the other couples dancing to the smoochy number the band was playing.

Gently she focused on Griff's face, noticing that he looked tense and anxious, her disappointment fading quickly as she realized that whatever he wanted to discuss with her must be serious.

Encouragingly, she waited.

Out of the corner of her eye she could see the head waiter heading purposefully towards them. Mildly curious she watched him. He reached the table, but instead of going to Griff as she had anticipated, he came over to her, bending his head discreetly towards her as he told her quietly, 'Mrs Crighton, there's a telephone call for you. If you'd care to go through to our reception...'

Mutely Maddy got to her feet and glanced uncertainly at Griff, but he, too, was standing up, and she was grateful for his comforting presence at her side as she hurried towards the exit. For someone, *anyone*, to telephone her here, it must mean that there was some kind of problem at home...with Gramps...with the children.

Her heart thumping heavily, Maddy crossed the carpeted floor to the reception desk.

'There's a small private office, just to the left, if you'd like to take your call there,' the woman suggested quietly.

Nodding her head, Maddy pushed open the door she had indicated. The room was furnished anonymously with a couple of chairs, some prints on the walls, a table and, of course, a telephone.

Nervously she picked up the receiver, conscious of Griff standing in the doorway, both protecting her privacy and refusing to intrude.

'Maddy? Is that you? It's Jenny....'

Maddy could feel her throat starting to tighten as she heard the uncertain, unfamiliar, fearful note in her mother-in-law's normally so calm and warm voice. Even without closing her eyes she could picture Jenny standing in her large, comfortable, comforting kitchen.

'Yes. Yes, it's me...what...something's wrong,' Maddy guessed. 'What...who...is it Gramps...?'

'No...not Gramps.'

Now Maddy could quite plainly hear the

tears in her mother-in-law's voice, but before she could force her taut throat muscles to form the names of her own two children, she heard Jenny telling her chokily, 'It's Jack...and...and Max. There's been an accident. Jon... Oh, Maddy,' Jenny wept. 'Max is dreadfully poorly and they don't know...they can't say... Jon has managed to get a seat on the next flight out to Jamaica from Manchester. It leaves in a matter of hours. Maddy...'

'It's all right, Jenny,' Maddy heard herself saying gently. 'It's all right, I'm on my way home.'

Slowly she replaced the receiver before turning to face Griff.

'It's Max,' she told him quietly. 'There's been some sort of accident. I don't know what... Both Max and Jack were hurt, apparently, but Max...' Very carefully she swallowed and then began to speak again, her voice calm and controlled as though somehow it belonged to someone else she recognized distantly as she marvelled at her own self-control.

'Jon is flying out to Jamaica. I...' She lifted her glance to Griff's face for the first time since she had picked up the receiver.

'I could tell from Jenny's voice that they

don't expect... I have to go home, Griff, Jenny needs me,' she told him with calm dignity.

As they exchanged looks, Griff knew without her saying anything that the news she had just received changed everything between them; that what they had shared, what they were going to share, would have to be shelved, to be put on hold, that for now and for as long as it was required of her, Maddy was Max's wife, and not in any hypocritical sense, but simply in the sense that being Maddy, she instinctively wanted to be there for those who needed her. As he himself needed her. Wryly he wondered what would have happened had he been able to put his plans into action and tell her about his inability to give her any children and the reasons why *before* she had received that telephone call. Would she have been torn then between her pity for her husband's family and him, her duty to them and to him? Outwardly he might seem to be a whole, healthy male, but inwardly, at least in his own eyes, he was just as maimed, just as likely to be a burden to her as Max might turn out to be. But it wasn't her *pity* or her duty that he wanted. What he wanted...

'What will you do?' he asked her. 'Go back to Luke and Bobbie's for the children?'

Quickly Maddy shook her head.

'No,' she told him decisively. 'It's Jenny who needs me now.'

'I'll drive you back to Haslewich,' Griff offered, but Maddy shook her head again.

'No.' When she saw his face, she touched his arm. 'It wouldn't be the right thing to do. Not now,' she told him softly. 'Not when... I'll have to leave Leo and Emma at Bobbie's, though, and... It would help if you could visit them tomorrow,' she told him. 'Bobbie has enough to do with her own family, and I'm not sure when I shall be able to get back over to Chester for them. Until we know how Max... Until we know what's happened. I can't...' She stopped, her eyes suddenly shining with moisture, and then ducked her head.

'Don't, please...' Griff groaned. 'I know what you're going to say.'

Quickly he came into the room and shut the door, walking purposefully towards her and taking her in his arms, cradling her body against his, as much a protector and a friend as a lover.

'This doesn't change *anything* between us, Maddy, at least not so far as *I* am concerned, but I know you, and I know you won't want... Go to Jenny. Do whatever you feel you have to, and when...when you feel able...you and I...for now, you and I will just be...friends.'

'Oh, Griff, you're so good. Too good,' Maddy protested.

'No, *you're* the one who's that,' Griff corrected her.

Maddy shook her head.

'I feel I'm being so selfish, for wanting to keep you in my life and for...for using you when...'

'You're not being selfish and neither are you using me. Don't you think I *want* to be here for you?' Griff demanded roughly. 'Don't you *know* how much I...' He stopped. 'One day, when this is all behind us...' he promised her, and then groaned softly before cupping her face and turning it towards his own.

Maddy knew that he was going to kiss her, and she knew, too, that she should stop him, but she didn't...couldn't...

Feverishly, she clung to him as he parted her lips with his own, returning the passion of his kiss with her own pent-up feelings and longings. Tonight, even if they had not ended up in bed together, they would have taken another step towards doing so. Maddy knew that, knew it, and had been not just prepared for it but wanting it...wanting him. Jenny's phone call had put an end to all of that, though, and brought her swiftly back to reality.

Jenny… Reluctantly she pushed Griff away.

'I must go,' she told him softly, looking up into his eyes, her own sad and already shadowed. 'Jenny will be waiting.'

They drove in silence back to Luke and Bobbie's, Maddy getting out quickly as soon as he had stopped the car and hurrying to the front door, which Bobbie opened to her knock.

Quickly she explained to Bobbie what had happened. Luke joined them.

'You say *Max* has been injured?' he questioned Maddy sharply.

'Both of them have,' Maddy confirmed, 'but it seems that Max received the more serious injuries. Jon is to fly out to Jamaica to see him. Bobbie, may I leave the children here for tonight?'

'Of course you can,' Bobbie assured her quickly. 'Just as soon as you…as there are any details, let us know, won't you.'

Hugging her tightly, Maddy turned to go.

'Are you sure you wouldn't prefer me to drive you?' Luke asked her, but Maddy shook her head.

She was grateful for their concern and their offers of help, and grateful, too, that they were not expecting her to lay claim to a grief she could not feel. She might be Max's wife, but she had no sense of feeling what a loved and loving wife should have felt in her shoes. Her main concern, her main *fear* was not for Max but for his parents, and most especially for Jenny, whom she truly loved.

'No, I'll be fine,' she assured him.

Another hug, a brief silent exchange of looks with Griff, and then she was gone.

She drove fast but carefully, concentrating on the road and the traffic.

She could tell from the sound of Jenny's voice just how seriously ill Max must be, but she couldn't visualize him alone and helpless in a hospital bed. Instead, the only mental image of him she could create was the anger and contempt on his face, the hostility that always seemed to emanate from him. The energy and restlessness that drove him made it impossible for her to imagine him lying still and pale…and close to death….

Automatically she increased her speed. She would soon be home now. She drove straight to Jenny and Jon's house, parking her car in the drive and then hurrying round to the back door, which was the door that the family always used. It was open despite the cold night air, and she could see Jon standing inside speaking into the telephone.

He looked older, smaller; somehow grayer.

As she walked into the kitchen, he was replacing the receiver.

'That was the hospital in Jamaica. They can't tell me anything new. Maddy...'

'It's all right, it's all right,' Maddy soothed him automatically, using the same tone of voice she might have used to one of her own children as she reached up and wrapped her arms around him, holding him.

'We never thought, never imagined... Max, of all people...' he said in a muffled, strained voice. 'He's always been so...'

'What time is your flight?' Maddy asked him, gently disengaging herself from him, still speaking to him as she might have done to a child. 'Have you packed yet? Where's Jenny?'

'My flight? I...it leaves at four in the morning.' He gave her a wary smile. 'I shall have to be at the airport at two...the death hour. I...I haven't packed...not yet. I'm not sure... Jenny and Joss have gone for a walk.'

'Would you like me to pack for you?' Maddy offered.

'Would you...that would be kind. I'll make us both a cup of tea, shall I? I...I haven't told

Dad yet,' he added as he moved about the kitchen like a sleep-walker. 'God knows what this will do to him…to lose Max as well as David.'

Maddy swallowed a lump in her throat as she saw the tears welling in his eyes.

Like Bobbie and Luke, he had said nothing about her own lack of emotional reaction, but then even more than them, he knew what her marriage had been…what Max had been….

Gently she touched his arm.

'It may not be as bad as you think,' she told him softly. 'Max is very strong…a fighter.'

'They've already had to give him an emergency operation to remove his spleen,' Jon told her bleakly, 'and they say that even if he does manage to survive, which they aren't holding out much hope that he will do, they may have to amputate one of his legs. Apparently the knife wounds to it have done so much damage…'

He stopped as he heard the shocked, distressed sound that Maddy had made.

'Oh, I'm so sorry,' he apologized remorsefully. 'I'm so sorry. Oh Maddy, forgive me, for a moment I'd forgotten that you…'

'It's all right,' Maddy reassured him shakily. 'I can't pretend to be, to feel, but the thought of

Max of all people having to… He would hate it so much.'

'Yes,' Jon agreed, and Maddy knew that they were both thinking the same thing, that Max would rather not live than to have to suffer what his father had just described.

An hour later Maddy had packed her father-in-law's case and had returned to the kitchen to discover that Jenny and Joss had still not returned.

'It's starting to freeze,' Jon told her fretfully, 'and she wasn't wearing a warm coat, neither of them were.'

'I'll go and get them,' Maddy promised.

'You know where they'll have gone?' Jon asked her.

'Yes, I know,' Maddy agreed.

The ancient church at the centre of Haslewich had been there as long as the town itself. Frost rimmed the path that led from it towards the graveyard, sparkling in the lights that illuminated the church. From the town square, Maddy could hear the faint voices of the teenagers who had gathered there. Somewhere in the distance, a car backfired. She paused, lifting her gaze from the path in front of her to the row of houses that bordered the church and its environs, elegant three-storey Georgian houses, one of which was the home of Max's great-aunt Ruth.

Ruth would have known what to do and say had she been here, but she wasn't, she was in America. She would have to be telephoned and informed of what had happened, Maddy noted practically before squaring her shoulders and walking quickly into the graveyard.

She knew exactly where she was going, and it came as no surprise to her to see the down-bent heads of her young brother-in-law and Jenny as they knelt together in front of one of the gravestones.

'Maddy!' Jenny exclaimed as she looked up and saw her. 'Why...what are you doing here?'

'It's time to go home, Jenny,' Maddy told her mother-in-law softly. 'Jon's got to leave for the airport soon and he needs you.' Automatically, as she reached them, she had put out her hand and placed it comfortingly on Joss's shoulder. He had grown so much these last couple of years and was going to be taller than Max, but right now, as she felt the tension in him and the thinness of his adolescent body, Jenny saw him not as the adult he would one day be, but the child he still was.

'Joss is getting cold,' she told her gently.

'I've already lost one child,' Jenny told her dully. 'I don't want to lose another. Oh, Max, Max,' she whispered, covering her face with her hands.

Watching her, Maddy felt her own eyes burn with tears. She knew full well how Jon and Jenny felt about Max, how much it hurt them that he was the way he was. How much *he* had hurt them. But at the end of the day, Max was still Jenny's child. She had still given birth to him, and to Maddy, as a mother herself, there could be no greater imagined pain than that of losing one's child.

Maddy knew that all her married life and before it, Jenny had always been the one who had been strong for her family, her friends, her children. She had been strong for her, too, Maddy acknowledged, giving her the love and support that Maddy had never received from her own mother. Now it was Maddy's turn to be strong for her.

Gripping her shoulder, she told Joss, 'Help your mother to get up, Joss.' To Jenny, she said firmly, 'Max isn't dead, Jenny. He's alive, and Jon...'

'He's going to die, though,' Jenny told her bleakly, but Maddy saw with relief that she was getting to her feet and allowing her daughter-in-law and Joss to lead her out of the graveyard.

'We don't know that,' Maddy argued. 'Max is very strong...and very...stubborn. He'll fight to live.'

'This is all my fault,' Jenny told her dully, without responding. 'If I had loved him more...properly... I did love him when he was born. We had wanted him so badly, but he wasn't...he didn't...'

'Joss, run and start the car engine, will you, and get it warm,' Maddy instructed him, handing over her keys. 'I've parked it in the square.'

It was no secret that there was discord between Jon and Jenny and Max, but Maddy felt it would do little good for Joss to listen to what his mother was saying.

'I suppose I thought he would be a replacement for Harry,' Jenny told Maddy painfully, stopping walking to turn to look at her, her hand going out to halt Maddy as she focused on her, her eyes bleak and tormented.

'But he didn't even look the same as Harry. He looked different. He was...bigger... noisier—he was...'

'Max,' Maddy supplied quietly for her.

'He was such a difficult baby. He wouldn't breast-feed. He... I felt so helpless, so inadequate. The nurse said that sometimes babies did reject the breast but... He would look at me sometimes so... He hardly ever seemed to sleep. He was walking at nine months, you know, and talking at eighteen, properly, not just baby-talk, but if I tried to pick him up or cuddle him he would simply freeze. It was such a difficult time. Jon was so very busy with the practice. I hardly ever saw him, and he and I...' She bit her lip. 'Things weren't very good between us then. The only person Max seemed to respond to was David. David desperately wanted a son, and I think it irked him a little that Jon and I had Max before he and Tiggy... The first boy in the family... I used to think sometimes that David deliberately encouraged Max to turn to him instead of Jon, and, of course, Jon being Jon, he never forced the issue. He always backed off and allowed David to have his way.

'Max hated it when the girls were born. The first time he saw them he said they looked like two blind kittens and that he wanted to drown them. I was terrified of leaving him alone with them. He was terribly jealous of them.

'I can remember him once telling me that I

didn't love him. I denied it, of course, and asked him why he should think that, and he told me that he had overheard David saying it.

'I *did* love him, Maddy. I *do* love him,' she added, her mouth trembling.

'Come on,' Maddy coaxed her, putting her arm around her shoulders. 'Jon will be worrying.'

'I wanted to go with him to Jamaica,' Jenny told her, 'but there was only one seat. Do you think that Max...'

'I'm sure he'll understand,' Maddy soothed her, relieved to see that they were clear of the graveyard and that she could see the car and Joss waiting for them several yards away.

As she carefully eased her mother-in-law into its welcoming warmth, she was sharply conscious of their abrupt role reversal.

'Oh, Maddy,' Jenny wept, and watching her start to shiver, Maddy made a mental note to call their family doctor in the morning. Shock did strange things to people, and old Ben still had to be told the news of Max's accident.

Jon had heard the car drawing up outside the house, and he looked anxiously at Jenny's set face and despair-laden eyes before turning towards Maddy.

'Don't worry,' she reassured him quietly. 'Jenny's naturally very upset and shocked. I'll ring the surgery in the morning and get the doctor to call round and see her.'

'Joss, put the kettle on, would you,' she instructed her brother-in-law. Gratefully, Joss seized on the opportunity to do something, anything, so that he didn't have to look into the frighteningly unfamiliar expression on his mother's face. He *still* hadn't quite come to terms with what was happening. Because of the age gap between them and the huge gulf in their personalities, Joss and Max had never been close, and the extent and intensity of his mother's grief over the brother who had never seemed to be really a part of the family had shocked him into an awareness that his mother, always so calm, so comforting, so much a solid, dependable part of the fabric of his life, was far more vulnerable than he had ever realized.

Now, instinctively, just like Jon, he found he was turning to Maddy for support, drawing strength from her calm, practical handling of his mother's despair.

'Jenny, why don't you go upstairs and get some rest,' Maddy suggested gently, but Jenny immediately shook her head.

'No. No, I can't. I have to drive Jon to the airport. I have to…'

'*I'll* do that,' Maddy told her firmly. She could see that Jenny's eyes were filling with tears, and tactfully she touched Joss on his arm and asked him, 'Joss, could you come out with me and guide me while I turn my car round? There isn't a lot of room on the drive.'

No one seemed to find her request suspicious, despite the fact that she had undertaken such a manoeuvre many, many times in the past.

Left on her own with her husband, Jenny fought the shivers that still racked her body.

'Oh, Jon, I can't believe this is happening,' she wept as she went into his arms. 'Oh, God, I don't want him to die,' she had sobbed. 'Please don't let him die. Is it my fault?' she asked Jon emotionally. 'It is…'

'Shush, shush…' Jon tried to comfort her, his own voice thick with emotion.

'It isn't anyone's fault, Jenny. It isn't anyone's fault.'

By the time Maddy and Joss came back, Jenny was a little more calm, her eyes, Maddy noted with relief, had lost that look of vacant despair, which had alarmed her so much when she had coaxed her away from the graveyard.

When Jenny had announced quietly but very determinedly that she was going with them to the airport, Maddy did not try to dissuade her.

Knowing just how she would have felt herself had it been her precious Leo who had been lying close to death somewhere where she could not be with him, Maddy waited without complaint until they had actually seen Jon's plane taking off, a silver arrow against the pure clear dark blue of the sky, its light disappearing into the bright starlit expanse of the crisp, frosty night.

As she drove Jenny home, Maddy acknowledged that, as yet, she herself had felt no emotion other than a certain sense of there somehow being a protective but invisible wall separating her from the reality of what was happening. She knew that Max had been badly injured; she knew he was close to death. But somehow, she simply could not make her brain accept the fact that she might never see him again, that he might never walk arrogantly and irritably through the front door of Queensmead, upsetting Leo, treating her with contempt and bringing with him that highly charged atmosphere that always seemed to be so much a part of him. His presence immediately quickened the pace of life, adding to it a certain *brio* and dangerous excitement that warned Maddy that Max was about, creating the kind of tension and hostility in the household that he seemed to enjoy causing so much.

She closed her eyes. Max was far too alive, far too…too Max…to be dying. Her throat suddenly closed and her body started to tremble. She put down the cup of tea she had just made for herself and walked across Jenny's kitchen to stand by the window. Upstairs Joss and Jenny were both sleeping. Maddy had just been up to check on them, but she had been unable to follow suit. Dawn had broken. Soon she would have to drive home to Queensmead and break the news of Max's accident to his grandfather, then she would have to shower and dress and go back to Chester to collect Leo and Emma.

Her hands wrapped around the warm mug, she stared out into Jenny's frost-crisped garden.

In Jamaica it would be hot, the air in Max's hospital room cooled by air-conditioning. He would be—'Oh, God, please let him live,' Maddy prayed. 'Not for my sake, but for his and for Jenny's.' Max wouldn't want to die. She tried to picture him, her husband, lying white and still in his hospital bed, surrounded by the equipment that would be keeping him alive, but she couldn't. All she could visualize was the way he had looked the first time they had gone to bed together, when she had woken up to watch him with the eyes and the emotions of a woman deeply and bemusedly, bewitchedly in love.

He had been lying on his back, eyes closed, his dark hair ruffled, one arm flung outwards, the warm sheen on it making her want to reach out and touch him, to press her lips with passionate intensity to the solid bulge of muscle and gently kiss the fingers that had touched her, caressed her, taken her to a place of such intense, unbelievable sensual pleasure.

Giddy, drunk almost, on the elixir of her own happiness, she had propped herself up on one elbow to watch him, still not quite wholly able to believe that this wonderful, god-like man should be hers. And then he had opened his eyes and seen her watching him, and the look he had given her had made the hot, self-conscious colour burn up under her skin.

'Go ahead, touch me,' he had told her. Then he added mockingly, 'Oh, you don't know how to... Want me to show you?'

She hadn't thought it was possible for her

face to burn even hotter than it had already been doing, but she had been wrong.

Max had been quite dispassionate and thorough about his instructions—and her education—but she had gone way, way beyond being able to copy his detachment by that point. Her response had been to the hot pulse of desire she could feel and see driving his body, and to the equally hot and uncontrollable pulse of her own thudding, frantic emotions.

The smell of him on her skin, the taste of him on her mouth, these were sensations she would remember forever.

As she raised her cup to her lips, Maddy suddenly realized that her face was wet with tears.

10

—▶ ◀—

'If you'd like to come this way, please.'

Despite the hospital's air-conditioning, Jon could feel the sweat dampening his skin as he followed the crisply uniformed nurse. Her neat, femininely curved body reminded him of Maddy.

The calm, confident way his daughter-in-law had taken control at home had surprised Jon at first. He was more used to seeing her take a back seat, be more hesitant and unsure of herself, but he had to admit that her new air of self-confidence suited her.

He could feel his heart starting to thump in heavy doom-laden strokes as the nurse stood to one side so that he could precede her into the office of the doctor in charge of the intensive care unit.

Grave-faced, the doctor stood up and offered Jon his hand.

'My son, Max…' Jon began as soon as the introductions had been completed. 'Is he…?'

'He is, I'm afraid, very seriously injured,' the doctor told Jon quietly.

'But he is alive,' Jon pressed, his voice a harsh whisper.

'He is alive, yes,' the doctor agreed. 'But I have to warn you...he lost a massive amount of blood. His injuries were extremely severe.'

'Can I... Can I see him?' Jon asked him numbly, trying to swallow against the huge, painful lump that was blocking his throat.

'He won't know or recognize you,' the doctor told him quietly. 'He is very heavily sedated. Perhaps in another hour...'

Jon looked away. He knew what the doctor was trying to tell him. Max was dying. The lump hardened, tears that felt like jagged pieces of glass hurt his eyes.

'If you would like to see your nephew...' the doctor suggested.

Jon blinked guiltily.

'Yes. Yes, of course,' he agreed huskily.

Jack was in a side room at the end of a ward, his face lighting up with relief and then visibly shadowing over with guilt and fear as Jon walked in.

'Max? How is he? Have you seen him?' he demanded as soon as he saw Jon.

He was heavily bandaged, his face anxious

and drawn as he told Jon, 'I wanted to see him, but they wouldn't let me. It's all my fault. I...'

Seeing his grief and his guilt helped Jon to sublimate his own. 'Jack, it *isn't* your fault at all,' he reassured him gently. 'You were *both* victims of a senselessly violent attack and...'

'But if I hadn't tried to walk back to the hotel along the beach, it would never have happened.' Tears filled his eyes, and immediately Jon shook his head, touching him gently on the shoulder, unable to hug him properly because of his injuries.

'I wish I'd never come out here. Max didn't want me around and I...'

Jack closed his eyes.

His longing for Jon's reassuring presence had been increasing daily and he recognized that David, the father whom it had been so vitally important for him to track down, had been nowhere in his thoughts. Indeed, a stranger in the street would be as much comfort to him as his father, and if David had, by some miracle, walked into his room right now, it would have meant nothing to him. Less than nothing, in fact, because the only people he wanted to see were the people whom, he realized, he looked upon as his parents in every emotional sense of the word. His uncle Jon and his aunt Jenny.

Right now he longed for the security, the safety, the haven, that was his aunt and uncle's home...*his* home in Haslewich, with a passionate intensity that far exceeded the immature urgency of his previous desire to find his father.

All the things that Jon and, to a lesser extent, Joss had said to him had come back to him. All of Jon's gentle advice to accept that he was loved by them as himself had echoed in his head as he lay in his hospital bed, and Jack had resolved that if his father had deliberately turned his back on him, then that was his, Jack's, gain, because the parenting, the fathering, the loving he had received from Jon more than made up for anything he may have lost.

He had been counting the hours, the moments, minutes almost, until Jon's arrival, but now that he was here Jack was achingly conscious of the fact that he was not Jon's son; that Max was Jon's son, and Max was lying somewhere behind the locked doors of the hospital's intensive care unit and very close to death.

If Max should die... The weight of his emotions was almost too much for Jack to bear. If he had not quarrelled with Max, if he had not stormed off, if he had not walked across the unguarded strip of public beach...if he had never come out to Jamaica in the first place... If, if, if, if... If only Max would live. If.

'I wanted to see Max but they wouldn't let me,' he choked out to Jon again now.

'They wouldn't let me, either,' Jon said gently.

'And Aunt Jenny, how is she?'

'She's...worried...about you both. She sent her love. She'll feel better when she's got you both back home.'

Briefly their eyes met, and then quickly looked away, both of them dreading to see in the other's eyes the belief that Max and Jack would not be going back together...

The door to Jack's room opened, and the doctor Jon had seen earlier came in and told Jon quietly, 'I think perhaps you should see your son.'

Before it was too late...while he still could, Jon wondered sickly as he followed him out of Jack's room and down the corridor. He was still sweating heavily, but at the same time he felt icy cold.

Any number of TV dramas both real and fictional ought to have prepared him...warned

him, Jon recognized, but somehow or other
they had not. The familiarity of the scene was
there: the sterile room, the whirr of the banks
of machinery, the grave faces and demeanour
of the nurses, the heart-ripping vulnerability of
the patient lying motionless on the narrow
hospital bed attached to the equipment that
was keeping him alive. There was also an
added dimension for Jon, a gut-wrenching, ap-
palling, unwanted recognition that this was
not an actor lying on the bed, nor merely a
stranger for whom one might feel pity and a
certain morbid awareness of the high theatre
being enacted: the silent, stealthy struggle between life and death, the awful grim silencing
of the humming life support systems.

Life support... How easily the words slid off
the tongue, how dangerously one took them
for granted...when it was not one's own flesh
and blood who lay dependent upon their emo-
tionless, mechanical care.

Once before he had seen a close relative lying thus, but the anxiety he had felt for David
in the aftermath of his heart attack was nothing when compared to what he was experiencing now.

There was a chair beside the bed. Shakily he
sat down on it, looking helplessly from Max's

waxen face to that of the doctor's. He could see no signs of life other than those resonating from the machinery. Max lay completely motionless, so motionless in fact that Jon's heart leapt and twisted, jerking in painful, involuntary spasms of sharp fear.

'Is he…?' he began to ask the doctor, but the other man shook his head and told him warningly, 'He *is* alive but…it would be unfair of me to raise false hopes for you. He is becoming increasingly reliant on the life-support systems.'

'I can't believe it,' Jon half whispered. 'He's always been strong…so alive….'

'It was a very savage attack,' the doctor told him grimly. 'The worst of its nature I have ever seen. His injuries…'

He stopped. It was pointless telling this grief-stricken father that when he had first seen the blood-soaked body of his son he had assumed that the man was already dead, or that they had already had to resuscitate him twice, or that the senior nurse in charge of the unit, who had many, many years' experience of such things behind her, had already come to him and told him that she did not expect her patient to live through another night.

'We are losing him,' the nurse had told him.

'I have seen it before. There is a certain...' She had stopped, but the doctor had known what she meant.

Now he touched Jon gently and indicated a bell beside the bed.

'When you are ready to leave, press that and the nurse will unlock the door of the unit for you.'

'How long can I stay?' Jon asked him. His throat felt raw, as though he had been shouting or screaming, and his whole body ached with a pain that was much, much more than merely the after-effects of his long-haul flight.

When the doctor simply shook his head without saying anything, Jon felt the savage, clawing pain tear at his stomach, but as desperately as he wanted to deny what he could see in the doctor's eyes and to seek the reassurance he needed, he knew that the other man could not give it to him.

Max was dying, and Jon could stay with him until... Until the monitors were switched off and the nurses came to take away the still, stiff form that was his son, and yet somehow, not his son.

As he sat down beside him, Jon did something he could not remember doing ever since Max had been old enough to reject him.

He reached out and covered his limp, still hand with his own.

When Max had been born, safe, alive, healthy, after the loss of baby Harry, Jon's first overwhelming desire had been to protect him, to keep him safe, to hold him, but Max had never been the kind of child who had liked being touched. Now, suddenly, Jon ached to be able to take hold of Max in his arms, to succour and protect him, to show him the love he could feel slamming through him.

Max was his son, his child, flesh of his flesh, and as he looked at him and knew how much he loved him, Jon could only wonder that he had never previously realized how deeply his feelings for Max went and how he himself had never fully recognized them—or acted upon them.

His eyes filled with tears.

Max had been having the most extraordinary colourful and vivid dreams about his childhood, each detail thrown into sharply clear relief, memories he had not even known he had flooding strongly through him like a spring tide. Here he could see the colour of his mother's dress, smell her perfume, feel the warmth of her skin; a thousand recollections he had not even known he had made him marvel at the intensity of what he was experiencing.

Beside his mother he could see his father, tall, austere, but as Max turned to look into his eyes he no longer saw the familiar shadowing of disappointment mingled with distaste that always seemed to be in Jon's eyes when he looked at him. Instead, they were bright with emotion...with tears...and with love.

His father was in pain, and Max wanted to reach out to touch him and comfort him, but he was standing a long way away from his parents in a very special place, where he knew instinctively they could not be. This place, so wonderful, so bathed in pure, clear light, so different from anything he had experienced before, was having the most extraordinary effect upon him. In it Max felt safe, protected, at home, and at peace. In it he had the most profound sense of well being...of having a need that had burned deep down inside him met so totally and completely that it was like finding a missing piece of himself. In it he knew he was receiving something he had not even realized that he needed, something he knew instinctively he could not bear to be without ever again.

This place, so wonderful, so enlightening, was illuminated with a sense of love, of being loved, so intense, so benign and so pure that Max couldn't find the words to describe it. He knew that not only was he now receiving this love, but that he, too, was capable of generating it. He wanted to generate it; he wanted to reach out to his parents, to the whole of his family, and to share with them what he was experiencing, to let the love he was feeling flow through him to them. It saddened him unbearably that they could not be here with him to share in the wonder of this eternal love, this eternal knowing, that he could not reach out and wipe away his father's tears.

He could hear his father calling out to him, and through his love for him, Max felt the burden of a terrible deadening tiredness, a longing for his father to go quietly away so that he could enjoy the solitude of where he was, but, at the same time, he also yearned to be able to go to him and comfort him.

Somewhere down the long, dark tunnel that

now lay behind him, he could still hear his father's voice. He could feel an urge to turn and listen to it, to take one last look at the man who had given him life, but he felt so tired, his body felt so heavy, so cumbersome, so unwanted. Still, he must do this thing. He must try to comfort his father.

Down at the end of the tunnel Max could see his father, but not as he had ever seen him before. His father was crying, bereft, alone and in great emotional pain, and immediately Max knew that he had to go to him, that his father's need for comfort must come before his own desire to stay here in this wondrous place, despite his reluctance to leave it.

Sadly he gave one last, lingering look at the place where he was, breathing in the purity of its air, its light, the weightless, priceless gift of its love, and tiredly and painfully he made his slow, torturous way back down the dark emptiness of the tunnel. His body grew heavier and hurt more with each step. He could feel the heavy thud of his own heartbeat, feel the unwanted mortality of his injured flesh, and he cried out in protest, not at the physical pain but at the agonizing awareness of all that he had left behind him.

But at the end of the tunnel was his father, afraid, alone and in need. He could feel the weight of his father's hand reaching for his own. Tiredly he let him take it, and he tried to reach out to his father through his thoughts, to counsel him not to feel grief or pain, to tell him that in the place where he had just been there was no place for such feeling…no need. Yet he knew his father could not hear his thoughts or be comforted by them because he could feel Jon's tears warm and wet on the back of his hand.

Painfully he turned his head and opened his eyes to look at him.

'Jenny, it's Jon. Max… There was a crisis and they thought…but…he's going to pull through, Jenny. Yes, that's right…. No, I don't know when they'll let him come home. Certainly not until he's out of intensive care. He's still very poorly, but the doctor is much more optimistic now about his chances…. Yes, yes, I'll ring you as soon as I have anything more to report….'

He had been at Max's bedside for close on six hours and his whole body ached, but there was something he still had to tell Jenny, some-

thing he had to try to explain to her, that he
didn't even begin to properly understand himself, and in the end, because he simply didn't
know how else to try to tell her, he said shakily, 'Jenny, Max...he's...he's different....'

As he closed his eyes he could picture Jenny
at home in the kitchen at Haslewich, and
briefly he also had a superimposed image of
her, the memory of how she had looked after
Max had been born, her face crumpled with
exhaustion but her eyes alight with love and
pride...and relief.

'Different?' He heard her anxious question,
but he was too emotionally drained to try to
tell her what he meant. All he knew was that
he would remember for the rest of his life the
look, the love, the wisdom he had seen in
Max's eyes when he had opened them and
looked at him.

Looking back at his son, *he* had felt like a
child looking into the face, the eyes, of a caring
parent, but the abrupt about-turn in their roles
and the fact that it should be Max, of all people, in whose eyes he should see that comforting, benign look of tender, aware emotion was
still too much for him to be able to accept prop-

erly himself, never mind describe to anyone else.

'I must go,' he told Jenny quickly instead. 'Please try not to worry. Oh, and I nearly forgot, Max sends his love—to you, and to Maddy and the children. Oh, and yes, he asked me to ask Maddy if she would send a recent photograph of Leo and Emma.'

11

——▶◀——

'Max has asked for what?' Maddy stared at her mother-in-law in startled disbelief.

She had known the moment she opened the kitchen door that Jenny must have received good news, but to be told that Max had not only expressly sent his wife and his children his love, but had also asked for a photograph of Leo and Emma, caused Maddy to frown slightly and wonder inwardly if her mother-in-law was simply trying to be tactful.

'It's true,' Jenny assured her, correctly guessing what she was thinking. 'And Maddy—' she touched her on her arm, forcing Maddy to stop unpacking the bread and milk she had been out to buy and look at her '—Jon says that Max… He says he's different.'

'Different?' Maddy's eyebrows arched, but she kept her sceptical thoughts to herself. Max could certainly have a photograph of his children, but privately Maddy suspected that he probably wanted it more for the effect it would have on the susceptible emotions of some pretty nurse rather than because he wanted it for himself. Why should he when he had made it abundantly plain that he had not wanted either of his children. But now was not the time to tell Jenny of these facts.

'I've got to go over to Chester to pick up the children,' she said gently instead. 'Bobbie's kindly been looking after them again and...'

'You go,' Jenny told her immediately. 'I shall be fine...now. It's funny, I thought, felt...that I'd stepped back emotionally from Max years ago. He was still our son but...' She stopped and shook her head. 'When I thought that he could die...' She looked away, shaking her head. Compassionately Maddy reached out and touched her.

'I do understand,' she assured her.

Yes, she *did* understand, she reflected an hour later as she drove towards Chester, but understanding Jenny's feelings and even being relieved that Max was not going to die didn't alter anything else, especially not the growing awareness she had experienced recently of just how emotionally unfulfilling, how *empty* her marriage actually was.

Meeting Griff had brought home to her as nothing else could have done just what her marriage to Max was denying her, just what she was denying not only herself but her children as well. *Her* children, for that's what Leo and Emma were. Max might have provided the sperm, the seed, for their conception, but apart from that he had had about as much input into them and their happiness, their physical, emotional and mental welfare, as a bull who'd inseminated a cow, she decided with bleak self-awareness.

Max had never held his children, played with them, worried about them or shown them the slightest bit of interest, never mind any real paternal love, but she could still hear the uncertainty threaded through with hope in her mother-in-law's voice when she had told her, 'Max is different.'

Different... It didn't matter how *different* he was, though, did it? He would *still* be a stranger to her—perhaps a different kind of stranger, but a stranger nonetheless, because the truth was that the man she had married, the Max she had married, had never existed except in her own dreams and imagination. The Max she had fallen in love with had been a mythical hero created out of her own need, her own craving, her own love. Oh, she had tried to convince herself otherwise, had tried to believe that the cruel cynicism that was so much a part of Max's nature did not exist, and she had, at times, even tried to blame herself for being the one to provoke it, but that had just been a piece of pointless self-deception.

Since meeting Griff, she had come to realize many things, one of the most painful being that she had probably deliberately for most of her adult life attracted to herself people and situations that had robbed her of her self-respect and her pride, had thought so little of herself that a part of her must have felt that she deserved to be treated badly. It was not a very palatable home truth to have to come to terms with. It had been an extremely salutary experience indeed to realize that if her life was a locked cage, then she herself was the one who had walked into it and thrown away the key.

If Max was a bad husband and a poor father, then why hadn't she done something before now to remove his destructive effect from their lives, *why* had she so apathetically stayed within a marriage that she had known was damaging not just to herself but to her children as well?

Although the stretch of road in front of her was completely straight and hers was the only vehicle travelling along it, Maddy suddenly put her foot very sharply on the brake and brought the car to a halt.

If the metamorphosis within herself that had taken place recently had enabled *her* to change so much, then why was she so antagonistic towards the idea of Max having changed? Because Max was Max; because Max had so obviously enjoyed being the person he was. Because leopards, historically, do not change their spots.

Because she didn't *want* to have to think about the consequences of the fact that Max might have changed, not now, not when...

Quickly she put the car back in gear and depressed the accelerator.

'Mummee.... Mummee....' Emma screamed excitedly from Bobbie's arms when she saw Maddy walk into Bobbie's kitchen.

Handing her over to Maddy, Bobbie asked solicitously, 'How's Max?'

'Over the worst, according to Jon, although he's still in intensive care. Jon wants to make arrangements to have Max and Jack flown home, but the hospital there won't release him until they consider that he's fit to travel, which apparently will be some days yet.

'Jon's also told Jenny that the police have

visited the hospital to interview Jack about the incident, although it seems unlikely that they're going to catch the men who did it.'

'Mmm...by the sound of it, Max has had a very lucky escape.'

'Yes. The doctor has told Jon that it's a miracle that Max survived.'

'It's not going to be easy for you once Max does come home.'

Maddy looked sharply at Bobbie.

'What do you mean?' she asked her defensively. 'I...'

'I... I just meant that there...it's going to be hard work for you,' Bobbie told her hastily. 'Having both Ben and Max to look after as well as the children. If it would help, I could have Emma and Leo over here more often.'

Maddy's face flushed with mortification. Just for a second she had thought that Bobbie had been warning her about her friendship with Griff.

'I... I may very well take you up on that,' she accepted huskily, unable to completely meet Bobbie's eyes.

'Where *is* Leo, by the way?' she asked.

'Griff took him out.'

Now it was Bobbie's turn to avoid Maddy's eyes.

'He rang to speak to Luke, and when he found out the children were here, he came round after breakfast and asked Leo if he would like to go to the zoo.'

'Oh, Leo would love that,' Maddy said. 'He's animal mad. He's desperate to have a pet, preferably a dog, but with Ben the way he is and Max…'

'Oh, I nearly forgot,' Bobbie added. 'Luke asked me to tell you that the Ericsons have put forward a couple of dates for your charity "do." They're very keen to go ahead with the idea. Sue says she can't think of anything that would be more worthwhile, and she's told Luke that she can't understand why they haven't done something like this before. They're such a lovely couple. Sue mothers everything and everyone.'

'Have they got a family?' Maddy asked her interestedly. She knew the couple to be in their late fifties, but no mention had been made about their having either children or grandchildren.

Bobbie shook her head.

'No. I think that Lewis has a son from an earlier marriage, but I don't think that they have very much contact with him, and I rather suspect, although neither of them have ever said so, that it was more a matter of them not being able to have children rather than not choosing to do so, so there will be a certain poignancy for Sue in supporting this kind of charity. I don't suppose you've been able to make much progress in getting additional sponsorship from local businesses, not with Max's accident.'

'Well, I had started to make several approaches to local companies,' Maddy told her. 'Really more by word of mouth at this stage— I had planned to make a more concrete approach after I'd spoken properly with the Ericsons. It struck me that it might be a good idea to try to get some corporate interest in our Gilbert and Sullivan night.'

'Mmm…I know what you mean. Oh, and by the way, Ruth rang the other night. She sends her love.'

'I hope I'm not going to let her down. She's worked so hard to make the charity what it is,' Maddy grimaced.

'You won't. Griff is terribly impressed, you know. He's told both Luke and me that he thinks you're wasted on such a small charity and that he thinks you should be running the country.'

Both of them laughed, but beneath her

laughter, Maddy was aware of a tiny stab of pain. No matter what her own burgeoning feelings for Griff, or his for her might be, until everything else was back to normal, until Max was back to normal, they would have to be put on hold. Pointless to wish that Max's accident had never happened; that she was free to allow what was happening between her and Griff to develop into...

Into what? An affair? Maddy shuddered at the thought.

No, never that... What then? A separation, a divorce from Max, which would leave her free to start again with Griff.

'Griff and Leo are back,' Bobbie informed her, breaking into her thoughts.

Guiltily conscious of her still-flushed face, Maddy stepped back as Griff walked into Bobbie's kitchen, Leo at his side.

'Mum, Mum, I've seen giraffes and hippos...and I've seen a real me,' Leo told her, almost stammering in his excitement as he left Griff's side to rush towards her.

'A real you?' Maddy questioned, bemused as she looked over his head towards Griff for enlightenment.

'A lion...' he explained with a rueful smile.

'Yes, and he was called Leo...just like me,' Leo informed her proudly.

Maddy laughed as she hugged him and buried her face in the still-sweet baby scent of his neck.

Wriggling, he started to push her away. Just recently he had started to become much more of a little boy and less of her baby, but Maddy knew that inside he was far more dependent on her emotionally than Emma—and far more easily hurt.

She closed her eyes for a second. Unlike Jenny, she was dreading Max's return home. It was difficult enough sometimes balancing the needs of an irascible and sometimes very selfish old man with those of two young children, and Ben could be just as jealously perverse and demanding as either Leo or Emma when the mood took him. To have Max at home and in need of her care as well wasn't just going to put a lot of additional pressure on her and her available time, it was also going to create a good deal of stress and tension.

Slyly, the thought slid into her mind that Jenny might enjoy having Max, her son, under her roof for her to cosset, especially since unlike her, Jenny seemed totally convinced that

Jon was right when he claimed that Max had changed.

'What's wrong?' she heard Griff asking her gently. 'Has Max's condition deteriorated?'

Immediately Maddy shook her head. 'No, actually he's doing very well,' she began, until Leo interrupted her, tugging impatiently on her sleeve to ask her curiously, 'Mummy, what is a deter...det...what Griff just said?'

'Deteriorated,' Maddy repeated slowly for him. 'It means to get worse, Leo,' she explained simply.

As yet she hadn't said anything about Max's accident to the children. What was the point? They were too young to understand, and Max had been away, anyway. However, Leo, it seemed, had a much keener grasp of the situation than she had expected, because he said clearly, 'My daddy is very poorly, isn't he? Does that mean he's going to die...?'

After exchanging a quick look with Bobbie, Maddy explained quietly, 'He is poorly, yes, Leo, but he isn't going to die.'

'Does that mean he's going to be coming home?' Leo asked her, suddenly anxious.

Maddy hesitated. Over his head Griff gave her a compassionate look.

'Yes, but not for a while yet,' she told Leo.

Changing the subject, she added firmly, 'So, tell me what other animals you saw at the zoo.'

An hour later, when both children were safely installed in the car and Griff had accompanied her out to it to see her off—Bobbie having tactfully and discreetly suddenly remembered an urgent telephone call she had to make, which left them alone—he had touched her arm gently and told her softly, 'I know that things aren't easy for you right now.' He stopped and shook his head, then said fiercely, 'No, this isn't the time to burden you with my feelings. But, Maddy, if there's *anything, anything* I can do to help...as a friend...then promise me that you won't hesitate to ask.'

Close to tears, Maddy reached out and touched his arm, then withdrew her hand as she saw the tortured longing in his eyes, and her heart started to thump with deep, heavy strokes.

Max had certainly never looked at her like that.

Max... Max... Max...

'Thank you, Griff' was all she could manage to say before she had to turn away from him and get into the car.

It felt like another lifetime ago, not merely a matter of days...hours...since she had dressed

12

As Jon paused outside the open door to his son's hospital room he could hear him talking with Jack, the board game they had been playing lying discarded on the bed.

'No, Jack, you mustn't think that,' Jon heard Max saying firmly to his young cousin. 'You were not the cause of your father's disappearance or of his problems. No one was, as I'm sure that David himself would be the first to tell you if he was here.

'He was extremely proud of both Olivia and you, you know,' he added gently. 'He often used to talk to me about you. As I've had good cause to learn recently, we are each of us responsible for our own actions and our own reactions. David's problems, whatever they may be, are his, and my feeling is that when, and only when, he feels he has dealt with them to his own satisfaction will he start to think about coming home.

'However, if you still feel that you want to

stay here in Jamaica and look for him, then of course I shall stay here with you.'

'No. No, I don't,' Jon heard Jack replying in a low voice. 'Max… I… I want to go home. I do want to find my father and to talk to him but… I'm afraid of meeting him…of…'

'Don't be,' Max interrupted him gently. 'There's no need, but I have to admit that I'm relieved to hear that you don't want to stay. I must say that I'm looking forward to going home…but not before I've beaten you at this wretched game!'

Both of them were still laughing when Jon walked into the room to join them.

He still hadn't fully come to terms with the change in Max, although now, some weeks after they had been attacked, Jon was beginning to accept that the dramatic about-face in his elder son's behaviour and beliefs wasn't just some peculiar effect of the drugs he had been given to keep him alive, but a totally genuine inner change in the man himself.

'Dr Martyne says that he's prepared to allow you to fly home at the end of the week,' he told Max as he returned Jack's warm hug and sat down on the chair his nephew had pulled out for him.

'Mmm…so soon,' Max grinned, giving a lighthearted sideways look at the games board beside him. Both Jon and Jack laughed.

No matter how often he had tried to explain over the telephone to Jenny just how different Max was, Jon knew that he hadn't been able to convey to her the dramatic change that had taken place in him. Sometimes, even though he himself had witnessed it, and was witnessing it every day, he still found it hard to comprehend that the kind, warm-hearted, compassionate and sensitively understanding man whom he had come to know during these last days was actually *his* son, Max, the same Max who had grown from a withdrawn and resentful boy into a cynical, cold and very often cruel man, who had seemed to delight in hurting and manipulating others.

This Max, the new Max, couldn't have been more different from the old. Jon had witnessed the change in him and marvelled at it, marvelling, too, at the way that people now responded to him. Look at the rapport he had established with Jack, the understanding with which he had addressed the teenager's confused feelings towards his father, the sensitivity with which he had gently encouraged Jack to vocalize those feelings and to unburden himself to him.

'Can I go and ring Aunt Jenny and tell her that we'll soon be home?' Jack asked eagerly.

Nodding his head, Jon waited until Jack had gone before looking searchingly at his son.

'Dr Martyne also said that he wanted to be sure that you felt up to travelling such a long way before he gave his final agreement.'

'I'm up to it,' Max assured him, adding, 'and I'm not just saying that because I know you want to get back to Mum and Haslewich. In many ways it must have been far harder for her and, of course, for Maddy than it has been for us here. Have you heard from Maddy at all, by the way?'

The careful way in which he asked the question caused Jon to give him a look of concern.

'Maddy has rung every day to see how you are,' Jon informed him. 'I assumed that she must have spoken to you. I didn't realize...'

'I expect she's worried that Gramps will start complaining about his phone bill if she speaks with both of us,' Max smiled lightly, but Jon continued to frown. He hadn't realized that Max hadn't actually spoken to his wife.

'Well, at least Dr Martyne agrees that you've recovered enough to go straight home instead of having to spend any more time in hospital in England,' he comforted him.

'Yes, that is a relief,' Max agreed quietly, lying back against the pillows and closing his eyes.

'You're tired,' Jon apologized. 'I'll go and leave you in peace for a while.'

Max waited until the door had closed behind his father before opening his eyes. He wasn't tired at all, really, but the knowledge that he was shortly to be allowed to return home had raised several spectres in his conscience that he knew had to be addressed.

He had seen, in the days since his return to consciousness, the astonishment with which his father had greeted his metamorphosis, his originally wary disbelief giving way to cautious acceptance and then, these last two days, a more relaxed and almost joyful recognition of the fact that Max wasn't simply indulging in some kind of macabre joke. But despite the new closeness that was developing between them, there was still something that Max couldn't bring himself to confide to his father or, indeed as yet, to anyone. How did you explain such a total and dramatic change in one's personality? Max certainly couldn't.

All he knew was that he felt...*was*...different; that it was as though his slate of life had been wiped clean with a gently compassionate hand and he had been urged to try again, to be the person he had recognized that he could be when he had stood bathed in that pure, shining light, absorbing that pure, intense love.

But not all the shadows, all the dark places, had been banished from his memory or his consciousness. There was still the question of Maddy and the way he had treated her, the atonement he must make for those past cruelties and the problem of where their future might lie.

The new Max, the Max he had become, knew that he could not, would not, ever be able to hurt Maddy again, but he also knew that he had to be true to himself. He had married Maddy for all the wrong reasons and treated her so badly that he was amazed that she had stayed with him. He might now be aware of the wrong he had done her and be deeply regretful of it, but...

But, guilt was *not* love. He had married Maddy without loving her. To leave her now unhappy and in emotional pain was something he ached not to have to do, but to stay with her when there was no real love between them would be even more cruel. And then there was the question of their children. *His* children. He looked at the photograph Maddy had sent to him of Leo and Emma. Out of it his son looked at him, his body tense, his eyes shadowed and wary. Max knew he had a duty to Leo to wipe away that look and to replace it with one of openness and joy.

He and Maddy would have to talk, to be open and honest with each other. Hopefully, with tenderness and care and compassion, he could help her to understand that to end their marriage was the best thing for them both.

'Have you heard anything from your...from Max yet?' Griff asked Maddy quietly as they drove back from a meeting with the Ericsons that Luke had arranged. Griff had picked Maddy up at home, and how on earth he had resisted the temptation to take her in his arms when she had opened the front door to him, he still did not know. He risked a sideways glance at her as she sat beside him in the car.

Dressed in an elegant trouser suit, gold studs in her ears, a pair of loafers on her feet, she looked both elegantly smart and at the same time so femininely vulnerable that he literally ached with longing for her.

'I... I haven't spoken to him myself,' Maddy responded in a low voice, turning her head away so that Griff couldn't see her expression. 'I *have* spoken to Jon, though, and it seems that the doctor over there has said that Max can come home at the end of the week.'

'*Home?*' Griff questioned her. 'Does that mean...'

'He will be coming home to Queensmead,' Maddy interrupted him as calmly as she could but still kept her face turned away from him. The last thing she needed right now was the complication she knew would follow as surely as spring followed winter, if she allowed Griff to see the anxiety, the despair, the *pain* in her eyes that the thought of having Max home was causing her.

If he had been coming home to go into hospital, it might have been different. Then she would have had time to adjust to...to prepare herself for the role that would be expected of her.

Not even to Olivia, Tullah or Bobbie, her closest women friends, had she been able to confide her real feelings, and most especially not the ones that concerned Jenny.

Whereas before Max's accident, she had always sensed, even if it had never been put into words between them, that Jenny sympathized with her and felt for her, that Jenny was in a sense 'on her side,' now she was sensitively aware of the fact that Jenny was suddenly very much Max's mother and, like any mother, concerned for her child. Jenny's immediate instincts were to put Max and his needs first, and for that reason, it simply wasn't possible for her to confide in Jenny or to tell her just how little she was looking forward to Max's return home, how apprehensive about it she felt, how antagonistic towards it and towards him.

Nor could she confide such thoughts to Griff, who she knew would champion her cause just as blindly and lovingly as Jenny was likely to champion Max's.

Thank goodness no one but herself knew just how tempted she was to let Griff see how much she was dreading Max's return and how tempted she was to take the comfort she knew he wanted to offer her—practical and emotional and sexual. *That* was a bridge that once crossed she would have crossed forever, and much as she liked Griff, much as she knew she was attracted to him and by him, Maddy realized in her heart of hearts that her feelings for him were clouded and shaded by the unhappiness caused by her marriage to Max.

Along with her new self-confidence had come a much deeper self-awareness. It would be the easiest thing in the world to convince herself that she loved Griff. There were, after all, more than enough reasons for her to do so, not least the fact that both children, but especially Leo, already liked him.

But instinct and a certain sturdy independence that she was just beginning to develop urged Maddy not to commit herself until she was absolutely sure of her feelings. There was, after all, no reason for her to rush from her marriage into the security of Griff's love. It would be wiser, better, more adult by far, to wait, to distance herself first from Max and the past, to allow herself to be herself before she got involved in a new relationship.

That she must ask Max for a divorce was no longer in any doubt; the work she had been doing for the charity had proved to her that she had the ability, the capability of running and organizing her own life. She was, after all, fully qualified legally, even if she had never actually finished her pupillage. There was nothing to stop her from finding work, from supporting herself and her children, without the benefit of hers and their trust funds, if

Max's intransigence over a divorce should make that a necessity.

The allure of having her own independence, of occupying one of the pretty river-fronting houses she had seen in Chester, of living her own life, had never been stronger.

She would have certain regrets, of course. The prime reason she had agreed to live full-time at Queensmead had been because she had felt the children would benefit from the proximity of Max's immediate family, but surely Jenny and Jon would not turn their backs on their grandchildren just because she, Maddy, had chosen to divorce their father, and certainly neither Bobbie nor Olivia or Tullah would withdraw their friendship or support from her, she knew that.

Yes, she could build a good and happy life for herself and for Leo and Emma. She had the strength to do so, she knew that now, and she had the motivation, as well. Discreetly she glanced at Griff.

Oh, yes, she had the motivation, but her own strong moral beliefs meant that she felt unable to discuss either her plans or the future with Griff until she had spoken with Max, and that was something she couldn't do until he had returned home and he was well enough for her to be able to talk to.

Craven of her to wish that it was possible to suggest to Jenny that *she* might have Max to stay with them while he was recuperating. Craven and cowardly, yes, but oh so tempting as well.

The plane was a silver streak way up in the cloudless blue of the sky. The man glanced up at it and then away again, his attention momentarily distracted from the article he was reading.

The newspaper was well over a week old. Father Ignatius had brought it with him on his return from Kingston several days earlier. Newspapers were a luxury up here in the hills in the small hospice that the priest ran—a haven, a lost hope, quite literally, a last stopping place for many of the island's drug addicts and 'down and outs' on their voyage into eternity. Supported almost entirely by charitable donations, the facilities the hospice offered in material terms were pathetically meagre, but what the hospice offered in terms of love and caring, what it gave to those the priest gathered up protectively within its shelter, was truly beyond price.

He knew that from his *own* experience. The priest had quite literally picked him out of Kingston's gutter, an emaciated drunk, covered in dirt and cuts and bruises, and he had taken him home with him to this haven in the mountains, caringly nursing him back to health and sobriety.

Once he had ceased to curse him for refusing to either let him die or supply him with the drink he craved, he had watched in grim silence while the priest went about his daily business of succouring his patients.

Once, the priest had dreamed of following in the footsteps of famous missionaries, copying their dedication and zeal, but with maturity had come the wisdom to understand that if God chose not to impose his love and his beliefs on his children, then who was he to do so in his place? He had, for a while, worked at the front line of the order's equivalent to the Red Cross and the French Médecins Sans Frontières in the famine-ravaged lands of Ethiopia before making his home and his mission here in Jamaica.

It was hard to say quite what age the priest was. Certainly older than he was himself. Seventy, at least, maybe even older.

Frowning, he studied the front-page story of

the newspaper for the umpteenth time. Two tourists savagely attacked and in danger of having lost their lives had it not been for the timely interruption of a local sportsman. There was a photograph of them. Max, lying in his hospital bed, his face thinner than *he* remembered it and his eyes older and wiser. Jon, slightly stooped, his hair greying... Jack...

His heart thumped heavily against his chest wall. He had hardly recognized Jack, just as the boy would perhaps hardly have recognized him. He had grown thin, sharing the priest's meagre diet. Thin but whipcord strong from all the manual work he did, repairing the mission, lifting the patients, and his shoulders and arms and torso were heavily muscled. He had also grown a beard; it was cheaper than shaving. The priest, whose order had Jesuit leanings, scoffed that he was too spoiled by his rich Western life-style. The sun had darkened his skin and bleached his hair, but despite all this, the similarities between him and the man staring wearily back at him out of the grainy photograph could not be denied.

A shadow fell across the sunlight. He turned round and watched as the priest watched him.

'Your brother?' the older man asked him gently, indicating the photograph of Jon. There

were no secrets between them. What he had
not poured out to him in his drunken ravings
he had confided to him later.

'My brother,' David agreed quietly. 'My
brother, my twin, my guilt...'

But these were words he did not utter. Self-
pity was an indulgence the priest and the work
that David now shared with him did not allow. Instead, he pointed to Jack and added
softly, 'and my son.'

'A fine boy,' the priest told him, with a
small, ironic smile. 'He has the same look in his
eyes as your brother. They are two of a kind, I
would think.'

'We always used to say that Jack should
have been Jon's son and Max mine,' David
agreed.

Not even to the priest, his closest, his only
confident, did he want to talk about the trip he
had made down the hill and into Kingston,
into the hospital where his son and his nephew
had lain recovering from their injuries.

He had watched beside his son's bed while
Jack slept. He had looked so young...so vulnerable...that David's heart had ached for
him. He had lingered so long that a suspicious
nurse had eventually come over and chal-
lenged him.

He had seen Max, too, his condition much more serious than Jack's, and then, just as he was on the point of leaving the hospital, he had seen Jon. Pressing himself into the shadows of the half-open doorway, he had watched as his twin had walked past him, close enough for him to have reached out and touched him.

Jon.

David closed his eyes against his pain.

Jon was the one Jack needed now, the one he wanted, the one he would turn to. Jon had earned the right to Jack's love, while he...

The priest watched as David carefully folded the paper. He knew better than to ask if he wished to seek out his family. He was far too familiar with the act of doing penance for that. When David was ready, when he had worked through the guilt he carried with him, then perhaps he would return to his family, his home.

When he did, the priest would miss him. He was an intelligent man, well read and entertaining.

Once, in the initial stages of recovery from the alcoholism that had almost killed him, the priest had asked David if he did not feel that he should return home for the sake of his children.

'My daughter has her own life,' he had told him bleakly, 'and as for my son... He is better off without me. My brother Jon will give him a far better fathering than I ever did.'

Later, in the privacy of his bed that night, David reread the article. It detailed extremely graphically the injuries suffered by the two tourists who had come to Jamaica on holiday and been foolish enough to ignore the warnings posted by their hotel.

The expensive resort hotels and their guests were a world away from the life *he* now lived, David reflected, as the angry mutterings of one of the priest's new patients grew to a threatening roar. But it was a world that he no longer had any desire to be part of, nor was there any way he could ever go back. Not after what he had done.

It wasn't the legal consequences of his actions he knew he couldn't face, or even the shame and despair of his father. No, what he couldn't face was having to look into Jon's eyes and see himself reflected there.

Jon! He missed his twin more than he had ever imagined it possible to miss anyone. The roar became a full-scale howl. Automatically

David threw back the thin blanket that covered him and got out of bed.

'I told Jen that we'd make our own way back from the airport,' Jon said to Max quietly as he saw the way his son was discreetly searching the crowd waiting beyond the barrier as they came through customs.

Silently Max nodded his head. He was tired after the long flight, far more tired than he himself had expected to be, he acknowledged as he ruefully accepted the arm that Jack put out protectively to support him. The wound on his leg still bothered him at times and had now begun to ache ferociously. What he really needed more than anything else right now was a quiet, cool bedroom and a couple of strong painkillers, not an emotionally draining reunion. But he still couldn't stop himself from searching the waiting crowd again, looking for Maddy's familiar features.

There was no way she would be there, of course, not if Jon had said not to. Maddy wasn't like that. She was biddable, dependable, obedient. As an adult she was as firmly controllable as a small child.

The sky was already beginning to darken,

icy pelts of rain stinging their skin as they made their way towards the waiting taxis.

Max shivered beneath the protection of his clothes. He had lost weight and muscle from lying in his hospital bed, and he was suddenly acutely conscious of how fragile his physical strength now was.

The drive to Queensmead seemed to take forever, but at last they were there, driving in through the gates as the gloom further darkened the sky, the taxi's headlights picking out the familiar outline of the house.

The taxi drew to a halt, Jon paid him off, and Max stepped down into the cold, raw air just as the front door opened, and in the light from the hallway he saw his mother and his grandfather.

Since the accident, Jack had attached himself to Max like a guard dog, fiercely protective of him and his own new relationship with him, refusing now to allow him to carry any luggage, fussing over him as they made their way towards the house.

Jenny detached herself from Ben's side and took a few hesitant steps forward.

'He's changed,' Jon had said, but she had had no real comprehension of just what he'd meant, just how enormous and powerful that

change was until the light from the open doorway fell sharply across her son's face and she
saw in his eyes that which she had long ago
abandoned any hope of ever seeing there.

Her own eyes filled with sharp, shocked
tears, the practical words of greeting and anxiety she had been about to utter forgotten as
she crossed the distance that divided them and
went into the arms he had opened out to her.

'Oh, Max... Max...' was all she could manage to say, so profound were her emotions and
her realization of just *how* different her son
now was.

There was a local expression, 'touched by
God,' used to describe a person who was in
some way mentally damaged or retarded, but
now as she looked at her son, Jenny felt that he,
too, in a very different way, had been quite literally 'touched by God.' Ruth, she knew,
would understand just what she meant, even if
she herself could not as yet fully comprehend
the breadth and depth of the change that had
taken place within Max.... She only knew that
the Max who had gone to Jamaica had been a
man she had, at times, disliked and even despised, and that the Max who had returned
was a man of whom she already felt, in some
sense, slightly in awe.

As he released her and she looked at him, she saw from his expression that he knew exactly what she was feeling.

There was a small commotion in the hallway. Max held his breath, his body tensing as he recognized the small form of his son followed by the slightly more solid shape of his younger sister. Over the distance that separated them, Leo looked up and saw his father, his own expression immediately watchful and wary, his body poised for flight.

Gently disengaging himself from his mother, Max moved slowly through the front door and into the hall, then dropped down on one knee, ignoring the pain screaming at him from his injured leg as he called out softly, 'Hello, Leo.'

Afterwards, trying to describe to the rest of the family just what had happened, Jenny could only shake her head, lost for the right words as she told them simply, 'It was just like something out of a film. I thought that Leo was going to run away, but the moment he heard Max speak, his whole expression changed. It was like watching the sun come out from behind a cloud. He looked at Max and then he smiled. I've *never* seen him smile like that before, and then he ran over to his father and almost threw himself into his arms.'

'Daddy,' Max heard Leo breathe blissfully as he burrowed as close to him as he could get. And then more shakily, 'Daddy,' before Max turned his head and kissed him.

To Jenny, who had planned to keep the children out of Max's way until she had ascertained his mood, her initial emotion on discovering that the children had left the kitchen and were in the hall was one of trepidation. So the sight of Max kneeling down on the floor, his arms wrapped around Leo's small body as he cradled him lovingly in his arms before lifting his head and extending one open arm to Emma who was watching with her mouth open and her eyes rounding, was one that shocked Jenny so much that she could only stare at the small tableau in mute disbelief.

'Maddy...'

Maddy, who had also now come into the hall, could see Max standing up, emotions she was too shocked to register or analyze darkening his voice as he called her name and took a step towards her, Emma in his arms and Leo clinging determinedly to his side.

Maddy was aware of the expectant look on Jenny's face as he turned towards his wife, but

it was impossible for Maddy to respond, to re-
ciprocate the warmth she could see in Max's
eyes, to play the part she could sense that
everyone was willing her to play in his home-
coming, and instead of answering him, she
turned swiftly on her heel and almost ran the
length of the hall before disappearing into the
kitchen.

Before the kitchen door closed behind her,
she could hear Leo asking shakily in the silence she had left behind, 'Where has Mummy
gone?'

'I expect she's gone to put the kettle on,' Max
comforted Leo, but his head was bent over
Emma's so that neither of his parents nor his
grandfather could see his expression.

It had been a shock to see Maddy and for a
moment, when she had first walked into the
hall, even though he had known that it *was* her,
his eyes had almost refused to recognize his
wife.

She had lost weight, and her hair was done
in a different style, but those things alone
weren't responsible for the change he had immediately sensed in her. There was a new determination about her, a new strength, a resistance to him, which he had felt as strongly as
though she had physically pushed him away.

But more than all of those things, what had shocked and disturbed him even more had been his own reaction to her.

In place of the regret and indifference he had expected to feel, his body was reacting as though he, *it*, wanted to pick her up, carry her up those stairs in front of him, lay her down on their bed and—

The intensity of his desire for her, his *need*, was something that had nothing to do with the outward changes in her appearance, attractive though they were, Max knew. It was as though his body, his senses, had immediately recognized in Maddy their soul mate, and the sharpness of his sense of deprivation, the keenness of his yearning for her, were so strong that Max knew that what he was feeling for her now wasn't something new and untried, something he had never experienced or known before. At some deep and previously unrecognized level, he had *always* wanted her like this...*loved* her like this.

'Daddee...' Emma protested, wriggling in his arms as he involuntarily tightened his grip on her.

'Sorry,' he apologized, giving her a smile and a kiss before putting her back down on the ground.

'You must be worn out,' he could hear his mother saying. 'Let's get you upstairs and into bed.'

'I'm not an invalid, Ma,' Max started to protest, but inwardly he knew she was right. Walking was becoming extremely uncomfortable, and Jack, solicitous as always, leapt to his side as he noticed the way Max had started to drag his injured leg slightly as he headed for the stairs.

Escorted by his parents, his grandfather, his cousin and his children, Max allowed himself to be borne upstairs on a tide of loving concern. Escorted by his parents, his grandfather, his cousin and his children, but not by his wife...his Maddy...his love....

13

'So, you're quite happy with the date the Ericsons have come up with for the Gilbert and Sullivan charity evening, then, are you, Maddy...?'

As he waited for her response and recognized that she wasn't paying complete attention to him, Griff followed her line of vision through the sitting room window of Queensmead and onto the lawn where Max was walking with Leo and Emma.

Max had been home for close on a month now, during which time Griff had watched Maddy go from being distinctly wary towards him to...to what? When he had arrived earlier for their meeting, she had been in the garden with Max and the children, and Griff had seen the openly possessive and warning look Max had given him behind Maddy's back when he had reached out his hand to remove an early pussy willow catkin from her hair.

'Maddy,' he repeated, a little tersely now,

causing her to turn back quickly towards him, her eyes dark with contrition.

'I'm sorry, Griff,' she apologized. 'I didn't catch what you were saying.'

'I was asking you if the date the Ericsons had suggested was okay.'

'The date... Oh, yes,' Maddy agreed quickly, but Griff could see that her attention wasn't really on him or their meeting. He preferred it when she came into Chester and they met at his office. At least that way he had her all to himself and didn't have to compete for her attention.

'Max is looking very well,' Griff commented abruptly.

'Yes. Yes, he is,' Maddy agreed.

'Having him at home full-time must be quite a strain for you.'

Maddy looked away from Griff before replying to him. Outside in the garden Max was swinging Emma round in his arms, and she could see from the expression on both his and hers and Leo's faces just how much they were enjoying themselves.

Max had changed so much in his behaviour, not just towards the children but towards everyone else as well, that some days Maddy felt as though she had to pinch herself to make sure she wasn't simply having a dream. It was Max now who did the school run, taking Leo to his play school classes, Emma to her play group, and even driving his grandfather to and from the hospital for his appointments.

The change in him was so dramatic, so complete, that virtually everyone he was now coming into contact with had commented on it. Even Luke had remarked that his transformation had a certain awesome, almost biblical quality to it.

'Do you think he's just…that it's just something he's doing to amuse himself with at our expense?' Maddy had asked him quietly.

Luke had frowned before replying, but when he did his response had astonished her a little.

'No, as a matter of fact, I don't,' he had told her.

'Difficult though it is to take on board, and I must admit that I *have* found it difficult, bearing in mind my knowledge of Max's personality, I think we all have to accept that Max has been through an experience that has changed him at the deepest and most personal level of his psyche.'

Maddy knew what he meant. Max, the Max who had returned from Jamaica, might *look* the same as the Max she had previously known, but in every other way he was completely different.

Every day since his return he had gone over to his parents' house, where, according to a pink-cheeked Jenny, he had spent hours with them talking about the past, and not just the past but the present and future as well.

There was no mistaking the closeness that now existed between Jon and Max, nor mistaking, either, the tenderness and love that Max was now exhibiting towards his own children. Leo in particular had blossomed under the warmth of his father's love and attention.

Only *she* seemed to be excluded from the magic charmed circle that now surrounded her husband and those he loved.

Maddy swallowed the hard, painful lump that had become sharply lodged in her throat.

It wasn't that Max was unkind to her; quite the opposite. It was just that…just that…

Quickly she turned away from the scene outside the window and smiled shakily at Griff.

'The children love having Max at home,' she told Griff in response to his question, and without her having to say so Griff knew that what she was telling him was that for her, the children's needs would always come before her own.

Broodingly Griff looked back through the window. The man he was watching playing with his son and daughter was not a man who was going to give them up willingly or easily. Max's paternity, his fatherhood, only seemed to underline to Griff his own lack.

He would never be able to play, as Max was doing, with the children he had fathered. Not with Maddy, not with any woman, because—

'I was wondering if you were free to come into Chester one day next week to have lunch with me,' he asked Maddy quietly.

She looked helplessly at him. She wanted to be able to say yes, but her conscience simply would not let her. Her tender heart ached for the pain she knew she was causing Griff, but until she had resolved the situation with Max, talked with him about their marriage, she was simply not free to embark on the kind of relationship she knew Griff wanted with her.

But ironically, now that she had developed within herself the strength and independence, the sense of self-worth that she knew would have been powerful enough to sustain her through a divorce from Max and beyond it— even through a separation from his family if that should have to happen—she was heart-achingly aware that to separate Leo in particular from his father now could do untold damage to the little boy.

Every day she was confronted with fresh evidence of how much Leo must have secretly craved and needed his father's attention, of how strong the bond that passed from male to male down the family line actually was.

Emma loved her father, too, of course, the new Max who teased and played with her, who allowed her to flirt outrageously with him with a kind, loving tenderness, but Emma was far more emotionally sturdy than Leo. Emma did not *need* Max's approval and love, his presence in her life, in quite the same way that Leo did.

Maddy's head drooped slightly. Sometimes she felt as though she was the only person in the world, or at least in Haslewich, who was on the outside of this circle Max had created around himself, the only person to warily question the permanence of his change of personality.

'Maddy, what is it, what's wrong?'

She looked up quickly and shook her head at Griff as she forced a brief smile.

'Nothing,' she denied quickly, too quickly,

Griff noticed as he took an instinctive step towards her, lifting his hand to place it comfortingly on her shoulder.

From the garden, Max watched, pausing in the act of fastening Leo's shoelace as he saw Maddy's head incline towards Griff's down-bent one. There was nothing remotely outwardly sexual in what they were doing, but Max was immediately and instinctively aware of the emotions flowing between them. And he knew, without having to overhear a word of what they were saying to each other, that Griff was in love with Maddy...and her with him?

He wasn't sure. The new, composed, self-sufficient, self-confident Maddy who had greeted him on his return from Jamaica intrigued him very much, and he was well aware of the irony of the situation he found himself in. To recognize that he loved his wife after years of neglecting and yes, in many ways, abusing her, would have created a big enough hurdle for him to overcome, even without Maddy having undergone her own personal transformation, and Max knew that there was no way he could blame her for the manner in which she was now holding him at a distance.

It was for that reason that he had deliberately not tried to rush or push her. He might now know that he not only loved her but respected her as well, but it was Maddy he had to convince of those feelings and not himself, and he had decided that the best way to show her just how much he had changed was to withdraw from the kind of behaviour the old Max would have immediately engaged in; that was to say, rushing her into bed and overwhelming her with passion and sex.

What he was trying to do was proving inordinately sexually and emotionally frustrating, though. Watching her now, seeing the sad droop to her head and her mouth, he had an urgent desire to push Griff out of the way and take her in his own arms; the desire was so compelling that he was on his feet and heading for the house before he managed to call himself to order.

What had happened to the man who had told himself that one of his first duties on his return home would be to free his wife from the paucity of their marriage? There was, he recognized ruefully, enough of the old Max left within him to make him determined not to give up Maddy without a fight. He could see that Griff loved her, yes, and he sincerely felt for the other man, all the more so since he now

recognized just how painful loving a woman
you couldn't have could be, but Maddy was
his wife, and he intended to play that advantage for all it was worth.

He had two other advantages as well, he acknowledged as he looked towards his children, but his love for them was far too profound, far too deep for him to want to use
them as pawns in any fight to win Maddy's af-
fections.

It made his heart thump with fear and pain
to recognize how easily he could have lost out
on the miraculous wonder of loving them both
and in learning just how much he did love
them. Max had come to understand the truth
of what his parents were saying when they
told him that they had always loved him.

'No...you were *never, ever* just a substitute
for Harry,' Jenny had objected fiercely when
he had told her of how he had felt as a small
child. 'I... I always wanted you, loved you, for
yourself, Max, but I was ill after you were
born, and it was three days before they allowed me to have you with me. Now, when
we understand how important it is for a
mother and baby to be allowed to bond, that
would never be allowed to happen....'

'I always felt that neither of you really

wanted me,' Max had confessed to them both, 'and that you wished that I had been David's child.'

'I felt that I wasn't a good enough father for you,' Jon had told him in turn.

The old wounds had been properly cleansed and allowed to heal now, and Max felt a very protective love towards his parents, both of whom he could see had suffered very much in the early years of their marriage from his grandfather's obsession with David, to the exclusion of Jon.

'Did you have a successful meeting?'

Maddy tensed a little, turning her back to Max before answering his question.

He had returned to the house with the children just as Griff had been about to leave, but despite his perfectly pleasant manner towards him, Maddy had been almost physically aware of Max's distrust of Griff, and she had immediately rushed to protect the other man from any display of unkindness on Max's part.

The old Max would have shown his feelings by making some kind of cruel comment at the other man's expense, but the new Max had simply smiled and shaken his hand before escorting him to his car.

Now he was back, following Maddy into the sitting room, where she had gone to gather up the papers she had left there.

'Yes, I think so,' she agreed a little huskily. 'The Ericsons have given us a date for the charity operetta.'

'You know, I've been thinking,' Max commented quietly as he went to the other side of the table and started to help her gather the papers. 'I know that the main purpose of the charity is to provide safe and comfortable accommodation for single mothers and their babies, but it occurred to me that it might not be a bad idea if a communal sitting room be put aside in each property where, with the agreement of everyone concerned, the fathers could see their babies.'

Maddy was so startled that she dropped the papers she had been holding.

'I know what you're thinking,' Max told her before she could speak. 'In the majority of cases the boys who have fathered these babies have very little interest in them—a fault in the main of their youth—and who knows what effect their inability to recognize just what they are turning their backs on might have both on the child involved and the father at a later stage in their lives. But the chance to talk perhaps should be given to them. It's only a suggestion,' he added slowly. 'I'm not trying to interfere. Anyone can see that you're doing an excellent job, Maddy. My mother was commenting only yesterday about the amount of progress the charity is making with you on board.'

'I... I'll put what you've said to the committee,' Maddy told him a little breathlessly, ignoring the second part of his statement.

He *did* have a point, she had to admit that, and in fairness both to the babies and their fathers, it was one, now that he had raised it, that ought to be given proper consideration by the committee.

'I can guess what you're thinking,' Max told her softly as he bent to gather up the papers she had dropped.

His hair had grown quite long since his return home, and as she looked down at the top of his head, Maddy had an overwhelming urge to reach out and touch it. It looked so silky, thick and clean, so...so...

Quickly she took a step back from him.

'I wasn't thinking anything at all,' she denied quickly, too quickly, she recognized as Max looked gravely at her.

It was extremely disconcerting to discover

that the sexual hunger that the old Max had so easily and so emotionlessly evoked within her should have translated with such spectacular ease to the new Max, even if in his new personification her husband was behaving entirely and unexpectedly courteously with regard to her decision not to have sex with him.

He had given her a rather thoughtful and wry look when he had arrived home to discover she had made him up a bed in one of Queensmead's many spare rooms, but he had made no comment when she had quickly and a little nervously pointed out that while he was recovering from his injuries it made sense for him to have his own room.

It was now well over a week, though, since their local hospital had given him a completely clean bill of health, and for a couple of days Maddy had held her breath, half expecting him to announce, as she knew the old Max would have done, that he was moving back into their shared bedroom.

However, he had done no such thing, and now, unwantedly, she was suddenly acutely conscious of him as a man. In that respect, he had most certainly not changed. Max always had been, and she suspected always would be, the kind of man whom women looked at twice, probably never doubting that he would be a wonderful lover. With her he had been an extremely selfish lover, if *lover* was the right word to use to describe his sexual behaviour towards her.

Instinctively she knew that with Griff she would find all the tenderness, the caring, the selfless love she had not found with Max, but Griff, for all his good looks and obvious love for her, did not stir her emotions, did not stir *her* in quite the way that Max had always done.

Had done?

Hastily, Maddy averted her gaze from him. Living the life of a nun when Max wasn't around was easy enough to do, but living it when he was there... Only this morning she had snapped at Emma totally without justification just because the sight of the little girl laughing up at Max as she snuggled into her father's arms had awakened within her, sent jolting through her body, a teeth-gritting surge of such intense envy and such taut need that she had had to whisk herself out of the kitchen and away from Max's too-keen scrutiny before he could guess what she was thinking...feeling...

'If you want me to change Gramps' library books this afternoon, I could do it when I go into Haslewich to see Dad,' Maddy heard Max offering as he placed her papers neatly on the desk.

'You're going to see your father again? That's the third time this week. You had dinner with them last night and...'

'You could have come with me,' Max reminded her, giving her a surprised look.

'At such short notice? What about Leo and Emma?'

'You know that Ma would be only too happy to have them there as well....'

He was frowning now, studying her in a way that made her step defensively back from him.

'You're losing even more weight,' he told her quietly. 'I think I'd better have a word with Ma. Now that you're doing all this work for the charity, you really need to have someone here at Queensmead to help you with Gramps and the children. I should imagine that Guy Cooke must have a niece or second cousin who'd help out....'

For a second, Maddy was almost too taken aback to answer.

No one, not even Griff, had noticed that she had lost weight in recent weeks, and certainly no one had even suggested before that she might need some help, and yet, illogically, the fact that Max had noticed made her feel defensive and angry and even a little panicky, rather than pleasing her. She felt driven to retaliate quickly, 'Don't you think you're overdoing the good father bit just a touch, Max? After all, it wasn't so very long ago that you couldn't have cared less what happened here at Queensmead, and if I have lost weight...' She gave a small shrug. 'It isn't fashionable to be plump.'

'Fashionable?' Max's eyebrows lifted, and to Maddy's shock, before she could guess what he was going to do, one hand shot out and fastened determinedly around her wrist as he pulled her firmly towards him, the other hand spanning the narrow curve of her waist.

'You feel as fragile as a bird,' Max told her shortly. 'I can virtually count your ribs.'

Count them. From the way her heart was banging against them, Maddy was more concerned that it might break them.

'Maddy...'

Uncertainly, she looked at him, her breath suddenly rattling in her throat as she saw the way he was looking at her...at her mouth.

'Max...' she began shakily, but as though he had interpreted the words as an invitation rather than a denial, he closed the distance between them, keeping the hand he still held imprisoned between their bodies so that her palm was resting against his heart while his hand rested just above her breast.

As his lips stroked her mouth, his other hand caressed the curve of her waist.

Helplessly, Maddy felt her head starting to swim. She hadn't been this vulnerable to him even on that first, never-to-be-forgotten date. He was leaning back against the desk, drawing her with him so that she was held in the open space between his legs.

She could feel herself starting to tremble as she felt the warmth of his body, the hand she had put out to ward him off resting instead on the familiar muscled hardness of his thigh.

'Max,' she was still protesting, but he wasn't listening to her. His eyes were closed, his lashes, dark fans against the smooth tan of his skin, spiky and soft and making him look so heartachingly like Leo.

The fine tremor agitating her body had become an open shudder of female arousal, but she could have pulled back, could have resisted him if he hadn't chosen that moment to open his eyes and look straight down into hers.

What she could see there made Maddy catch

her breath. Only once before had she seen Max's eyes blaze like that with the heat of desire, but even then...this was different...this was...

'Maddy...'

She could hear the urgent longing in his voice as he probed her lips with his tongue, teasing them apart, kissing her with quick, hungry, biting kisses.

Beneath the fine wool of her jumper she could feel her breasts starting to swell, her nipples hardening, aching.

God, but she felt so good, Max acknowledged as he tried to hold back his body's response to the feel of Maddy in his arms. He had promised himself that this was something he just would not do, that he would be patient, careful, caring. But now, the moment he had her in his arms, the moment he could feel her close to his body, such noble intentions were immediately subordinated by the tinder-dry vulnerability of his emotions...his need...his love...

'Maddy...' He could hear himself repeating her name like some lovesick teenager as he kissed her over and over again, not daring to lift his hands from her body in case she ran away from him and in case, if *he* moved them, he wouldn't be able to resist the temptation to touch her more intimately. But while he kissed her, his imagination, his memory, was tormenting him with mental images of the way they had once been, the soft, smooth, cool paleness of her moonlit skin, the feel of her trembling against him as he touched her, the excitement, the enticement of knowing just how much he had aroused her.

Now, though, she was the one who was arousing him, and he was the one who was getting dangerously out of control, who yearned to hear the words she had once, in what now felt like another lifetime, begged him to say to her.

'Do you love me? Tell me you do. Tell me...show me...love me... Maddy...please, please love me....'

'No... Max... Max, the children are coming.'

Frantically Maddy pushed against his chest as she dragged her swollen mouth from beneath his.

She was trembling from head to foot, aching from head to foot, inside and out, and her face burned as her attention was caught by the old-fashioned fleecy rug in front of the fire and the images that were running riot through her head. If Max had chosen to pick her up and carry her over to lie her down and touch her...take her...

Thankfully the children had pushed open the sitting room door, clamouring for attention before her errant thoughts could betray her even further, and, in the busyness of listening to them and sorting out the source of their small quarrel, she was able to push aside the sharp pangs of tormented female sexual hunger that Max had aroused inside her.

Max watched her silently as she dealt with Leo and Emma's noisy urgency. His body ached, throbbed still with the need, *his* need for her, and he knew that if he was to see her looking at Griff or indeed any other man right now with that same compassion he had seen her watching Griff earlier, he would probably have torn him limb from limb, so primeval and savagely male were his feelings towards her.

Maddy checked the street leading from the Chester car park before setting out to cross it. Since the afternoon when Max had kissed her, their lives had settled into a new and rather tantalizing routine, with Max becoming more involved in not just the children's lives, but the lives of the whole family as he deferred the date for his full-time return to his chambers in London.

Their evenings were spent mostly on their own together, a departure so diametrically at odds with Max's previous life-style that Maddy was still slightly overawed by it.

To come home as she had done last week after a particularly gritty meeting with the financial director of one of the companies she was trying to persuade to sponsor the purchase and re-fit on another set of flatlets, soaking wet after being caught in an icy cold rainstorm, her hair hanging round her face in rat's tails and feeling thoroughly bad-tempered and hard done by, to find that not only had Max bathed and fed the children, but that he had also prepared their supper, had left her too stunned for speech. Or for any argument when he had insisted that she was to go upstairs, have a hot bath and then come down again, when they would eat in the warmth and comfort of the sitting room. It had been a breathtakingly, dangerously sweet incident, made even more so by Max's arrival upstairs, where he had found her rubbing her still-damp hair with a towel in their once-shared bedroom.

Firmly pushing her down into a chair, he

had taken the towel from her hands and started to dry her hair himself.

All too conscious of the way she must look and the fact that she was wearing her comfortable old towelling robe, Maddy had pulled a little nervously at the edge of it, causing Max to totally misinterpret her thoughts and tell her gruffly, 'Maddy, it's all right. I might be aching in every muscle and bone, not to mention all the other bits of me to take you to bed, but I promise you I am not going to jump on you when you're plainly far more in need of a bowl of hot soup and a warm fire. So be a dear and please stop tugging so protectively at the neckline of your robe, because what I can also promise you is that if you don't...' He had stopped and given her a heart-jerkingly rueful smile. 'Well, let's just say that while I know you well enough to acquit you of doing anything remotely provocative, my body finds that enticing little vee you're struggling to conceal more tantalizing and alluring with every breath you take.'

She had stopped, of course, feeling as absurdly excited and self-conscious as a young girl of sixteen and not a very well-married woman in her own bedroom with her own husband.

Her own husband. Maddy's thoughts shook her, her skin suddenly glowing a very fetching pink. In truth, Max was now much more of a husband to her and a father to the children than he had ever been in the days when they had actually shared a bed, and the trouble was that perhaps because of that, her body... But no, she wasn't going to think of that. Her body, her emotions, might yearn for a much more intimate relationship with Max than the one they were presently sharing, but her brain, her instincts as a mother, warned her that she could not afford to allow herself, and much more importantly, her children to be hurt by Max a second time.

'When do you plan to go back to work?' she had asked him tentatively earlier in the week.

'Why?' he had parried. 'Are you anxious to get rid of me?'

'No, of course not,' she had denied hurriedly. 'It's just...'

Her voice had trailed away self-consciously. How *could* she tell him that she was finding his constant presence at Queensmead increasingly disturbing and that her nights were being increasingly broken by her feverishly passionate dreams about him, dreams in which…

Quickly she shook her head and reminded herself of the reason why she was here now in Chester. She had a business meeting with Griff, and afterwards he was taking her out for lunch. She flushed again. Sooner or later she was going to have to make a decision about Griff's place in her life. Sooner or later she was going to have to talk with Max.

Max… He had come downstairs, formally dressed in a dark grey pin-stripe suit this morning, looking extremely distinguished and heartstoppingly, dangerously attractive. Since his attack, he had begun to develop just the beginnings of very sexy fine grey hairs at his temples, which, oddly, had the effect of making him look somehow younger rather than older.

'Work,' he had told her briefly when she had gazed at him in some astonishment, but he hadn't elaborated and she hadn't asked, assuming that he must have decided to go to London without feeling it necessary to discuss his plans with her. Ridiculously, she had felt hurt and excluded, especially when Jon had telephoned just before she herself had left, to speak to Max, telling her cheerfully that he was simply ringing to wish his son 'good luck.'

Jon had obviously been privy to Max's decision and so, too, no doubt, had Jenny. But Max had quite obviously not felt it necessary to tell her.

She had left without saying anything to him, driving rather faster to Chester than normal. She had no idea how long Max intended to spend in London. Obviously, though, he must be intending to remain there overnight.

'Are you all right?' Griff asked her when his secretary had shown her into his office.

'Yes, I'm fine,' Maddy responded tensely.

'Something's wrong,' Griff started to insist, but Maddy immediately shook her head.

'Nothing's wrong,' she told him irritably, and then regretted her small loss of temper when she saw the look in his eyes.

'Griff, I'm sorry,' she apologized immediately. 'It's just...' She paused.

'Maddy, you know how I feel about you,' Griff began fiercely, reaching for her hand. But Maddy shook her head and moved away from him.

'It's all right,' he assured her. 'I do understand... You and Max... All I want to say to you is that… I'll always be there for you,' he told her simply.

Maddy's eyes filled with tears.

'Oh, Griff, you mustn't say that,' she protested. 'You need…deserve…someone who…' She stopped, shaking her head, knowing that it was impossible for her to give him the comfort or the reassurance he wanted.

For several minutes after Maddy had gone—their business discussion had been kept brief and both had decided it was probably best to pass on having lunch—Griff stood silently in his office. Against all the odds, Maddy had aroused within him the kind of protective, possessive, masculine and very intense love that he had always thought himself too emotionally controlled to experience. A love that he was now beginning to reflect had, perhaps, been too intense. So intense maybe, that it might ultimately have burned itself out…. The logical, analytical side of his nature was warning him that he had fallen in love too quickly and too deeply, that such emotions might not have stood the test of time.

Already, beneath the pain he was feeling, there was also a tiny frail thread of something that could one day become strong enough to be called relief—or reality? This morning he had received a letter from an old friend, inviting him to visit him in his new home near Vancouver. Perhaps he should go?

14

—————◄—————

Maddy was on her way back to her car after her meeting with Griff when it happened. She was just walking past the Grosvenor when she saw a familiar figure standing in its shadow, his back towards her as he leaned over the woman standing in the curve of his arm.

Her heart in her mouth, Maddy watched as Max, her husband, bent his dark head over the blonde one. A feeling of sick nausea started to rush over her, combined with an urgent need to escape, a sense of panic that had her turning quickly on her heel, afraid that he might see her, and then colliding with a woman walking the other way.

As she started to apologize, she could hear the woman asking her uncertainly, 'Are you all right, love? You look awfully pale....'

'I'm fine...fine,' Maddy lied, knowing that she was anything but.

As she drove back to Haslewich, the sun came out, shining down warmly on the tender green of the newly growing grass and the golden yellow of the daffodils in people's gardens, a sight that would normally have automatically lifted Maddy's heart, but today she could barely see the beauty of the flowers because of the tears burning her eyes.

How *could* she had been such a fool as to believe that Max had genuinely changed? Of course he had not changed. How *could* he? He was still the same old Max, lying, deceiving, cheating.

The stoicism that had seen her through the countless affairs and betrayals their marriage had imposed on her suddenly seemed to have deserted her, and in its place was a coiling, writhing, torturing serpent of jealousy and feminine fury. How dared he? How *dared* he?

'So, how did it go?' Luke asked Max as his cousin stood in his office, looking down into the street below.

'So-so,' Max told him. 'In my opinion, she is still very much in love with her husband, and although she swears that she wants a divorce, I suspect that, in reality, what she wants is no such thing. Some counselling might be of far more benefit to her than litigation.'

'Mmm...' Luke steepled his fingers together. 'Mmm... I agree, but she insists that she intends to divorce him. I've told her that we don't have anyone specializing in matrimonial law here in our chambers...which is why I suggested to her that she might be better off seeing you.'

'Well, it would certainly be an interesting case to handle—from a legal point of view—but I still think she should give her marriage another try.'

'You're getting soft in your old age, Max,' Luke derided him mockingly.

'Mmm... I think you might be right,' Max agreed with a smile, refusing to rise to the bait.

'Have you thought any more about what I said to you about there being a definite opening for a matrimonial counsel here in Chester?'

'I *have* thought about it,' Max acknowledged, 'but at the moment my future in terms of my career is not the most important thing on my mind.'

Luke's eyebrows rose.

'Oh?'

'Stop fishing, Luke,' Max told him with a grin. 'You won't catch anything.'

'I don't *need* to fish,' Luke said truthfully. 'And if you want my advice...'

'I don't,' Max told him hardily, glancing at

his watch before telling him, 'Look, I must go,
I'm picking Leo up from play school at three.'

'Duty before pleasure, is that it?' Luke
teased, but Max shook his head.

'Being with my children *is* a pleasure,' he
corrected him truthfully.

Ten minutes later, standing at the window
where Max had stood earlier, watching him
stride purposefully down the street, apparently oblivious to the interest he was attracting
from a group of giggling young women, Luke
could only marvel at the change that had taken
place in him.

Max had just made it plain to him, without
putting it into so many words, that his priority
right now was his relationship with Maddy.
Luke wished him luck. Maddy, he suspected,
would not be easy to win over. She had developed an unexpectedly strong personality over
the last few months, and Luke, who was very
much an observer of the human mind, had noticed that Maddy was still holding back from
Max. Well, he couldn't blame her for that. He
had had his own doubts about the man. He
hadn't had much time for the old Max. But he
had to admit that he was finding it extraordinarily easy to relate to the new one. Even if the
offer he had recently made to Max to have him

join his own set of chambers had come as something of a surprise to Luke himself, he was still wholly convinced that having Max working alongside him would be a very definite asset—and not just professionally. He was discovering that he and Max were, if anything, even more on the same wavelength than he was with his own brother and fellow partner in the practice, James.

He frowned as he glanced at his watch. Max's comment about having to collect Leo had reminded him that Bobbie had charged him to get home early this afternoon. Not that he had any objection to that, and he certainly had none to what he suspected his wife had in mind as a means of passing the rest of the afternoon. He could think of nothing he would rather do than lie in bed making love to his wife while their room was bathed in the clear, bright sunlight of an early spring day. At over six feet tall, Bobbie had a physical presence, a physical magnificence, that still turned him weak simply to think about it, and her pregnancy somehow made her even more exciting. Firmly he rang through to his secretary, telling her, 'Janet, I'm going home and I don't want any calls....'

*   *   *

Maddy was still sitting at her desk, pretending to work but in reality rehearsing what she intended to say to Max when she heard him come in.

Strangely enough, despite the fact that she was convinced that seeing him with another woman meant that he was still very much the same old Max, it had never occurred to her to doubt that he would honour his commitment to collect Leo. As her son rushed into the sitting room ahead of Max to hug her and tell her excitedly about his day, she bent down to pick up Emma, who had been playing contentedly on the floor but who now insisted on wriggling free of her hold to run over to Max as he followed Leo into the sitting room.

'Maddy, what is it, what's wrong?'

The fact that he had noticed that something *was* wrong, coupled with the concern she could see in his eyes, threw Maddy for a moment, but then she forced herself to recall the mental picture she had stored of his dark head bent so protectively, so...so sexily, over the blonde one of his female companion.

Drawing herself up to her full height and positioning herself determinedly behind her desk, Maddy took a deep breath.

'I saw you this afternoon in Chester,' she

told him pointedly, adding just in case he tried to avoid the issue, 'with your...friend....'

Max's eyebrows shot up. He knew immediately what Maddy was trying to say, and hot on the heels of his initial sense of injustice at being so wrongly accused came a small, sneaky feeling of pleasure that Maddy should be so angrily jealous of the fact that she had seen him with what she had assumed was another woman.

'My friend?' he questioned, pretending not to understand, before allowing his brow to clear as he explained. 'Oh, yes...you mean the client who Luke asked me to see.'

'The...the client...'

'Yes,' Max continued gently. 'Luke seems to think that there's an opening in his chambers for a matrimonial counsel, and he suggested to me that I might like to consider moving from London to Chester to work. This particular woman he wanted me to see had consulted him about her desire to divorce her husband, but as Luke and I are both agreed, a spot of relationship counselling might prove to be more in her interests than a divorce. I strongly suspect that she still loves her husband, even if she feels aggrieved with him, and Luke concurs...'

'You're…you're thinking of working from Chester?' Maddy demanded weakly, unable to find anything else to say.

'It had crossed my mind,' Max agreed cordially. 'It would certainly give me more time to spend with these two,' he told her, indicating the children. 'And…' He stopped. Her pale face and sunken eyes touched not just his heart but his conscience as well.

'Maddy…we need to talk,' he told her gently. 'Why don't I ring my parents and ask them to have Leo and Emma…'

'I…' To her own consternation, Maddy felt her eyes starting to fill with tears. What was the matter with her? She was behaving like a complete fool.

Without waiting for her reply, Max had picked up the telephone and was dialling his parents' number. He was right, they did need to talk, but Maddy wasn't sure that her susceptible emotions were up to an evening spent alone with her husband, and yet, stupidly, after he had confirmed with his parents that they would be delighted to have the children and he turned to Maddy and asked her if she would like to go out for a meal, she found that she was shaking her head.

'Yes. I think you're right,' Max agreed soberly before she could change her mind. 'What I need to say to you is better said in privacy.

'My parents have offered to have Leo and Emma overnight,' he added as Maddy got up and walked round from behind her desk. 'I'll go up and pack their stuff, shall I?'

'No, I'll do that,' Maddy told him huskily. Better for her to have something to do, to have something to take her mind off what lay ahead.

'More wine...?'

Maddy shook her head. She had already had three glasses, and her head was starting to swim a little.

In any other circumstances she could have found it an extraordinarily intimate thing to be preparing a meal with Max, as he had insisted on her allowing him to do once Jon and Jenny had left with the children, but she had been so nervously aware of what lay ahead that in the end she had virtually left Max to cook their supper by himself. Then, to add insult to injury, she had barely touched the food he had put in front of her, her stomach churning sickly as she tried to guess what it was he wanted to say to her.

It hurt badly, knowing that he had discussed his future with other people and not with her.

'What is it? What are you thinking?' he suddenly asked her, surprising her not just by his question but with the intensity of the look that accompanied it.

'No, Maddy...don't look away from me,' he urged her, reaching across the table to take hold of her hand before turning it over, playing with her wedding ring.

'You've got lovely eyes,' he told her abruptly. 'They're very expressive. The first time I made love to you I could see each and every emotion you were feeling registering in them.'

'You didn't make love to me,' Maddy told him stiffly, trying to retrieve her hand and failing as he tightened his grip on it. 'We had sex.'

There was a small silence, and then Max said quietly, 'I know I deserved that, Maddy, but *you* certainly didn't, and neither did the reality of what we shared that first time. We *did* make love...even if...'

'You didn't love me...you said...'

'I lied...' Max told her simply. 'What I said wasn't what I felt...not then and certainly not now. I love you, Maddy, and I think somewhere deep down inside me I've loved you all the time, even if I've been afraid to admit it to you and even more afraid to acknowledge it to myself.'

'I... Max, you've changed so much' was all that Maddy could find to say.

'Yes,' he agreed simply, 'I have.'

Maddy looked uncertainly at him.

'How?'

'I don't know, Maddy,' he answered. 'I only know that there was a time just after I had been attacked when I went to a place where I knew unequivocally and forever that nothing mattered so much as love. Oh, I don't mean sexual love, or even the love of a parent for a child...simply the love that exists all around us, the love that we are unable to see and that I had so...so stupidly and foolishly denied myself and others. For a brief, magical space of time, I saw that love, felt it, knew it...and I knew, too, that I never wanted to be without it again, that I couldn't imagine how I had ever lived in denial of it.

'I didn't want to come back, you know, Maddy. Being there felt so right...so... Oh, I can't describe it to you,' he told her huskily, shaking his head. 'I just...but I could hear my father calling to me and he sounded so desperately unhappy. I turned round to comfort him, and then suddenly it was gone and I was coming back, even though…'

Maddy moistened her lips, her heart was thumping and she could hear the emotional tremor in her own voice as she told him, 'It sounds like a near-death experience. I've read about them. They say that people who experience them are…that they…'

'Yes,' Max agreed gently. 'It's because love has touched their soul, for want of a better word, because they, *we*, know. I know how much you doubt me, Maddy, and why, but I promise you this isn't just some act…some game I'm playing. This is real…this is *me*. I can't undo all the damage I've done. I can't turn back time and change what's been said. All I can do is to ask you…' He curled his hand around hers, rubbing her wedding ring.

'Not to forgive me for the past, Maddy, and certainly not to forget it, but…' He paused and lifted his head, looking straight into her eyes, the brilliance and emotion reflected in his own causing hers to widen in instinctive recognition of his honesty.

'But *allow* me…give me the chance to prove to you that what I am now…what I feel now… I'm asking you to give me…our marriage…a second chance, Maddy. Tell me it isn't too late for us...' he begged huskily.

Maddy looked away from him. She couldn't find the words to express just how much what he had said had touched her own emotions. When he said that love had touched his soul, she had known that he was speaking the truth, had seen it, witnessed it in the extraordinary change in his behaviour...in his attitudes and beliefs, but this plea he was making for her, for their marriage... It was too much, too soon, and she was too confused, too unsure....

'Tell me it isn't too late for us, Maddy,' she could hear him begging her.

'I don't know....' She bit her lip, and then forced herself to meet his eyes. 'Max, you say you love me and that you've changed...that you want our marriage to go on, but...please try to understand... I know that you *believe* you mean what you're saying, and I wouldn't want you to think otherwise, but...'

She had to stop to gather up her courage before she could go on. What she needed to say to him was bringing back, resurrecting, so many painful memories that she would rather not have exhumed, but they had to be. He had to understand why she simply could not just comply with what he was asking from her.

'When we married, I loved you so much, Max…too much… I… If you made me unhappy, then I know now that I colluded in that… I allowed you to treat me badly. I've only just begun to be my real self, to *know* my real self, and I feel… I think…' She stopped and shook her head.

'I need time, Max…time to learn to live happily in my own skin, with my own self and…'

'Are you trying to tell me that you're in love with someone else?' Max interrupted her quietly. 'I know that Griff Owen loves you, Maddy.'

Immediately she shook her head and told him truthfully, 'No… I like Griff and he's been a very good friend to me. Perhaps if you and I had separated and…' She paused. 'This doesn't have anything to do with Griff, Max. This is about you and me and…'

'And the fact that I don't deserve to have your love,' Max finished for her, but Maddy stopped him.

'Don't you see?' she told him passionately. 'It isn't about deserving, it's about… I don't want either of us to turn round in years to come and feel that we opted to stay together for the wrong reasons. You out of a mistaken sense of compassion and duty, in the belief that…' She stopped and sighed before continuing in an even lower voice, 'and me because…'

'You because of what?' Max prompted her when her voice trailed away.

Screwing up her courage, Maddy lifted her head and told him proudly, 'And me because, despite the fact that in bed…sexually…it was never very good for you—you told me often enough how hopeless I was—for me…sexually I still want you, Max, very, very much, but that isn't enough to build a marriage on…a life….'

For a moment Max was too bemused to respond. He had always known, of course, how vulnerable Maddy was to him sexually—the old Max had, at times, been amused by her loving sensuality—but he had never expected to hear her admit it, because he had always known, too, just how desperately ashamed she was of wanting him to such an extent. Now, immediately, the love he already felt for her was deepened with additional respect and pride. Unlike him, Maddy had not needed to undergo a life-threatening experience to recognize the value of self-honesty.

As he moved to stand up, releasing her hand, Maddy gave him an alarmed look.

'Don't worry,' he told her softly. 'I'm *not* going to. Oh, yes, Maddy, as I've already indicated to you, I want you and it hurts like hell, more than enough for the old me to be sorely tempted to take hold of you now and lie you down right here and now and show you just how much I care, just how very, very good it could be between us, but I know that it wouldn't be right, not for me and certainly not for you, and that it isn't the right basis for the relationship I want us to have together.'

'Max,' Maddy protested, her skin starting to burn as she saw the way he was looking at her, and she recognized that he was speaking the truth when he spoke so openly of wanting her.

'Not now, Maddy. My self-control is just about stretched to its limit,' he warned her gently. 'All I'm going to ask of you is that you give us a chance...'

'I... I need time...' Maddy began, but Max obviously hadn't finished speaking, because he touched her hand very briefly and added rawly, 'Oh, and by the way, it was never true, you know...'

'What wasn't?' Maddy asked him, confused.

'What I said about you being hopeless in bed,' Max told her.

Maddy watched him warily, her heart

crashing dangerously into her ribs as he gave her a ruefully sweet smile.

'If you want the truth, Maddy, even though I denied it to myself at the time, the truth was that what you lacked in experience you more than made up for with the warmth and generosity of your response. You'll never know how many times I came dangerously close to losing myself completely in your arms....

'How the hell do you think you managed to conceive my child...twice,' he added softly. 'I hadn't wanted that...them...but...'

Maddy's skin burned even hotter as she looked away from him.

'It's been a long day, and if you don't mind, I think I'll go up now,' Max was telling her.

Maddy could see in his face that he was tired. Despite his determination to deny it, there were times when the effect of his attack could still be seen—times like now when he was under stress—and watching him, Maddy was immediately reminded of how very, very close he had come to dying...how very, very close they had all come to losing him. Even so, when he turned towards her as she stood up and asked her gravely, 'May I kiss you, Maddy?' she could feel her body instinctively tensing defensively as she shook her head.

'You still don't trust me, do you,' Max sighed gently, entwining his fingers with hers and then releasing them. But as she watched him walk slowly towards the door, Maddy acknowledged inwardly that it wasn't Max she didn't trust so much as herself.

She waited until she was sure he had gone before allowing her tormented imagination to remind her of just what it felt like to have Max's mouth on her own.

It was a long time before Maddy had made her own way up to bed. She had worked ferociously in the kitchen, cleaning out cupboards, washing and polishing utensils that were already spotlessly clean, in the despairing hope that by physically exhausting herself she would be able to sleep without being tormented by memories, images of Max, but an hour after she had crawled into bed, she was still wide awake...wide awake and...

Pushing back the covers, she slid out of bed. They had the house to themselves virtually apart from Gramps, who never stirred from his own suite until Maddy had taken him a cup of tea in the morning, but old habits die hard and she waited until she had gently turned the handle of Max's bedroom door and stepped inside before shrugging off the robe she had donned to walk the length of the corridor from her own bedroom to Max's.

Max had omitted to close the curtains, and in the moonlight she could see the shape of his sleeping body beneath the covers.

He was lying on his side on one half of the large double bed, and where the duvet had slipped away, she could see the smooth, hard muscles of his arms and shoulders beneath his skin.

Her stomach tensed in sharp sensual awareness. How many times in the past had she watched him while he slept, stroking her fingers over his skin as she snuggled closer to him, taking, while he slept, the intimacy he always denied her while awake, pretending in her imagination that he loved her as much as she did him.

From beneath his half-closed eyelids, Max watched as Maddy approached the bed, hardly daring to breathe in case he frightened her away.

He had been lying there unable to sleep when he had heard the soft creak of her bedroom door, and, at first, he had assumed automatically that she was going to check on the children—and then he had remembered that

Leo and Emma weren't there—and so he had lain where he was, hardly daring to hope...hardly daring to breathe.

When she reached the bed, Maddy stretched out her hand. Her fingers were shaking. Very gently she touched Max's exposed shoulder, stroking her fingertips along his skin. It felt hot, silky, the muscles under it bunching and quivering slightly, her own stomach tensed and quivered in immediate response.

'Max...' She wasn't sure whether she had spoken out loud or not, but suddenly Max reached out and took hold of her hand.

In the moonlight she could see the dark gleam of his eyes as he carried her fingers to his lips, very gently kissing each one in turn before sitting up in bed and drawing her down into his arms, into the bed, against his body, his naked, warm, so familiar and so well-beloved body. Maddy felt her own body start to tremble helplessly in mute response, not just to the feel of his but to all the memories it evoked.

'Maddy.'

She heard him whisper her name between kisses, over and over again, like a refrain; a chant of love and adoration. A rash of goose bumps lifted her body as he kissed her throat, the soft curve of her shoulder.

It was like letting herself slide into deep, luxuriously warm water, the sensation of his skin, his body, against her own evoking a thousand images of past caresses. Only now, instinctively, Maddy knew that she was free to give herself to him, to what she was feeling, totally and completely, safe in the knowledge that the gift she was giving him would not be rejected.

Even the touch of his hands on her body felt different, slower, gentler, giving as well as demanding. But the old familiar excitement, the hunger, the need, the desire she had always felt for him were still there. Still there, and if anything, enhanced by her awareness of just how much he had changed, Maddy recognized as she shuddered in quick pleasure as his hands cupped her breasts, his thumbs rubbing erotically over their sensitive tips. She could hear Max's breath catching in his throat as she arched her back and the moonlight from the window silvered her body.

'Maddy... Maddy...'

She could hear the need, the hunger in his voice as his lips caressed her throat, his forehead hot and beaded with sweat, his body shuddering violently as he opened his mouth over her breast, suckling gently on her nipple at first until she started to push herself rhythmically against him.

She could feel the hard bite of his fingers against her skin, but she gloried in it and in his primitive response to her, his open need for her.

As he knelt up in bed beside her, she could see how his sweat dampened the silky darkness of the hair that arrowed down his body.

'Maddy, don't look at me like that,' she heard him groaning feverishly as she saw the way he was watching her.

She had seen him aroused before, but never, never quite like this. Never had she been so intuitively aware that the very strength of his male body was also his weakness; that beneath the sexual power she could see so awesomely and openly displayed lay a vulnerability that for the first time he was allowing her to see.

Slowly she reached out and touched him, tentatively at first and then more confidently, stroking the silky damp hair, shuddering in response to the heated male scent that surrounded and enveloped her. The urge to touch him, taste him, was so strong that she couldn't ignore it, a compulsion that had her bending towards him, tracing the shape of his body with the delicate butterfly, explorative touch of her lips, until he reached out and clasped her head, moaning frantically,

'Maddy, Maddy, for God's sake, what are you trying to do to me? You know...'

But whatever he had been about to say was lost as she pushed away the bedclothes and pressed her open mouth against the inside of his thigh, drawing in the scent and taste of him, filling her senses, herself, with the sweetly heavy sensuality of her own liquid response to him. The gentle insistence of her fingers caused him to open his legs and catch back a thick sob of tormented pleasure, her fingertips drawing delicate circles on the inside of one thigh while her mouth slowly caressed the inside of the other.

Lower down his leg the scar from where his leg had nearly been severed gleamed whitely in the moonlight.

As her slumberous, heavy-lidded gaze caught sight of it, Maddy felt a surge of emotion, of love, so intense that her eyes filled with tears at the strength of it.

'Max...'

As she whispered his name, her voice thick with those tears, Max knew that he had reached the limit of his self-control. Sweat seemed to spring from every pore of his body as he leaned back against the bed, unable to find the strength either to resist or to encourage her, his body, his senses, his whole self no longer under his own control but instead given wholly to hers.

He was hers, completely, utterly hers to do with as she wished, hers to love or to abandon....

As she heard the words tumbling from his lips, Maddy felt the most immense, intense wave of love for him wash over her. Very gently she reached out and touched the scar on his thigh with her hand, and then, moving her head, she caressed it with her lips.

Her tears felt hot against his skin. Hot and oh so infinitely sweet, Max recognized as he reached out and drew her up in his arms, up against his body, holding her close while he cupped her face and kissed her with slow sweetness. Then, with hunger-aching passion and need that had been building up inside him for what felt like a whole lifetime, before moving her very deliberately underneath him, his hands swept down her body, caressing her breasts, holding her hips, parting her thighs.

She felt hot and tight and oh so belovedly familiar, his body filling hers so perfectly and so completely that the thought filled his mind that they were not just made for each other but were almost two halves of one perfect whole.

The feel of him inside her was so much more than Maddy had imagined, so much more than she had remembered, and yet she had thought, during the long and lonely nights when she had daydreamed, fantasized feverishly about his lovemaking, that she must surely have exaggerated the intensity of it...the pleasure of it. But now she knew that she had not done so, that if anything, she had not allowed herself to remember just how good it had been.

But now, it was different. Now it was more than merely sex, now with each thrust of his body within hers, with each frantic, eager response of her own hips to the rhythmic surge of him inside her, she felt a little closer to immortality.

The words of love and hope and longing that poured from his lips, caressing her senses in the same way that his mouth was caressing her skin in between uttering them, were like balm to her soul and much, so much more.

The pleasure he was giving her seemed to last forever, to reach a pitch of such intensity that she cried out instinctively, half afraid of what she was experiencing.

Later she must have slept, exhausted by the intensity of her own release, because when she had woken up she was lying cradled in Max's arms while he gently kissed and caressed the soft, rounded swell of her belly.

Once he knew she was awake he moved lower, his touch, his mouth, becoming more insistent, more hungrily passionate.

'Max...' Maddy protested as he parted her thighs and she felt his lips, the tip of his tongue slowly start to caress the soft warmth of her sex.

'I want you so much like this, Maddy,' she heard him whispering thickly to her. 'I want to store up every tiny touch and taste of you....'

She could hear him groan as his emotions, his desire, overwhelmed him, the hungry insistence of his mouth against her body causing her own to jerk in a fierce feminine spasm of intense pleasure.

But it wasn't her but Max who later wept tears of emotional pleasure as he held her wrapped tightly in his arms, his heart thudding fiercely against her while he told her over and over again how much he loved and valued her. But despite his pleas, Maddy had refused to stay with him, sliding naked from his bed as she told him huskily, 'This doesn't change what I said before about needing time, Max. What just happened was just...'

'Sex?' Max supplied wryly for her without taking his eyes off her face.

'No,' Maddy denied at once.

'Why, Maddy...why did you do it?' Max asked her softly.

'I don't know. I just.... I just wanted to know what it would be like with you now,' she told him gravely.

Max looked away from her, and when he looked back, the expression in his eyes nearly made her break her resolve.

'And what was it like, Maddy?' he asked her quietly.

Now it was Maddy's turn to look away.

How could she tell him that she now understood what he had meant when he had told her that love had touched his soul. What she had just experienced, what they had just shared, was too much...too soon...and she was too confused, too unsure...too reluctant to trust it with the total and complete acceptance that she knew it demanded of her.

'I need time, Max,' she repeated.

'It isn't over between us, Maddy,' Max

warned her as she started to walk towards the bedroom door still naked.

He ached to go after her, to pick her up and carry her, drag her, back to his bed if he had to, but he knew much better than to do so.

Holding her in his arms, making love to her...with her...had shown him so very clearly just what he would lose if he lost her. He couldn't afford to prejudice his own case now by giving in to the possessive and passionate demands of his body.

She had come to him of her own volition once...maybe, just maybe, she would do so again, and if she did...if she did...then the next time he most certainly would not let her go, and he fully intended to tell her so.... But not yet...not now...and besides...

She had conceived easily before, perhaps if he had given her a child this time that might persuade her to stay with him, but he didn't want her with him for the sake of any child they had conceived, but for his own sake...for the sake of loving him and wanting him.

He ached so much for her that he had to grind his teeth together and close his eyes to stop himself from calling out to her as she slipped out of his room.

* * *

In the early morning light of her own bedroom, Maddy shivered in the chill of the cool air. The bed, her bed, felt empty and unwelcoming without Max in it as she crawled between the covers.

She could have stayed with him...should have stayed with him? She closed her eyes, and her mind was immediately flooded with images of what they had just shared, sensations, feelings...needs.

Sexually he had always had the capacity to arouse and to satisfy her when he chose, but tonight there had been another dimension to what they had shared, something quite separate even from his own previously unexpressed and very erotic desire for her.

Her hand touched her stomach. They had not planned on having Leo and Emma. What if this time...? Panic started to flood through her. She didn't want another baby...not now.... She needed time to herself...for herself...and if Max thought she might be carrying his child, he would pressure her to stay with him.

What would it be like to carry a child that they both wanted...to give birth to that child with Max there beside her, to know that he exulted in its conception, its birth, just as much as she did herself?

She knew how much he loved Leo and Emma now, but this child... This child bearing the gift of his or her father's love...

This child?

Maddy started to tremble.

She had other things she needed to give her time and her attention to—the charity, Leo and Emma, Max's grandfather... This was not the right time for her to have another child, and these were certainly not the right circumstances.

This child... A small, secret smile curved her mouth when she finally fell asleep, and it was still there later in the morning when Max walked into the bedroom carrying the breakfast he had made for her.

There will be more to come
from the Crighton family
in future books from
Penny Jordan

A trilogy of warm, wonderful
stories by bestselling author

DEBBIE MACOMBER

Orchard Valley, Oregon

It's where the Bloomfield sisters—Valerie,
Stephanie and Norah—grew up, and it will
always be home to them.

When their father suffers a heart attack, they gather at his
side—the first time in years they've all been together. Coming
home, they rediscover the bonds of family, of sisterhood.
And, without expecting it, they also find love.

ORCHARD VALLEY

MIRA

On sale mid-June 1999 wherever paperbacks are sold!

By the bestselling author of *Romancing the Stone*
and *Elusive Love*

CATHERINE
LANIGAN

THE LEGEND
MAKERS

The steamy jungles of the Amazon offer the perfect
escape for geologist M. J. Callahan, a woman running
from her own haunted past.

But the jungle has a dangerous secret of its own—of a
past expedition from which there were no survivors. As
she and the two very different, very compelling men in
her party approach the heart of the jungle, truths are
revealed, betrayals uncovered, and M.J. is forced to
confront her own demons before history repeats itself.

MIRA®

On sale mid-June 1999 wherever paperbacks are sold!

From one of the world's most popular authors
comes a novel that masterfully explores one
man's attempt to climb beyond his station in
life and the tragic consequences it will have
on his family.

THE UPSTART

CATHERINE COOKSON

Businessman Samuel Fairbrother wants a home more in
keeping with his recent wealth. The thirty-four-room
mansion he purchases comes with a staff—a headstrong
staff. In particular, butler Roger Maitland considers his
new boss nothing more than an upstart. Soon Samuel and
Roger are locked in a battle for supremacy of the
household and for the loyalty of Samuel's own children.
And Samuel is at a disadvantage.

As the years pass only Janet, the eldest daughter, remains.
In her lies the only hope of reconciling the scattered
family—even if she has to defy both her father and
convention to do so.

MIRA

NOT FOR SALE IN CANADA

On sale mid-July 1999 wherever paperbacks are sold.

SHE WOULD GIVE HIM EVERYTHING...BUT THE TRUTH.

MARY LYNN BAXTER

ONE SUMMER EVENING

One summer evening, Cassie Wortham's life changed forever.
Now she's returned to Louisiana: to her childhood home, to
her parents...and to Austin McGuire.

Nine years later, Cassie must face the man she brazenly
seduced. The man who fathered the son he doesn't know
exists. He's still as desirable and disturbing as ever...and still
as forbidden.

When danger follows her home, Cassie must risk everything to
protect her son by turning to the only man who can save them.
She came to Louisiana seeking safety and peace. Instead, she
found the man who first gave her love.

MIRA

On sale mid-July 1999 wherever paperbacks are sold!